✒

The Sorrows of Young Alfonso

Chicana & Chicano Visions of the Américas

The Sorrows of
Young Alfonso

Rudolfo Anaya

UNIVERSITY OF OKLAHOMA PRESS : NORMAN

Library of Congress Cataloging-in-Publication Data

Names: Anaya, Rudolfo A.
Title: The sorrows of young Alfonso / Rudolfo Anaya.
Description: Norman, OK : University of Oklahoma Press, [2016] |
Series: Chicana & Chicano visions of the Américas ; volume 15
Identifiers: LCCN 2015035651 | ISBN 978-0-8061-5226-4 (hardcover :
acid-free paper)
Subjects: LCSH: Young men—Fiction. | Accident victims—Fiction.
  Self-realization—Fiction. | Self-actualization (Psychology)—Fiction.
  GSAFD: Epistolary fiction.
Classification: LCC PS3551.N27 S67 2016 | DDC 813/.54—dc23
LC record available at http://lccn.loc.gov/2015035651

The Sorrows of Young Alfonso is Volume 15 in the Chicana & Chicano Visions of the Américas series.

The paper in this book meets the guidelines for permanence and durability of the Committee on Production Guidelines for Book Longevity of the Council on Library Resources, Inc. ∞

1 2 3 4 5 6 7 8 9 10

This book is dedicated to all the good people

who have helped me in my journey:

To my parents, Rafaelita and Martin

To my wife, Patricia

To my extended family and friends

To my ancestors

To my teachers and healers

To my readers

The Sorrows of Young Alfonso

"The world is full of sorrow."
That's what Agapita told Alfonso.
That's how it begins. Alfonso's story.

Dear K, although you don't know me well.

You asked me to write what I remember of Alfonso. As you know, he didn't write an autobiography. He said his life was contained in the books he wrote. Isn't that true for every writer? I wish he had kept a journal, at least a travel journal. He and his wife enjoyed their excursions abroad. They loved México. Over the years they attended numerous conferences in Europe, where they developed many lasting friendships.

Take my letters with a grain of salt. It all happened so long ago.

Alfonso's biography starts on the New Mexico llano, that flat grassland that gets flatter as it spreads into the West Texas prairie and beyond. Land of scrubby grasses where cattle and sheep graze, a horizon broken in places by mesas, those tabletop hills that rise a few hundred feet to meet the azure sky. A few ancient river canyons cut across the barren land—these arroyos, or gulches, carry water only during summer thunderstorms. A land dotted by juniper and piñon trees, mesquite, yucca, cholla, and prickly pear cactuses. Vaqueros work cattle and sheep on the plain; hunters in search of deer climb the rocky slopes of the mesas.

The "old country," Alfonso called it. The landscape was in his blood.

Llano. The word sounds like "yano." It rolls softly off the tongues of Spanish-speaking Nuevo Mexicanos, my gente, poor as hell but full of pride. His story is the story of a proud people—guess they got that from their Spanish ancestors. Nuevo Mexicanos have spoken the language of Castile since it arrived in New Mexico in 1598, when Oñate and a group of families came up from México and settled near present-day Española on the banks of the Rio Grande. Those hardy people farmed the valley floor and hunted buffalo on the plains east of Santa Rosa de Lima. Later some followed the Pecos River south, and small villages began to dot the river all the way to Puerto de Luna.

Americans from the East started arriving in New Mexico as fur trappers and traders at the beginning of the nineteenth century. In 1848, after the war with México, the Nuevo Mexicanos had to learn English and begin abiding by the laws of the United States government. This clash of cultures became a theme in their lives.

The next influx of Anglo Americans came during the Homestead Act of 1862. Anglos were given land if they settled on the allotments. Most were too poor to meet the requirements of the act, and that's where the speculators come in. Moneyed cattle barons who dreamed of setting up empires purchased foreclosures on homesteaders who went broke. When the Civil War ended, Southerners—mostly Texans—moved into the New Mexico llano.

English was laid over Spanish, and a new history was laid over an existing history. It took a generation for Nuevo Mexicanos to learn the Queen's English, and by that time they had lost many of their land grants to greedy attorneys and politicians. The same thing happened to Native Americans, who were first on the land. They suffered the conquests.

The llano of eastern New Mexico was first peopled by Clovis hunters, those intrepid first Americans who crossed the Bering Strait into the Americas around 11,000 BC. They roamed across the land hunting elephants, horses, camels, giant sloths, lions, cheetahs, and mountain goats in the Grand Canyon. They must have been good at what they did; those animals didn't survive. Clovis people left their bones and large stone spear points buried in shallow ravines that eons before had been carved out by glacial ice.

Their crude spear points were first identified near Clovis, New Mexico—thus the name. They spread all over North America and South. What a story. We don't know what they called the llano, so we adopted the Spanish word used by the españoles who in the late sixteenth century came north from México looking for gold.

Legend tells us that those so-called Spanish conquistadores called the land "la Nueva México," the New Mexico. The name stuck. Most of those colonists came up the Rio Grande, but a few ventured across the llano. In order not to get lost on the flat plain, they drove stakes into the prairie earth, signposts to mark their passage—posts to help them find their way back to México if need be. Thus the name "el Llano Estacado," the Staked Plains. Sky, empty land, and the wind whispering its message is all there is.

A man can get lost on the llano, as happened to Cabeza de Vaca when he wandered across the land. Shipwrecked on the Gulf Coast in 1527, he and two companions walked across what is now Texas and into the llano of southern New Mexico. They finally made it back to México City. De Vaca told the viceroy there that cities of gold waited in the northern lands called New Mexico. He lied. El Río Bravo del Norte, today the Rio Grande, held no Aztec cities made of gold, only Indian pueblos made of mud.

After Cabeza de Vaca reported that there were cities of gold, expeditions began to be sent from México to establish settlements and to spread the Catholic religion among the Native Americans. Ain't proselytizing the way so much history is made? Often a lot of gory history.

But you want me to write about Alfonso. Since you asked, I'll share what I remember. It might be good therapy for me. The days are long for an old man. A lot of time spent staring out the window. Seasons come and go, birds migrate, my bones seem to respond to the changing seasons. Yesterday a lovely monarch butterfly landed on my windowsill. She's going to México for the winter. I feel my soul migrating.

You asked specifically about Alfonso's birth. Here's what I pieced together from what he told me. Remember, though, this is through the filter of an old man's memory—stuff he told me when we were students at the university.

Agapita held the baby up, squirming and bloody. He had come slipping and sliding down the birth canal but paused at the door. "No you don't," the old midwife said, and she pulled Alfonso into this life, all the time puffing away at her cigaro, ashes falling and creating runes on the baby's sensitive skin.

She gave the baby a whack, and he cried. She sucked mucus from his nose, wiped the blood from his face, and looking into his eyes, she whispered, "The world is full of sorrow."

Damn! Why would she say that? Did she stamp those words into his destiny? Is leaving the womb the first sorrow in life? Alfonso's mother, Rafaelita, reached out to hold her son, but Agapita hurried out into the night, the baby dangling from one hand, the bloody afterbirth and umbilical cord dragging.

She stopped in front of the forked juniper tree, where the owls sat waiting. She held the baby up to the starry night sky and cried, "A son of the llano is born. He will know sorrow."

Was she crazy? Or was there truth in what she said? Agapita didn't mince words. Everyone born of woman will know sadness one time or another.

Coyotes heard the baby's cry, and they filled the dark hills with a loud wailing. Cautiously they came down from the mesa, yellow eyes shining in the pale moonlight. Smelling the blood of the newborn they came, as near as they dared because now the village dogs were also howling up a storm, and horses were neighing in the corrals, welcoming the baby. Cattle turned from sleepy, cud-chewing dreams to look upward, where a falling star etched an arc across the sky, like a diamond cutting a deep line across a pane of glass.

Did the baby hear the cacophony exploding in the night? Was this the first poetry he heard, the voices of the llano? Tumult might be a better word.

Agapita called the owls in the juniper tree, the ancient tree half-green, half-dry, entre verde y seco, and they came whooshing down, their huge wings fanning the air that the baby sucked into his lungs.

They cried his name, Awwol-foon-sooo. He was baptized in the village church a few days later, but the owls were the first to call his name.

In the village cantina, where they were playing cards and drinking, Alfonso's father, Martin, and his vaquero friends heard the clamor. "Your wife has given birth," one of his compadres said. "Pray it's a boy," said another. "You better get over there," Moises Anaya said. Martin smiled. He was holding a full house, and two hundred dollars in crumpled bills lay on the table. The baby could wait.

Moises sensed that Martin held a good hand and folded. Carlos Ortega set a bottle of rotgut whiskey on the table and pocketed ten dollars, and he and the vaqueros toasted Martin. That was how a birth was celebrated in that simple, common time.

"Mi hijo, mi hijo," Rafaelita cried when Agapita placed Alfonso to her breast. He drank the milk of his mother, his first nourishment, but as he said, it was the owls that had fanned the breath of life into his lungs. The sounds of the night were his poetry; the juniper tree would become the center of his life.

He was tied to those two women. The mother because he was of her blood, and the old woman who whispered that the world is full of sorrow. Why would the old bitch say that? Was it a warning? Why tell the just-born there is sorrow in the world? Only women truly understand sorrow.

Who was Agapita? A curandera, a healer. She had lived on the llano for centuries, people said. She was as old as the llano of eastern New Mexico. Healer, witch, or doppelgänger, it's all the same. For generations she had been there when the women of the llano gave birth. Her brown, gnarled hands had known sorrow. Her touch passed sorrow into Fonso.

Hands are responsible for all the sorrow in the world, but they can also give love.

What else did she tell him that night? When he looked up into her wrinkled face, did he see a reflection of the earth furrowed by time? Her face told ages. Her eyes were dying stars, rheumy with time.

They would eventually explode inward, like a collapsing giant star burning down to a small core of gravity.

She lived alone in a hut away from the village. When he was seven, Alfonso was already hunting rabbits. He was an expert with his father's .22 rifle. In late winter, when the llano was frozen over like the Siberian tundra, he followed rabbit tracks across the snow. He shaded his eyes and looked into the clear, cold sky, spotting circling hawks. There were sure to be rabbits in the sights of hungry hawks. The trick was to get there first.

He listened to nature's secrets. The wind spoke to him. The screech of a hawk he could interpret; a coyote hunting was his rival. Every smell in the wind told a story. He took Agapita the rabbits he killed. No one in the village visited her. Women only went to her when they needed a cure for one of the many curses that ill winds visited upon them.

She could fly. In those days, the old people could fly. In their eyes were reflected owls, hawks, eagles, and vultures. All kinds of birds. Those elders only had to wish themselves in a distant place, and suddenly they were there. Such was the power of mind and body they possessed. They could fly. With their eyes they could fly.

You read the story Fonso wrote about a man who could fly. Was the man a brujo, a shaman? Did Alfonso learn to fly? "It was different for me," he told me. "Writing stories was like flying." No, it *is* flying.

Then came strangers on the land who didn't believe in miracles, and everything changed. The mystery of faith was broken.

Agapita thanked him for the rabbit. She was burning dry cow chips in the cast-iron stove because wood was scarce when the snow was deep. It was too cold to go to the arroyo and gather dry tamarisk branches. The thick, acrid smoke made his eyes water. That's when she leaned close to him and said, "The dead grieve for the living. They mourn for us."

A weight fell on poor Alfonso. What a dreadful thing to tell him.

"The dead are always with us," she whispered. "Crying their hearts to pieces for us left on earth."

There it was. A truth the old witch had gleaned from life. Not wisdom, just a simple truth. Everyone knew. Now Alfonso knew.

Perhaps he had known before, she told him. Day after day he trekked across the desolate llano, with wind his constant companion, blowing all the time, from gentle breeze to roaring storm. Wind carried the voices of the dead. Walking alone on the vast land he heard voices, he saw images in the gathering clouds.

His uncle Santiago Bonney had been thrown from a horse that tripped in a prairie dog burrow. His legs cracked on impact; he would thereafter walk with a limp. The image of his uncle played over and over in Alfonso's mind, like pictures on the movie screen he was later to see when the family moved to Santa Rosa de Lima.

"Pastura del Santo Niño," the mother prayed. "Pastures of the Holy Child, the wide, grassy land. Santo Niño, take care of my family. Keep my family safe."

His mother's first husband was Salomon Bonney, a handsome, well-built man of French stock, so the genealogies of later years noted. Like many other Anglo and Irish Americans who traveled down the Santa Fe Trail, he had come seeking a new life in the New Mexico Territory.

Such men married the young and lovely Mexicanitas, girls whose forefathers had founded La Villa de Santa Fe, Española, Taos, a hundred villages along the Rio Grande from Las Cruces up to the northern Sangre de Cristo Mountains. Bonney wound up in Puerto de Luna, married Rafaelita, and died shortly thereafter, during the great influenza epidemic of 1918, leaving Rafaelita with a son and daughter to raise. She turned to Martin, a widower with a daughter of his own, and the two were married. Such were the unions in that common time. Expedient and convenient.

Bonney left behind his son, Salomon, and daughter, Elvira.

Martin brought Suzanna to the union. Their family would grow.

Arable land became scarce along the Rio Grande and the Chama. The Nuevo Mexicanos moved south along the Pecos River into the llano, land of the Comanches, tierra incognita. They established villages and tapped the river to grow their crops. Anton Chico, La Loma, Colonias, Pintada, Santa Rosa de Lima, Puerto de Luna. Poetic names began to fill the space.

Everyone was seeking land; it was the era of Billy the Kid and the Lincoln County Wars. Anglos fought each other for land that had already been settled by Mexicanos, land first christened by the hooves of Comanche horses. Tumult! War! Blood and thunder! White Protestants were God's chosen race, ordained to rule the ill-bred Indians and Mexicans, or so the doctrine of Manifest Destiny proclaimed. Racial tensions exploded. Anglo Americans insisted that the Territory of New Mexico must become English-speaking. Reformation Protestants clashed with Catholic New Mexico, politicians in Washington didn't trust brown-skinned Catholic New Mexicans. Those roots of racial prejudice still live with us today.

Alfonso heard stories about Billy the Kid from his grandfather, Liborio Mares. The Kid liked to show up at dances in the village of Puerto de Luna. Singing, he rode up the Pecos River to sweet-talk Mexican girls in the villages of the llano.

Martin was a quiet, plainspoken man—Rafaelita's burden if the bed's creaking springs told the story. The family grew. Was there some joy or passion in her conceiving? Or was Rafaelita's destiny only to have children and create family? That's how it was in those days, in that llano, and I guess all over this land in that common and difficult time. Children brought joy, they were her future. She would care for them; even in the poverty of that land, she would care for them. There was no poverty in her heart. She slept peacefully. She had a purpose not of any man's making.

Alfonso heard the coughs of a dying man asking for a drink of water with his last breath, asking absolution. Who? A man shot in the village cantina. They dragged him out and laid him on the dusty street. Everyone ran to see, his wife hysterical, crying into the dust-driven wind. The ghost of the man was already grieving.

The voices of the dead, crying in the wind.

Alfonso walked into the llano, a child alone. His mother watched from the door of the adobe house they called home. He became a speck in the immense land, then disappeared. Her heart filled with sorrow. Why him? Why her youngest son? Her older boys were in their teens, already helping their father, bringing in piñon wood from the mesa, gathering the pieces of coal the fireman threw from the train as it passed by the village. They carried wood and coal home to burn in the cast-iron stove where their mother cooked meal after meal, ad infinitum.

Her older sons, Salomon, Laute, and Martinito, were strong, agile boys, but what of Alfonso? What had he heard when he lay curled in her womb? One warm night she had stepped outside for some fresh air and walked to the owl tree. The owls called as usual, but the movement in her belly surprised her. Had he heard the owls?

A summer thunderstorm came down like a wolf, full of sound and fury. She felt serene until the first blast of thunder, and she felt him move to the sound.

A vaquero was bringing in Tapia's bull when suddenly it broke the lariat and came charging at her in the garden, where she was weeding—the old bull grunting, tearing up clods of wet earth as it charged. She froze for an instant, then threw the bucket she was holding in its face. The angry bull turned and ran off. Trembling, she ran her hands over her full belly; he had felt her fear.

He was aware; the sounds and emotions of the world passed through the thin membrane of her womb to him. A realization. Her blood nourished him, as did her emotions. He heard the varied songs of nature and responded. She felt joy in her heart, and thereafter she would sit alone in the shade of the juniper tree and sings lullabies.

Duérmete, niño lindo, en los brazos del amor . . .

Mientras que duerme y descansa, la pena de mi dolor.

A la ru, a la me, a la ru, a la me . . .

a la ru, a la me, a la ru, a la ru, a la me.

New Mexico's rivers aren't navigable, but traders used the old river trails to get from Taos to the southern pueblos like Isleta, trading deer leather and apples for corn. They followed the Pecos as far south as the Ruidoso area. Men eager to trade goods or to see a querida in a distant plaza walked to Alburquerque, Santa Fe, Española, Chimayó, Embudo, and Taos. There was commerce along the New Mexico rivers, especially during fiestas. If the Matachines were dancing in Bernalillo or if Santo Domingo was celebrating a corn dance, then young men from the far-flung villages were sure to saddle up and ride to the fiesta.

Such commerce spread the songs and poetry of the people. Musicians with guitars or fiddles were always ready to play. For birthdays they played "Las Mañanitas," for dances la varsoviana or polkas, and during Christmas "Los Pastores." A song for every occasion, poems recited on the spot if a young man was courting his novia. Romances, inditas, corridos, canciones, décimas, and the alabados of the penitentes. Songs, stories, and poems passed down in the oral tradition that nurtured the people.

Many a summer afternoon, Martin would sit under the juniper tree and sing for his children: "Delgadina" or "La Cautiva Marcelina," and a variety of inditas. Not only would Edwina, Angie, and Alfonso sit listening raptly to the music, but a few neighborhood kids would gather, too. Then a vecino might appear with a couple of cold home-brewed beers, and later his wife would arrive to visit.

Historical continuity alive in the folksongs, scales the medieval church had employed centuries before, were heard in the mountains and llanos of New Mexico, modes going all the way back to ancient Greek music. The world was full of music for Alfonso, from his days in the womb and on.

Rafaelita often saw a look in his eyes, a gaze that stared beyond the present. Where did that come from? Were those her secret dreams that shone in his eyes?

"Let him go," her husband said more than once. "There's much work to do."

He was right. Her children needed her, the man who lay beside her at night needed her; she worked, cooking, washing, saving what little money her husband brought home to buy staples: flour, sugar, lard, coffee, pinto beans, potatoes. There was much work to do. And there was Alfonso. She knew he went to see Agapita. "Maybe he belongs more to her than to me," she whispered to herself. The old woman had touched him. She gave his soul to the owls. Perhaps her touch runs in his blood.

"I will never know," she thought, and turned to go into the house. So much to do. The strain of hard work was already clawing at her body.

"My destiny brought me here," she whispered, "away from the safety of my father's home, to marry and raise children, to work until my back aches and my fingers are bruised. I accept my destiny, for my children I accept my fate. I accept my burden as every woman before me has accepted. I pray to God and all the saints, I accept."

He walked into the immense landscape, summer land of gramma grass, yucca, flowering cactus, there where the eagle cried and marked his way. He looked at every object in his path: birds, insects, the crying cicadas, the lizards called escupones, rattlesnakes, rabbits, jackrabbits, quail, coyotes hiding, and above, the ever-circling buzzards. In a land where death came often, the buzzards left carcasses picked clean to the bone, testaments to what once was.

Everything was a miracle to the child. My child. My young Alfonso.

In the ever-reaching arch of sky, clouds gathered and rose, and the child stood in awe.

"I came from there," he told his mother. "From clouds and sky, from a faraway place. I came from there," he said, and pointed at the majesty of sky.

"Yes," she said, and called it heaven. "You came from heaven." He went on believing in heaven as children believe, until later sorrow entered his heart, and he knew he would have to find heaven all over again.

Dear K,

It's hot, but I'm not going to talk about the weather. I want to concentrate on what I remember . . . I have trouble remembering details, you know, one of the consequences of getting old. In his last books Alfonso spoke a lot about memory. We are all haunted by our memories. Am I writing memories when I write these letters? Yes, I think that's all that's left. But where do I start?

You're too young to remember, but Fonso and I shared a tumultuous transition into our manhood years during the time we were at the university. We enrolled the same year, 1958; Fonso graduated in 1963. The fifties and the sixties, rock-and-roll years, great years. Why did he wait two years to start at the University of New Mexico after graduating from high school? I'll get to that.

There's so much to write about. Why does one remember certain events, brief images left from those events, and not others? So one writes fiction. Everything is fiction, isn't it? Fonso said everything that's ever been written is fiction. All the bibles and histories and biographies of the world, fiction. Records of all the wars fought, civilizations conquered and those destroyed, fiction. Was that realization a sorrow? Can we live in a world composed of fictions?

He made an exception for mathematics. Maybe there was some truth in the Hubbell telescope's photos of faraway galaxies and mathematical equations that got closer and closer to describing the nature of the universe. He was no mathematician, but he had a keen love for science and its march toward revelation. And might those revelations cause our eventual destruction? The march of computers, which would someday compose their own reason for being. Especially the quantum computers. They're here, you know.

He meant by fiction that whatever one writes is filtered through the personal, and therefore by its very nature is a world composed by self, a fiction. Solipsism. Something like that. More and more he believed that what our senses call reality is illusory. The world as illusion. Was it because he had gotten older, and the old seem to understand the vanity of things that once seemed so real and important? Or was he heir to those eastern philosophies that came to Spain and then to México and finally to his little world in New Mexico?

Cada cabeza es un mundo, thus spake his ancestors. Each mind is a world. If each mind is a world unto its own, then the worlds that others imagine must be illusions because we can't know them. Another person's mind can't be quantified. There are a million thoughts, desires, and dreams buzzing in every mind at any given time.

In this universe we can't know both the speed and the location of a particle at the same time. The mind is like that, traveling through space, never in the same time at the same place.

His early worldview was constructed from his Catholic upbringing, his mother's deep faith. This world is a vale of tears, and we can know Truth only in heaven. God or the Logos is the truth, but we can't really know the Divine Mind as long as we're clothed in flesh. We go on believing that what we read, see, touch, hear, and smell is real, and all of that is gone in a flash. He would have made a good Buddhist. Or Plato unclothed.

The sun was shining so strongly, it turned the grassland into a burning plain. El llano en llamas, the plain on fire. Then clouds appeared in the brilliant blue clear sky, and rain pelted the earth with large, glistening drops. "The devil is chasing his wife," the village children sang when it rained while the sun shone. The devil had a wife, and she could be as full of mischief as her mate. What was her name?

"The devil is a trickster," his mother said. "Don't fall for his tricks. He will lead you down a slippery slope. Stay close to the saints, they will protect you. Jesús, Virgen María, San José, Santa Ana, San Martín, Santo Niño de Atocha." She prayed by owl light late into the night, the holy rosary, novenas, prayers her parents had taught her, penitente alabados, old prayers from Catholic Spain. Her sleepy children knelt around her, plodded into the Hail Marys, *Diós te salve*

María . . . She prayed in Spanish, that ancient language of the Nuevo Mexicanos.

Stay awake, the devil makes you sleepy. Haven't I told you, he plays tricks. *Santa María, madre de Diós* . . .

In the heat of summer, dust devils rose up from the dry earth, swirling storms running across the searing land, lifting dust and tumbleweeds into the air, choking man and beast.

"The devil's in the wind! The devil rides the whirlwind. Run! Run!" sisters Edwina and Angie called. "If the dust devil sweeps over you, the devil will grab you!"

Make the sign of the cross! Hold your thumb over your forefinger to form a cross and hold it up to the whirlwind. It will turn away! The devil can't face the Jesus cross! Jesus died for your sins!

The wind came down like a ravenous coyote ready to break the rabbit's neck, but Alfonso stood his ground. He didn't make the sign of the cross. He waited for the dust devil to strike. It came upon him with the roar of a train, blasting him so hard he almost fell over, but he held on. He heard a voice in the rushing wind. "Son," the wailing wind cried, stretching out the word. "Saaaaaaa-on." Then the whirl-wind passed over him, leaving him smitten, trembling, pelted by the dirt and weeds of the great grandfather storm.

"Grandfather," Fonso answered, his eyes burning with tears, smil-ing.

He could smile. Even as he pulled together his tattered shirt and wiped his eyes, he could smile. He had heard the voice in the wind, and it was good. The whirlwind went racing across the llano, and everything in its path took cover. A cold silence filled the vacuum the wind left. He had heard the voice in the wind, devil or no devil.

"Crazy Fonso," the kids cried. "The devil got him!"

"No," Agapita said. "Everything in our body and out there on earth is God, not the devil. The devil is only what evil men do."

One time as he was approaching the old woman's hut, a hailstorm rose in the west. It came suddenly, dark clouds, flashes of lightning that turned neon-blue, then yellow and red; thunder blasted the harsh rain into his face, hail as big as ping-pong balls. There was no place to hide. A storm like that could injure exposed man or beast.

Agapita ran toward him. In one hand she held a knife, in the other her scapular. The image of Our Lady of Sorrows on the scapular had long since faded, erased by the old woman's sweat, grime, and sloughed-off skin cells.

"See," she told Alfonso. "Our Lady's face. She is here. See. La Virgen giving birth to Jesús el Nazareno. Ponte a pensar. Think on it. The Virgin Mary knew that her only son would be tortured and crucified. Think, Alfonso. She was a girl, maybe just eighteen. She gave birth to God, and holding the baby in her arms, she knew He would die on the cross. That is why we call her Our Lady of Sorrows. The village church carries her name. All women know sorrow."

"How many sorrows are there?" Alfonso asked, a serious question for one so young. Did he already carry sorrow in his heart? Did he know? Were his dead ancestors already mourning his passage through life?

"Seven," she answered. "Pray to God."

Alfonso looked skyward. The old woman laughed. "Yes, clouds and rain fall on this earth that runs in your blood. That's all you will ever know of God. God gives and He takes away. He is the instrument of sorrow."

Alfonso looked perplexed. It was clear he didn't understand.

Agapita didn't care. Her owl eyes were fixed on her journey. The mourning of her ancestors grew louder with each passing day. The wind carried their grief.

She blessed the boy. "¡Véte!" she said. "Go. Your life will not easy. Gracias a Diós."

As the first hailstones began to fall from the dark cloud, Agapita jumped in front of the howling wind and sliced the air with the long knife. She prayed, "Our Lady of Sorrows, we beg you, cut the storm in two. Save this boy. He has a destiny. God of ice, do not press close on this boy. Santo Niño de Atocha, his mother loves this boy."

Agapita stood like a rock of ages, cutting the storm in two, just like

---

Moses when he parted the Red Sea. Maybe he had a knife like Agapita's. The dark, dangerous storm parted and turned away, thrashing and groaning like a wounded monster, howling a death cry and bleeding red lightning. The two halves turned away from the boy and disappeared down a river canyon.

He had felt the power inherent in the old woman. The same hands that had pulled him from his mother's womb had parted the storm and left him in the calm middle, the eye of the storm, which was the eye of God. Only soft, cold rain fell, silently, wetting him to the bone. He opened his mouth and drank the raindrops on his tongue.

"A blessing," the old woman said. She placed her scapular around his neck. "Go and suffer the devil," she said.

So it had been when the giant dust devil swept over him. He had heard a voice in the wind, groaning as if in pain. The child born of woman was a thin stick the powerful whirlwind could have lifted and dashed against the ground. But the child had been blessed countless times by his mother. He bore the mark of her sorrow. The wind had turned away, leaving the boy shaking but unhurt.

Rafaelita, who had seen the dangerous whirlwind approaching, ran to call her children to safety. She stopped when she saw her son standing in the vacuum left by the wind. Her fear subsided. Her son was of the wind, but so were all who were born on that desolate land.

The sorrow she had felt at the birth of her son was lifted from her heart. He was bound to live a tragic life, and he would leave sorrowful footprints along his path as he journeyed through life. Still, some kind saint might watch over him.

She passed her nervous hands across her apron and called him to supper.

He was baptized in the village church, Our Lady of Sorrows. Neighbors attended, the wind-worn rancheros of the area, their work-worn wives and thin, stringy children. The priest who came from Santa Rosa de Lima to give mass only once a month splashed holy water on the baby's forehead.

Alfonso? Why Alfonso?

It is the name the owls gave him.

In the old and fragile bell tower, the wind grieved and cried. Pigeons cooed and flew away. A last angry gust of wind made the dry boards rattle, then passed on, joining the greater winds of the open plain, the wind that circled the universe.

A joyful day, lots of drink and good food set out on tables in front of the church. Some of the men drank too much; a guitar and a fiddle appeared, and the people danced. Dust and loud cries rose from the merriment. Even the priest danced, then fell, drunk. He would sleep it off in the church that night, wake up, ask forgiveness, and go home.

A respite from the daily toil. When the fiesta was done, the invited drifted away. Tomorrow was a day of work.

Maybe a different name would have saved him from sorrow. Is our destiny wrapped up in our names? Alfonso I am, and Alfonso I will become. Would being named José, Tomás, or Carlos have saved him? No, I don't think a name can save you from the blows that come from living. Hercules was not saved, and neither was Prometheus, both strong names. We are bound by our names.

Every event passes into the cycle that is the life of a man, and each new experience blends into a greater cycle. Life passes from birth to death; the child born today will die tomorrow. This is the awful truth we know deep in our hearts.

All is transient. Women know this intuitively. They bear the greatest sorrow. The mother and the old midwife passed their sense of sorrow along to Alfonso. Of that, I'm sure.

I, too, have known sorrow, and sometimes I think I am Alfonso. Like him, I learned that sorrow is a gift. Without that deep emotion of loss, we cannot fully appreciate life. Living depends on suffering. Sorrow is our guide through life's illusions. A heart that has felt loss lives fully. Perhaps that's what those philosophers who preached the dark night of the soul meant.

Or the Buddhists. Erase the past and the future. Live in the present moment. Alfonso had written something like that. "The past is a memory," he said. "We are truly alive only in the thin instant that is the present, before we pass into the future that no one can know. We have only that split second in which to peer into the Absolute. Only in that precious moment can we erase suffering and sorrow.

"The goal is to be authentic, real to oneself and others. Real in a universe that is indifferent to us. Stand alone in that immense and brooding mystery and shout, I am real! I am here! The earth decays and passes away, and I too will pass away! But now I am here!"

"No, mijito," Agapita counseled. "The universe is not indifferent to us. We are little bits of light in nature's bosom. We are made of the same energy as stars and earth. Yes, flesh dissolves, but our souls grow on."

Fonso was learning about the organic universe that at first had seemed so far away. The universe wasn't only in sun and stars, it was in the leaves that fell from trees in autumn, the apples he tasted, the air he breathed, the water he splashed on his face in the morning.

I'm sorry, I didn't mean to get carried away. I don't want to write bullshit. I'll stick to what I know about Alfonso. Write from a distance. Even the stories documenting the life of Jesus were written from a distance, many years after his death.

The passage of time haunts us all, and all that's left in the wake of time are vague memories.

So it is with the life of my friend, my crippled Alfonso.

Dear K, hope you're well.

The wheel of fortune spins without mercy, but once in a long while it stops at an interval that blossoms with ecstatic joy, a revelation that transforms, an epiphany that reveals the authentic soul, the true purpose of life. Such moments bring joy beyond comprehension or critical thinking. This kind of joy fills soul and flesh.

The wheel can also stop at moments of misfortune. Not joy, but punishment of soul and flesh as fate decrees. Fate, fortune, or destiny, call it what you will. Nuevo Mexicanos call it el destino, a belief as old as the ancient philosophers from Iberia: Moors, Jews, and Christians. Or maybe belief in destiny is not taught by the culture, but comes bound in the bloodstream, generation after generation, an archetypal intuitive feeling that resounds in the travesties life brings. Feelings become images, become beliefs, and such beliefs have worked their way into Nuevo Mexicano culture. Faith. This ancient land is ruled by faith.

Alfonso recognized the role of el destino, destiny embedded in thought, music, poetry, everyday language, unto death.

Martin, Alfonso's father, believed that Fonso's accident was the working of destino. What could he do when they brought his son's mangled body home? It was God's will, and God wrote each man's destiny.

It was Rafaelita who clutched at Alfonso as if trying to right the wrong. Knowing the accident was meant to be, in one way or another she had mourned his fall.

Not fall from grace, no, just one of those accidents, such as happen every day to sons and daughters. Long ago his mother had acknowledged the fragility of the flesh that once rested in her womb. She may not have known the specific time when fortune's heavy weight would fall on one of her children, but from the beginning she had felt that inner sense of sorrow. Destiny would unravel the lives of those she loved most.

Intuition? Did Agapita know? She who ate rabbit meat and tossed the carcasses to the owls. She had cursed Alfonso by telling him the dead mourn for the living.

She had pulled Fonso into the breath of life and offered her owl wisdom to the just-born baby. He was her son, and to prepare him for life, she gave advice clothed in metaphors that not even Vilmas, the local village poet, could decipher. Vilmas sang poems at every village celebration and at the cantina on Saturday nights. He was the only one from the village who had traveled to California, but he was no match for the old woman.

Agapita didn't just mouth the old Spanish dichos everyone knew: cada cabeza es un mundo, el diablo no es diablo por ser malo, es diablo por ser viejo, una mujer con un diente que llama a toda la gente. No, she spoke directly to the heart of the boy, using the language of the llano, using the direct metaphors of the world in which they lived. Nature's language.

As he drifted in and out of consciousness, Fonso remembered her warning: Don't chase the snake.

She loved him and had taught him reverence for nature. Nature was to be his church. Honor all creatures. For her the chain of being was a unity, a continuous energy. The villagers called it God. Insect, beast, or fowl, all had a purpose, and man was not to interfere. Man was not given domain over the world; he was but one link in the chain of timeless energy that stretched from earth to the heavens.

Fonso didn't understood why she had cautioned him about snakes. The snakes of the llano, because they slithered across the face of the earth and lived in dark holes, were closest to the earth's energy. Snakes felt the pulse of the earth as few other creatures could.

He was to honor snakes for their wisdom. They brought rain to the parched grassland. When he ran across the llano, the rattlesnakes he disturbed did not strike at him. He was learning to live in harmony with nature, as the old woman had predicted.

The trains that carried the nation's goods passed by the village, awesome monsters whose steel wheels screeched against shiny rails laid on oily black ties that lay like ribs on raised earth and gravel berms. Spewing columns of smoke and sparks, and bawling like the devil, trains seemed out of place in the grassland, infringing on the peaceful silence of the llano, spooking the ranch animals.

Pulling a long line of dark boxcars, pregnant and bulging with goods destined for foreign markets, trains had to slow down on the wide curve around the village. Pasty faces stared out through the soot-covered windows of the passenger cars. The children of the village liked to run alongside the trains and wave at the faces, and sometimes the faces waved back. Americanos, the people said. Where were they going? The faces stared at Alfonso standing by the track. A child in a car waved, then the train moved on.

"Those in the train are dead," Agapita said. "Don't believe in them. Only we live." She laughed. "I have lived for centuries. See, my skin is wrinkled like dry earth cracks. I was here before trains and cars and barbwire. I could fly everywhere without getting tangled in that damned wire. Cuando llegó el alambre, llegó el hambre. When wire came, hunger came. They came and fenced the llano into little squares. Like their souls, fenced in. Our freedom on the llano is dying.

"Late one day I'm sitting quietly, and some vaqueros stop to make a campfire. They think I'm an old juniper stump, dry enough to burn. If they throw me in the fire, I would burn down to ashes. I thank God for that. From ashes we come and to ashes we go. Like the cigaro I smoke, the tobacco becomes ash, but the smoke rises to heaven. One vaquero reaches for me and I jump up. Scare the hell out of him. '¡Bruja! ¡Bruja!' the vaqueros shout, and I disappear. I laugh many days.

"I burn green juniper boughs and wash myself in the sweet smoke that rises. Like this." She was burning juniper branches and cleansing not only herself, but also the village and the llano. The thin, bluish smoke curled across the land.

"'Why didn't you come and get your ashes on Ash Wednesday?' the priest asks me. I laugh at him. I am already ash, pendejo. Can you see? There's no grease left in this bag of bones. Not even good to start a fire."

"You're not old," Alfonso said.

Agapita puffed on her cigaro. Marijuana smoke flowed from her nostrils. Ashes fell to the ground. With her foot she rubbed them into the earth and they disappeared. See.

The wail of the train floated across the llano, reminding Alfonso of La Llorona, the Crying Woman, who cried at night along the arroyo, looking for the children she had drowned. One afternoon when the boys were jumping in and out of the water tank, refreshing themselves, La Llorona appeared. Fonso saw the frightful figure standing by the windmill. He shivered.

The dark figure approached the boy standing on the edge of the tank.

"Fermin!" Alfonso tried to shout, but his throat was dry.

She pushed the boy, and he went flying into the tank. He hit the bottom and broke his neck. One moment, in the heat of the day, they were splashing and having fun at the tank under the windmill, the only water for miles around. The next moment she pushed Fermin, and he dove in headfirst. Fonso's best friend.

La Llorona, creature of many stories, had snatched him away. Her son, one of many. The water parted for Fermin, then gathered again, and his body floated lifeless to the top, rolling in the water like a piece of deadwood, never to breathe again.

The faraway scream of the train seemed to grieve for him, like La Llorona cries for her children. But the old bitch hadn't cried; she gave no warning, she came as a silent shadow. The boys stopped their splashing, opened their mouths wide, dripping with water, sputtering, crying, "Damn! Did you see? Pull him out! Pull him out!"

Too late. La Llorona sat quietly in the shade of the windmill, eating piñon, cracking the small nuts with her sharp teeth, spitting out the shells and chewing the delicate meat.

"I warned them," the phantom woman said. "I cried to scare them away from the water tank. They didn't believe. Or maybe the train drowned out my cry. Ah well. Just doing my work. Kids don't listen to their parents."

Who is she?

A story creature. Make-believe. No, she's real.

From where?

From the stories our parents tell. She was Medea who killed her sons, or maybe an Aztec goddess who went up and down the streets of Tenochtitlán, crying because she knew the Europeans were coming. Millions of her Indian children would die. Now she lives here by the water tank. She needs water to drown her children, and in the llano the water tank is all there is. Don't go swimming in the water tank.

But it's only a story?

Yes, but stories grow flesh and come alive. Creatures in stories become real.

Is La Llorona real?

Maybe in the old days, when people believed in stories. Video games killed her, thus killing part of the culture.

K, I've been thinking of the day Fermin died. Every man in his life-time must create a revolution. This is what Fonso remembered as he helped pull and tug and finally push the dead body over the edge of the tank to the ground. The earth received it with a dull thud.

Was this another curse from the old bruja, she who was always near, beside him, always pointing to a deeper connection with nature, prodding Alfonso into God knows what secret knowledge? He was just a boy! Let him play baseball with his friends, ride his bike down the dusty roads, look longingly at the girls, play hopscotch with them. Let him feel the warm touch of Delfina's hands—the girl who in his dreams taunted him with her kisses.

Let him be a normal kid!

Oh no, there she was at his side, whispering through cracked teeth, "Every man must create a revolution."

What did she mean? What possible meaning could the cryptic phrase have for Alfonso? Why tell him life is full of sorrow? Curses I call them, yet they were good preparation for him who was to be a cripple.

Damn! He dove in! Why?

He hit bottom!

Broke his stupid neck.

They cried and called for help, except Alfonso, who bent to touch the forehead of the dead boy. Cold and lifeless. Still wet. He knew he had to say a prayer, but was it too late? Prayer could not save him.

A couple of vaqueros coming in at the end of the day to water their horses lifted the boy onto one of the horses and took him into the village.

The boys scattered, full of fear, running to tell what had happened, to repeat the story over and over, how he stood at the edge of the water tank and dove in.

Sometimes a spirit infuses a man, telling him to act even though he does not know the consequences of his action. His destiny at work. I am God-like, he tells himself, and he does things he would never otherwise do. A revolution is always tragic because it changes the course of one's life.

What was the shadow? Alfonso asked himself. He knew. La Llorona playing tricks, acting like her sister La Muerte.

He was alone with the lapping water in the tank, the slow churning of the windmill's fan, and a trickle of water flowing from the rusty pipe and splashing into the tank. A silence had come over the land.

"It is the spirit of God," a voice said, and Alfonso didn't know if it was La Llorona who had spoken or Agapita, she who had pulled him from his sac of water into the world.

Or was it the wind that spoke? The wind of the llano was full of spirits. The voice of God whispered across the land, blessing all creatures great and small. She had taught him to listen to the voices in the wind, the old woman who ate rabbit meat.

And his mother told him stories. "When you were just a baby growing in my womb, I walked in the llano and listened to the wind. I exposed my belly so you could hear the wind. I sang beautiful songs my parents had taught me. Lullabies in the wind."

The cicadas sang. Across the llano their cries rose in exaltation. Grasshoppers chirped, chewing grass, spitting tobacco, humping each other.

"I prayed the prayers our ancestors brought to this land. Bendito sea Diós. Creo en Diós Padre. Diós te salve María. And the wind carried me away, like a kite into the clouds. This is what I gave you as my inheritance. Your father will teach you hard work, things of the world, but I gave you the songs in the wind."

La Llorona moved away. She had done her work. The boy from the Broken Wheel Ranch was dead. The cry of the train had receded into time past. The past moved on, captured only in Alfonso's heart. The dead boy, his friend. Death, a revolution without end.

That night they prayed a rosary in the village church, Our Lady of Sorrows. An hermano penitente led the mourners through the Hail

Marys and the alabados, prayers as old as Catholic Spain. He sang in a voice that sounded like a muezzin's call to prayers, the small, humble village church the minaret. Notes high and sorrowful, piercing the soul, reverberating against the ceiling timbers and flying out the open door, carrying this truth: We live for a brief moment en este valle de lágrimas.

Life in a valley of tears. That's what Fonso heard.

The next day they buried Fermin in the cemetery next to the church, the open grave a cavity in the dry llano earth.

The boy's mother had washed and wrapped the body. The blacksmith had hammered together a crude coffin from worm-eaten wood he kept in his shop. The prayers for the dead were sung by an hermano from the Puerto de Luna morada. Men lowered the coffin and covered it. A brief ceremony.

"I'm sorry," his mother said, laying her hands on Alfonso's shoulders, comforting him.

The following afternoon the boys were back splashing in the water tank, not knowing that the soul of their dead friend lay in the water. He had become a new form in the eternal recycling of forms in that harsh land. The energy of soul would not be denied.

Death is natural.

I know, but sometimes I get angry, knowing what Alfonso had to see, to feel, to experience—with the old midwife like a shadow at his side, and his mother's loving eyes trying to explain la tristeza de la vida, the inherent sadness in life.

The village boys played a game, "I dare you," chasing the train as it slowed down around the winding curve. The goal was to touch any part of the train, a game the boys practiced, an initiation. He who could run alongside the train, reach out, and touch hot black steel was no longer a boy. No longer a mocosito. He became a man. Bragging rights.

That day the brakeman shouted from his perch, cursed the crazy boys. "Get away! Get away, you sons of bitches! You're gonna kill you self!"

The boys didn't listen. They laughed and ran faster because the train was picking up speed, and soon it would be too late.

Alfonso was running that day. The older boys had dared him. "You little runt! You're always alone! Your grandma's a witch. You can't touch the train! Chicken! He got no balls! Witch ate them!"

The boys laughed, and Alfonso smiled. He would run that day, not because of the taunting, but because he was filled with spirit. It had come on suddenly, like the Holy Ghost descending. That morning he had seen a large white owl blinded by sunlight, fluttering down, swooping down in search of the juniper tree that was home. Why was it flying in daylight? Why was it lost? Why had the altar of the church crumbled to dust that morning, frightening the old women who knelt there? Why were so many signs not heeded?

Omens. A flock of geese flying south in January.

Alfonso ran to catch the train. He could run faster than all the other boys his age. Faster and faster he ran. He was filled with spirit. He would create a revolution!

The steam-scream of the whistle blasted the other boys away, exhausted, their sweaty bodies black with soot. The brakeman called one last time. "Boy! Stop, boy!"

Too late! Alfonso reached out to touch the train.

While preparing supper, his mother looked up from the meal and sighed. A shudder passed through her heart. She tossed her apron aside and rushed out into the lingering afternoon. The sun lay blood-red in the west. Why? She ran.

Agapita, searching along the arroyo for wild onions and other herbs, lifted her head and sniffed the wind. It is as I said, she thought. The world is full of sorrow. It will bend down at God's command and touch our lives, and there's nothing we can do.

Already the women of the village were coming out of their homes, dressed in black, lamenting.

K, this is what Fonso told me.

She tossed the sack of herbs aside and hurried out of the arroyo, sidestepping the huge rattlesnake whose rattler sounded like a Matachines dancer's gourd, those dancers who long ago danced on the feast day of San Lorenzo, before the village had begun to disappear.

The wind was blowing everything away.

"Madrecita," the old woman addressed the snake, "let me pass, hijita." The snake shook its rattle once more, blinking as if to say, It's too late. Pass, but it's too late.

Alfonso's father, herding a few steers toward the village corral, pulled softly on the horse's reins. I don't feel well, he thought. Something I ate. No, it was something that happened a few days ago.

He was riding home across the darkening plain after a hard day's work. Days were always hard on the llano. Made a man pure muscle and gristle, tough as railroad steel. He never complained. He fed his family, provided a roof for his children and his wife, the young woman from the Puerto de Luna Valley who had come to live with him on the llano.

Life was difficult but good. On Saturday afternoons, some of his amigos and compadres gathered under the juniper tree to talk about work, sing, and drink the bootleg booze Moises cooked in a still up in the hills. Many years later, Alfonso's cousin would take him there and show him the place, a rusted stove and scattered bottles. The cousin took him to a stash of sandstone metates that he said were once used by Comanches to grind buffalo jerky. And maybe to grind dry mesquite pods, wild grass seeds, or peyote buttons.

The children sat nearby and listened. Martin played the guitar, and Alfonso's older sisters, Edwina and Angie, sang Delgadina's song for the men. The men laughed and threw nickels and dimes at the girls' feet, which they scooped up, then ran to the village store to buy candy.

Fonso enjoyed those childhood days. He remembered the songs

his father had sung and the presence of the hard-muscled vaqueros and the gaiety and happiness the singing created. Neighbors
appeared with food and drink, and a spontaneous fiesta broke out.
The kids ran and played kick the can and hide-and-seek. It seemed to
Alfonso that the songs of his father went out across the land and beat
down even the cry of La Llorona.

"Death stay away," the songs said. "Comadre," they called to La
Muerte, "stay away, kind godmother, we are enjoying ourselves."
Doña Sebastiana, they called death. She, the godmother of every
person. "You can't come near when we sing. The fiesta is for the living, although we know that an ever-present God means ever-present
death. He gives and He takes away."

Alfonso took the songs to his heart, each song a story committed
to memory, a haunting. He memorized the faces of the men, their
laughter, the way they drank, the sound of their voices, their eyes
as clear as coyote eyes, always tearing, tortured by the wind of the
llano, their hands and arms tempered by work, their sneezing and
blowing into worn and tattered handkerchiefs. Everything he could
see, hear, smell, he saved in memory. The smiles of the women; they
too sang. They tapped their feet in worn-out shoes bought long ago
on credit, and they served up dishes of beans, mutton, green chile,
and tortillas.

A good time was had on those all too brief Saturdays when the
men gathered to drink and sing and talk about work. A brief respite
for the women, though each secretly worried that her man might
drink too much, for each man thought himself invincible. The bootleg whiskey awakened a restless spirit in some of the men, an angry
fire in the soul. If the drinking lasted all night, there might be consequences. A wife at home might be the way the angry demon was
appeased.

Alfonso lived a slave to that time, and everything that occurred
went into his heart and soul—and isn't that what time does? It molds
a man's soul. Especially one so young, when his soul is new on earth
and open to everything.

K, I wish I could change that part of his life. Why? Because he allowed everything to become part of him. I felt something bad was going to happen. But no one can change the formation of soul. Every iota of experience creates soul, like a tree growing from seed holds the essence of the seed within its bark. Some call it personality. We are containers into which life is dumped. Billions of us walking across the face of the earth.

Alfonso was an old soul, cursed, to be sure. He could hear the voices of the dead in the wind, see their faces in the clouds. His father's compadre, Isidro, was thrown from a horse. That afternoon Fonso saw him and a bunch of rip-roaring vaqueros riding across the sky, chasing a ghost herd of longhorns, shouting, "La vida no vale nada!" Lariats whistling, horns slashing the air, long skeins of frothy saliva glistening in the sunlight, shod horse hooves cutting open the earth.

Was it real or imagined?

Wait! Even if I could change what was happening to him, I wouldn't. His poetic sensitivity developed on that wide land, in that small village, within that circle of the people. Let each person be what they will be.

Alfonso's story, like the story of every man, is written only in summary. A million details are lost, buried in memory. Consider this. The life of Jesus was written long after he died. One of the apostles wrote what he remembered; the other three wrote pretty much the same story. A million details were left out of his life. One would need many thick volumes, twenty or a hundred books, to tell the real story of Jesus.

That's the way it is. We write the outline of a man's life, but the million details in every man's life are lost. So I write what I remember. We enrolled at the university, and destiny led us to literature and art classes. We became aficionados of the British, French, and Italian movies of the time. Saturday nights we drank beer at Okie Joe's, smoked cigarettes, then wound up at the Casa Luna pizzeria. The waitresses provided us with free pizzas. They provided other things, too, but I'll get to that later.

I try to write what I know of his story. During those times we played billiards or went fishing on the Pecos or just hung out with the pizzeria girls, talking and drinking beer into the night. We were poor as hell, so talk is what we had to share. Our stories, our dreams, art, poetry, movies, coffee-shop Beat poets denouncing America, listening to Bob Dylan and Joan Baez.

We felt we didn't belong. We were Mexican kids from the barrio, and very few doors were open to us, but art we could do. We read. Books saved us, saved Alfonso. He began to write poems, stories. The girls loved him. Would things have been different if he had dropped out, married one of the girls at the pizzeria, worked 8 to 5, raised kids, changed his destiny? What if he had given up his dream?

Every person's destiny is sealed in a jar kept by two angels: one is terrible, the other is good. Alfonso wanted to break that jar, like Pandora broke the box of secrets. He wanted to know! Know what? Why the hunger? He wasn't satisfied. A creative spirit moved in him, as such spirits move in all artists.

These letters I write you are disjointed. Time is disjointed. Fonso knew sorrow in that precarious time. So did the characters in the books he was reading. Pip had no great expectations; neither did the crippled boy in *A Christmas Carol*. Even distant Quixote, the knight of the Sorrowful Face, was a tragic figure. He didn't achieve his dreams. Sorrow comes not only from the loss that death brings, but also from realizing that one didn't accomplish one's goal. Life must be fully lived to overcome the inherent sorrow in living. We must be able to say at the end, I suffered, but by God, I lived my dream.

Could Philip Carey say that of his human bondage? Alfonso related to his story. Philip dragged his clubfoot through life. Hell, we were all in bondage. We read the Studs Lonigan novels, Thomas Wolfe, Dylan Thomas. We related to the characters, lived in their stories. That's what made Alfonso think he, too, could write. He would write his story. But who was going to be interested in the story of a boy growing up in the New Mexico llano who knew the language of owls and the mystery of a golden fish in the river?

The spirit and stories of our ancestors drove us. Their sacrifice, suffering, and hard work moved us. We were all crippled young men on a ship of fools, floating through life, without a compass to guide us, not knowing what port we were seeking. We slept with the pizzeria girls, thinking that in their arms we would find a degree of meaning. We wrote poems and thought we were cool. Deep inside we felt a disturbing sorrow, our wasted days and nights.

The stuff we read at the university helped; ideas made us think and drove us forward.

Stories reminded us that we are born to suffer loss. Not just to know sorrow, but at one time or another to feel it to the bone. The characters whose stories we read had suffered. That's a truth.

Dear K, back to Martin. Here's his story.

Martin rode into the gloaming, the ominous dusk settling over the llano, the time of bats, owls, the lonely cry of coyotes. He thought only of getting home for supper, a time to be with his wife and children.

He was proud of his children, especially his sons. His wife took care of raising the daughters; the older boys he took to work with him, or he hired them out to ranches around Duran, which in those days had the biggest sheep herds in the county. All that's changed now.

He kept his family fed and a roof over their heads. That's all a man could do. He was a hard worker. Work made him strong. Last year a bully foreman new to the ranch where Martin worked had called him a dumb Mexican and pushed him to the ground. Martin got up and knocked the man flat. The surprised Anglo foreman was new to the ranch and thought he could lord it over the New Mexican vaqueros.

The Anglo foreman had picked the wrong man to push. Martin knew he was equal to any man when it came to working cattle, and like any other self -respecting Nuevo Mexicano, he stood his ground. Even though the ranch owner knew Martin was a good worker, he fired him.

A poor man had to work, so that September Martin took his family to Texas to pick cotton.

The New Mexicans were becoming Okies in their own land. During the Depression, many families had packed their trucks and cars and headed for the cotton fields of West Texas, looking for work. They weren't afraid of hard work. Their ancestors had settled New Mexico's sparse river valleys and the northern mountains; survival had taught them the value of work.

But Alfonso? What did the father know of his youngest son? Too protected by the mother. He wasn't made for the hard work of ranching. For what? He didn't know, and right then he had something else to deal with. A menacing ball of fire had come bounding across the darkening plain. He knew what it was. He spurred his horse to a gallop, but the fireball followed alongside, frightening the horse. Martin felt the hair on the back of his neck rise, and his heart beat faster.

"¡Cosa del diablo!" he cursed. He made the sign of the cross and spurred his horse to a full gallop. Those fireballs that haunted the night were witches clothed in the devil's fire. This one was after him, jumping and bounding, keeping up with him.

He remembered when his compadre Emilio Luna had encountered a fireball years ago. It ran his horse to death, and Emilio only escaped because days before he had etched a cross on each of the bullets in his pistol. He shot the fireball, and the next day the villagers found old Trancito dead in his house, shot through the heart. What does that tell you.

There are evil people on this earth, parents told their children. Witches who praise the devil. They gather at night, dress a black goat in garlands of flowers, and they dance and sing around the goat. And they do things. Don't go out at night. Obey your parents. Some witches turn into owls and fly; some are coyotes that prowl the night. They do the work of the Evil One. They can turn into balls of fire. Remember Emilio Luna? He saw one.

"What happened?" Fonso asked.

"Pues, he went loco. All he does is talk about the night a fireball chased him. People say he's cursed."

"Can a horse run faster than a fireball?"

"No, a horse cannot run faster than those bolas de lumbre. An exhausted horse will fall dead. Have you ever seen a frightened horse? They pin their ears, their eyes roll white, you can't hold them. A horse can kill a vaquero by falling on him. Horses, like most animals with five fingers, can smell evil."

Alfonso trembled. "What else?"

"Oh, the devil is everywhere. In the whirlwinds that sweep across

---

the llano. He waits at the door of the cantina. He sends his witches to tempt you."

Temptation, Alfonso wrote years later. Did his father's encounter with the fireball have to do with temptation? Agapita said that all men fall.

The prior Sunday, a handsome woman in a black dress had attended mass in the village church. She was from a rancho where Martin had worked the previous month. The people whispered. Everyone knew.

Temptation. One disobeys the rules. Like the girl from the Milagro ranch who, or so the story went, disobeyed her parents and went to a dance without their permission. She danced all night with a handsome stranger who at midnight took off his white gloves. He had pig's feet instead of hands. The girl had danced with the devil.

Some of those stories scared the hell out of the children. That's how they learned to obey their parents. Today kids are free all over the place. No respect. They only love their electronic gadgets.

Had Martin's temptation taken the form of a fireball? Maybe. When you do something bad, the knowledge of what you did takes form and haunts you.

He spurred his horse, and still the fireball kept pace. He knew his horse would soon drop. The holy names he flung at the devil's fire didn't turn it away. He swallowed the dry fear that filled his mouth and pulled his horse to a sudden stop.

He carried a small-caliber pistol in his saddlebag, which he used to shoot coyotes. With trembling hands he pulled out the pistol, jumped to the ground, and fired point-blank at the fireball. Three times he fired, and at close range he knew he couldn't miss. He called the holy names: "¡Jesús, María y José!"

But his bullets weren't etched with the Holy Cross. The devil's demons can't be killed by human means. It takes a devil to kill a devil. The fireball screamed in pain and bounded away. That scream would haunt Martin's nightmares the rest of his life. The horse's fear-filled eyes would stare at him in nightmares.

You ask, why all this mumbo jumbo about fireballs, witches, the devil's demons, and old lady Agapita, who ate wild rabbit meat and whose cryptic messages cursed Alfonso?

Because of the stories. The witches in that fortuitous time lived in the stories, and as such they were more fearful than today's Hollywood's digital monsters. The stories were real, La Llorona was real, evil was real. Today's fantastic creatures in movies and video games are make-believe. The kids know that. It's not like listening to the old stories when magic was real. Children paid attention to the stories. Today they just flip off the video monster and move on to the next one.

The speed of the Internet is killing us. They say it's good to be connected, it serves the world—but is it making us complacent? Is it just a game?

Children no longer know the story of the Crying Woman. She's a quaint old lady compared to the latest bloodsucking vampire in the movies. There are so many monster shows and games to choose from that evil has been dumbed down. A new time with its own evil has arrived. Children around the world are being butchered by evil men who make war to stay in power.

Alfonso was raised in a time when people believed the devil was real. Folk stories were part of the mythopoetic, the communal sharing of beliefs. Such beliefs disappeared as people no longer told their stories to the children. Alfonso knew the stories; the folktales were ingrained in him. You can't erase childhood. What the child was, the man becomes.

What will happen when our stories die?

"I grew up in a house of prayer," Fonso once told me. His mother was a votary of the Virgin Mary, la Virgen María, la Guadalupana. When he was at the university, Alfonso wrestled with God, tossing him into and out of his life, but he never forgot his mother's prayers. He remembered kneeling through a thousand and one rosaries his mother prayed, night after night, for the safe return of her sons.

World War II had come to the llano; ranch and town boys enlisted and went over there.

Magic and miracles existed in our lives. I know, I grew up in a small village. I know what it was like.

Village cultures have existed since the beginning of time. All over the world, in small jungle communities, on lonely mountains or deserts, it's all the same. Folk wisdom is the content of village stories. People rooted in nature and the spirits that reside in nature create folktales, legends, myths. Read the ancient Greek epics, or the adventures of heroes from ancient Persia, Mesopotamia, India, the Old Testament. All those stories evolved in village cultures.

We wouldn't have folktales if it weren't for the storytellers from those communities. The folktales became the content of Fonso's soul. Soul is built from stories. People close to nature were our first storytellers. Long before we had books and libraries and electronic media, we had storytellers. A good storyteller knows how to capture your imagination. The old people Alfonso listened to were some of the best.

Those storytellers were creative. They understood the workings of good and evil, and they told the story to fit the crime. Yes, there's always a crime behind a story. A wrongdoing. Adam and Eve were tempted; so was Jesus. A need to be God-like drives the crime.

Desires of a restless heart.

From the beginning of time, families have gathered around storytellers and listened to moral tales, how good and evil came to humankind. The soul remembers how it came to earth, it knows the mysteries of nature and gods. In the beginning was the Word—or was it a lotus blossom? Storytellers gather the stories of the village, give them form, and return the epics to the people. Remember Homer?

After Fonso was married, he and his wife attended ceremonies along the Rio Grande, the Matachines dances in Bernalillo, fiestas at the Indian pueblos, where they sat attuned to hypnotic drumming, the chorus singing, the appearance of sacred messengers dancing in the plaza. I think he was rekindling what he had learned as a child. He wanted to keep alive the nature of village life, its sense of tradition and wisdom.

Do we need a rebirth of soul? If we do, does that mean we have lost part of our original soul?

Dear K, today I feel sad. I know I had to get to the train accident sooner or later. So here's my story based on what Fonso told me.

Running on the treacherous train bed, panting, leaping over the railroad ties, Fonso reached out to touch the moving train. You know what happened next. His hand caught on a bar of steel, and the force of the speeding train flipped him away like a rag doll.

He tumbled through the air and hit the ground hard enough to smash every bone in his body. Some guardian angel had kept him from falling underneath the sharp, churning wheels.

His friends watched in horror as Alfonso flew through the air. The train swept on, its long, mournful whistle taunting the boy who had won the dare. He had touched the train and lost. La Llorona had won.

His frightened friends ran, shouting, "He fell! He fell! The train ran over him! Help! Help!" A neighbor who had seen the boys racing after the train picked up Fonso's mangled body and carried him home.

Even before she heard the boys screaming, Alfonso's mother knew what had happened. A fluttering in her heart told her, a sinking feeling. She was a woman of intuitions. She felt accidents and deaths before they happened.

"Mi hijo," she cried softly. She made the sign of the cross in front of the statue of the Virgin Mary, then hurried out. It always came like this, a feeling of doom, a sudden knowledge, dread coursing through her blood. An image of a crumpled rag doll appeared, her youngest son, the one who walked alone on the llano. Something terrible had happened. All was in God's hands. "Diós mío, protect my son! Virgen María, take care of my son!"

She hurried outside, where she met the neighbor carrying Alfonso. Taking Fonso in her arms, she hurried into the house. She laid him on the bed, kissed his forehead, thanked God he was alive. Alfonso smiled, telling her he was sorry. She hushed him, reassuring him that all was well, what happened happened.

"Call your father," she told the girls. "Go for Agapita! Hurry!"

Fonso's frightened sisters ran out the door.

Pain was settling in, for both mother and son. Neighbors appeared at the door, offering help.

Alfonso's father rushed into the room and looked at his son. "Por Diós Santo, ¿qué pasó? ¿Qué pasó?"

"The train—"

"The train! The damn train! Chasing the train!"

"Go for Agapita." He understood that cursing the train wouldn't help his son. A panting Agapita entered.

"Alfonso," he said.

"I know," she answered.

She leaned over Alfonso. He cried, "My arm, my arm!" The pain burned through his arm, which had taken the brunt of the fall. "Bring me whiskey," she said, and Martin hurried to get the bottle. She took a small bag of marijuana from between her breasts and poured a handful of marijuana into the glass of whiskey Alfonso's father handed her.

"Sana, sana, colita de rana," she whispered, looking into Alfonso's eyes, gauging his pain, assuring the mother the boy would be all right. "Drink. You will be the town drunk," she said. "Drink." She helped Rafaelita cut away his shirt and pants. "See, his left hand and foot are bruised and already swelling."

"You won't wear these again," Agapita joked, tossing the shoes and clothes aside. "Drink." She made Alfonso drink the whiskey potion. "The town drunk," she said again. His mother prayed as she washed away the dirt and soot from his bruised face and arms.

She kept osha roots in a jar with water. The herb was one of the most efficacious of those she kept in her kitchen cabinet. It grew mostly in mountain regions and was bought and stored with great care. She dipped a cotton towel in the water and cleaned the cuts and bruises.

The terrible feeling in her heart subsided as she ministered to her son. A root of her life had suddenly been damaged, and she felt the pain. But life on the llano was full of accidents. All the women on the llano, at one time or another, had been witness to the broken bodies of their men. Now it was time to do what needed to be done. Trust Agapita. Martin, too, trusted the old woman. They knew the miracles she had worked.

Agapita lit a cigaro. As she smoked, she felt for broken bones, her old wrinkled hands softly running over his body. The hand and the foot were obvious; she prayed she wouldn't find breaks in the spine.

"The train?"

"Yes, the devil train."

His mother had heard the whistle, the long cry that marked the time of day, and she knew that some of the boys often chased after the train. Trains loaded with army trucks, jeeps, and tanks of that fortuitous time. Munitions of war to be shipped to distant places. She had seen her older sons gaze into the distance, a gaze past the llano's horizon and as far as Japan. They would soon be gone.

He would remain, sitting by her when she cooked or mended clothes. She would ask him to hand her the things she used in her work, and he learned the names of many different objects from the woman he loved.

"Gracias a Diós," Agapita said. "Un milagro."

Agapita leaned over Alfonso, dropping cigaro ashes on his stomach.

"No big bones broken," she said. "But . . ." She held his swollen hand. "No more baseball." She touched his foot. "No dances at la cantina."

Alfonso smiled through the giddiness of the whiskey.

"Con tiempo your hand and foot will get strong. Gracias a Diós . . . In the meantime you will walk in sadness."

43

K, where was I? I went to the doctor today. My bones ache. So, where was I?

Alfonso had stolen the train's fire, the coal-burning snake that rocked from side to side with its heavy load of war matériel. He had proven himself a boy of the village, but stealing fire did not go unpunished. Every initiation ritual has consequences. Fonso wasn't alone; all across the country boys were becoming men, each in his own way entering manhood in the customs prescribed by his village, his barrio, his family.

I'm sure girls go through as many tough times as the boys. I've read a few books. I can't write one.

The train struck at Alfonso, as steel monsters throughout the world struck daily at every working man who challenged them. Faith in a new technology had come of age, the New Industrial Revolution gone wild, digital, promising a new future, yet the poor kept getting poorer.

He cried when she pulled off his shoes.

"Ooh, not going dancing," she said, smiling, all the time feeling for broken bones in the feet, which were bruised red and puffing up.

"The ladies like a man who stomps the floor when he whirls them around in a polka. Look here. The wise doctor should see this."

Was she taunting him? Was this the first lesson in his new reality? Was she teaching a lesson called aguántate in Spanish? Suck it in. We're not there yet, so hold it!

Alfonso's mother sat at his side, feeling her son's pain, aware that this was but one day in his unrolling destiny. She trusted the old woman. Everyone knew the miracles she had performed. Her healing powers were as old as those of Ultima. You know that book.

She continued to give Alfonso sips of whiskey. The liquid burned his throat, but it numbed the pain.

"Not cooked yet," Agapita said. "The yerba buena"—that's what she called marijuana—"has to cook in the whiskey to be potent. But we don't have time. You have to take him to the doctor in town. I have done what I can."

Across the room, Alfonso's sisters sobbed in silence, gulping down heaves of worry and fear. They thought their brother was dying. No one could touch a moving train and live.

Alfonso looked around and realized that his pain was reaching out and becoming their pain, his mother's pain. She would feel it in her heart for as long as she lived.

"Pain means you are alive," Agapita said, rubbing the ashes from her cigaro on his stomach until an image appeared. "Ah," she said. "Look. It's clubfoot Jesus. Your patron saint."

The ashes had formed a crude face of Jesus, but Jesus nevertheless. See. She made the sign of the cross.

His mother leaned over to see, and she, too, crossed herself. Blessed be God.

Why did Agapita call him clubfoot Jesus? She believed the nails driven into the feet of Jesus had left him a cripple. Three days later, when he walked out of the tomb, he limped. He must have.

The large, rusty nails had torn apart tendons, muscles, and bones.

Mary saw Jesus limp. She cried out, as Alfonso's mother had cried out to see her son so battered and, she thought, near death.

Mary knelt at the feet of Jesus, poured oil on the open wounds, and lightly washed the crusted blood away with her long dark hair. Some say the wounds closed, but those who truly hold Jesus in their hearts know he walks with a limp. How could it be otherwise?

"Your patron saint," Agapita repeated, and Alfonso smiled. He was falling asleep. But he understood. The old woman had taught him life on the llano. Now she was preparing him for the days ahead by telling the Jesus story, a metaphorical whisper that only Alfonso understood.

Nails were hammered through the hands' bone and cartilage. The disfigured Jesucristo, God. Throughout history, different cultures have created gods who are very human. Not like the Greek gods in

Olympus, but down-to-earth gods. Gods who went fishing, hung out with regular folk, enjoyed a cup of wine at a fiesta, maybe even admired the dark-haired dancing beauties.

¡Sí! Why not?

Some say the tomb was empty when Mary had men remove the large boulder at the entrance. Some say it wasn't Mary, but a woman with long dark hair who went to the tomb and called his name. Was he gone? Had he risen as promised? No, he was just slow in walking out of the tomb into the rising sun. He limped, greeted his mother, and with battered hands he blessed her. "In the name of the Father and love everlasting, do not grieve. I still have work to do."

And Mary whispered, "Son."

Alfonso's mother wiped his hands with a cloth soaked in osha water, soaked with her tears. She would save the cloth and thereafter use it to wipe away future accidents her other children might suffer. She prayed that her son would live. The prayer of every mother when she washes away a son's pain.

Had Mary used a towel or the hem of her dress to wipe away her son's crusted blood? I don't remember the church saying anything about a blessed cloth with her sorrow imprinted on it. That would be a holy relic. Like the figure of the Virgin Mary was imprinted on Juan Diego's tilma when she appeared to him on the Hill of Tepeyac near México City in 1531. Or the face of Jesus on the Shroud of Turin. There are other accounts of holy people leaving traces behind, like the bones of St. James in Santiago Compostela.

Mary wept. Her sorrow. Her son had suffered, died, then moved on as promised. She used her hair to wipe his wounds; maybe that's why there was no cloth, no remnants left of that morning's meeting.

Alfonso's mother turned to the picture of Jesus on her small altar. She believed the heart of Jesus was alive with fire and compassion, burning away the sins of the world. Could it burn away her son's pain? Yes. She believed.

"Once an Anglo priest came to say mass," Agapita said, rolling between her lips the cigaro she had lit. "He asked my name. 'Agapita,' I told him. 'Agape,' he said. Agape! My comadres laughed. So I was given a new name. Agape. Oh, I have many names. The people call me bruja, hechicera, mujer que no ha pecado, curandera. Some call me loca. Mujer que no puede morir. The dead pray for me, but I cannot die. I think that gringo priest was smart. I liked my new name, Agape."

Alfonso smiled.

"A new name," she said. "When man or woman create a revolution, they need a new name. Even if they keep it secret from others. Alfonso of the Seven Sorrows," she whispered.

She forced the last of the last of the whiskey into his mouth, and he closed his eyes.

"I can do no more," she said. "This tragic day is just the beginning." She blessed Alfonso's forehead, making the sign of the cross, not from left to right but from right to left. As if the train's cruel steel were still stuck in the flesh and she had to be very gentle.

"We have to go," Alfonso's father said. "¡Vamos!"

Rafaelita threw a sheet over the boy. Martin picked him up and hurried to the truck. The mother grabbed some clothes and told her daughters they would soon be back, blessing them as she went out.

They flew down the two-lane road to Santa Rosa de Lima, the same road used by Mexican workers when they came to work on the cattle ranches. The Anglo ranchers prized them because they were excellent vaqueros, respected even by the cowboys from Texas.

Agapita shouted into the wind, "Those vaqueros from the deserts of Chihuahua could rope a steer blindfolded. See, they blindfold the steer." Her cry shredded the silence of the llano. Coyotes laughed and answered her lament. The woman who ate rabbit meat was in pain. She cracked the joke about the blindfolded steer, but inside her pain was as real as Alfonso's. "Diós bruto," she cried, and the coyotes slunk away out of respect.

Martin's eyes were fastened on the road, those eyes that could spot a defect in a horse or steer a mile away, his knuckles white from his grip on the steering wheel. He found it difficult to look at his son.

Alfonso lay cradled in his mother's arms, moaning from time to time. Soon the effects of the whiskey would wear off.

"We're almost there," she reassured him. "Hurry," she told her husband. "Hurry." The nightmare was beginning. "How could this happen? Diós mío, I trusted you. Why did this happen?"

Stories and legends describe mothers holding dying sons in their arms. Pietas repeat throughout the world. Now it was her turn, her story unfolding, full of pain and worry. The crippled Jesus. What did Agapita mean? It's true, a woman had gone to his tomb early the third morning following his crucifixion. Did he limp from the torture he had suffered on the cross? Why did pictures never show him using crutches?

She shook away the thoughts. She would trust the Blessed Virgin. She began praying a rosary. She would take her son's pain, she would restore him.

Later, Alfonso would wonder whether one had to suffer to be close to God. Why did God permit suffering? The age-old question.

K, I'll tell you the story of the demiurge later. A violinist who takes care of earth.

Finally they arrived and made their way to the office of the only doctor in town. El Tonsils, the people called him, because he had taken out the tonsils of every kid in town. Kids loved him; he always gave them ice cream. The people trusted him even though he had never saved a life. He was old beyond repair. The people forgave him because he loved to fish. In a town where every man was a fisherman, that garnered him respect. No matter that he always fell asleep in his small boat and had never caught a fish.

Martin burst into the doctor's office and laid Alfonso on a table. Rafaelita grabbed the startled doctor.

"¡Mijo! ¡Mijo!"

The doctor looked at Alfonso.

"He fell?"

"Sí."

"Where?"

"The train!"

"Let's see." He poked the bruised body. "Does that hurt? Ah, poor hand. Handy, handy. And this foot. No dancing tonight, young man. But look at me. I wear a brace on my clubfoot, and I can fish. Life takes some things away, but gives others. You can sit by the river and fish."

He injected morphine. Alfonso fell asleep.

"You need to take him to a hospital in Alburquerque."

"No money," Martin said, shaking his head sadly.

There never is. The doctor understood. He took x-rays with an ancient machine, bandaged the hand as best he could, and fixed a sling. He bandaged the broken foot. "He won't be able to walk for a month or two. I have some crutches." He gave them a pair of old wooden crutches. "Take him home. No more whiskey. I'm going fishing. That's all I can do."

Curse that old fool! If he had x-rayed the spine, he would have found the fracture in a neck vertebra that was to bug Alfonso the rest of his life.

I'm sure I've left out some details, but that's the way it was. Too many sick and broken people depending on one doctor. They thanked the doctor and drove home. Alfonso was turning a chapter in his life, like llano grass turns with each season, the green in the juniper tree rusting.

K, here's how I'll tell it.

A few days later, Rafaelita let his friends in to visit. The kids were fascinated by the bandages. "Can he play baseball?" "Does it hurt?" "You look like a mummy."

Agapita shooed them away. "¡Cabroncitos!"

"You were born with a gift," she said, comforting Fonso.

"What gift?" Alfonso asked.

"You will bring people good luck. Money, gold, or whatever they desire."

"How do you know?" he asked.

She tapped his head with the ear of corn she was shucking. "Didn't I tell you? I know everything."

Alfonso nodded.

"The night you were to be born, I went to the tree where the owls sit and talk. I found their fresh poop on the ground and rubbed it on my hands. I was on my way to deliver you."

"Owl caca?"

"Sí. It is special, for good luck. I spread it on my hands, silver and glistening like mercury. I looked to la Loma de las Golondrinas. The mesa was blue, the deer dancing, the moon waxing, growing full like your mamá. Lightning split the air en el Cañon de Pintada, and the echo rolled as far as China. ¿Quizás? Orange and red and gold, glowing like the neon signs in town. I like to go to town to see neon signs. Bats and owls played together."

"And my gift came that night?"

"Gifts come from God, who lives in the hills."

"Not in church?"

"Bah! A building cannot hold God. The soul of God is the soul of nature. Everything comes from Madre Tierra. I think God is a woman, always giving birth. That's why the universe continues to grow. Bendito sea la Diosa."

"Am I special?"

"No, Alfonso. You are common. All men are common. Born to work, suffer, and die. One in a million rises to do something special. Only because the mother gave him huevos."

"¿Huevos?"

"Sí. Even the prophets got their huevos from their mothers. Except Adam. Ese pobre had no mother. Never tasted the sweet milk from mamá's breasts. And the Bible said we descend from Adam? That's why we are the we way we are, because we came from a man who had no mother? We thank him anyway, he is our abuelo. Our great-grandpa. It's a sorrow of life to have no mother. No wonder he ate the apple Eve gave him. He had no mother to teach him right from wrong. Bless your mamá every day, hijo."

"I will. Are children special?"

"Sí. Every child is special. But the gift only develops if the parents pay attention to nature when the baby is in the belly. Most are too busy. On the day the baby is born, they need to look at the sunrise and sunset, where is the moon. The clouds are messengers, birds flying together or alone, the color of the earth—everything is being born that day."

"How do you know?"

The old woman laughed, chewed the butt of the cigaro she had been smoking, and swallowed. "Never waste a stub of marijuana," she said. Alfonso laughed with her.

He told me that some of his best times were spent with Agapita. And with his mother. But they were different. One gave him her DNA, her gift of intuition. The old woman filled his mind with stories. All he heard and experienced created soul.

Some say those things build character, but no, it is soul that is made brick by brick. Soul is deeper than character.

Late that afternoon, the doctor caught six of the most beautiful rainbow trout he had ever seen. He had never caught a fish until that day he bandaged Alfonso. He was so excited, he hurried home to show his wife his good fortune. Fresh trout for dinner! Upon reaching the front door he fell, clutching at this chest. He died instantly of a heart attack.

The trout fell to the ground, their red gills slowly opening and closing, their eyes turning gray with death's film.

"How did you know?" Alfonso asked the old woman.

"Ay, hijito. I know. I took you from your mother's womb. The moon was full. Lady Luna gave you her gift. The lunar on your back is her sign."

Yes. His mother had held a mirror so that he could see the round, dark mole on his back. Lunar.

"You are blessed," his mother said, and kissed his forehead. "My ancestors were farmers in Puerto de Luna. The Valley of the Moon, the Americanos call it. Puerto de Luna. A beautiful name for the valley. My father and my brothers grew the best chile and the sweetest corn. People came from all over to buy. In September their apple trees were loaded with ripe red apples, like Christmas trees. The trees bulging, like women ready for birth. Do you remember?"

Yes, he remembered. Some of his fondest memories were of visits to his grandfather's farm in Puerto de Luna. From his mother he inherited his love of farming, vegetables growing in straight rows, the dark earth opening to receive seeds, trees laden with apples, peaches, cherries.

"Your grandfather Liborio took his spirit from the earth of the valley. His soul was made of earth and water. Blessed be God. He and my brothers, Pedro, Zacarías, Blas, Pablo, and Gabriel, helped neighbors build an earth dam to turn the river into acequias to irrigate, and every year summer floods washed away the dam. But farmers do not rest. The next day they went with picks and shovels and built the dam again. They tamed the river, and the river gave its blessing. Do you understand, hijo? That is your inheritance."

He remembered his grandfather appearing like a prophet, a handsome man with spirited eyes, eyes full of vision, a soft voice that sounded like the green of his orchard. In his horse-drawn wagon he arrived in Santa Rosa de Lima to sell apples, corn, and green chile.

Apple love stirred in the hearts of women, who rushed out with a few dollars in hand to buy a basket of Liborio's apples.

"Ay, Diós," they murmured when they touched his hands, the hands of the man who grew the apples of Eden, apples bursting with sweet juice, creating havoc on palates, sensuous fruits picked right off the tree by Liborio Mares.

The women swooned, and each returned home to bake pies and make jellies and preserves, each carrying the aroma of apples in her hair, the touch of the prophet of apples.

A proud Liborio returned home to Puerto de Luna. With the money he bought his wife a dress at the general store. They would go dancing on Saturday nights at the local dance hall, a small, friendly place where they met neighbors and enjoyed the music, while the moon filled the valley with its lovers' light.

"I remember," Alfonso said, lost in his fantasy world where all men and women seemed like characters in the folktales he so loved. Nothing was real, everything was real. With extreme joy came pain. The pain flowed like warm caramel syrup in his veins, throughout his body.

"Is everyone like this?" he asked Agapita.

"Yes," she answered. "Men are common creatures. Once in a lifetime one of them has a great awakening."

"What is that?" Fonso asked.

"Men go through life asleep. Once in a while one wakes up. Suddenly he is born anew. The old self falls away, and a new person walks out of the shell."

"How?" he insisted.

"You will know!" she answered, clearly irritated. "Maybe it is the spirit of God striking the man. Or maybe the man realizes how pitiful he is in the face of the universe, so he casts off the old shadow and becomes new. A change of clothes. Like putting on a new pair of shoes. But it's not just the body that changes, it's the soul. A spirit strikes the old soul, and it awakens into something new."

"It happens to everyone?" he asked.

"Yes. The universe is fair. Everyone is equal. Everyone can become."

What did she mean? The becoming was not fully described. Many a poet has tried, and stories the prophets told hinted at the becoming. But how? Where? What epiphany or ecstatic joy filled the person who suddenly felt the change, from old soul to one shining with light? "Like a neon sign," she liked to say.

"Everyone?" he asked.

She chewed on her cigaro. "Most men are cogs in a machine. They keep the machine going, but nothing changes in the soul. El alma. Ánima. Each man must seize his awakening moment."

"Me?" he asked.

"Yes, you." She chewed on the stub of the cigaro she had been smoking. "Life gets dull if you don't wake up."

"You?"

"You ask too many questions. Come." She took off the bandages. His foot and hand were no longer swollen. She had prepared an ointment from rabbit fat,, mint leaves, osha, other wild herbs, and her home-grown marijuana. With this she massaged his hand and foot; working slowly and softly, she brought circulation back to the lifeless limbs.

Late that afternoon, as the nighthawks began to fly, Rafaelita massaged her husband's sore shoulders while he sat on an old Coca-Cola box under the juniper tree. She kneaded the tight muscles back to their normal tone, and he thanked her. There was magic in her hands, as there is in the hands of every woman.

Next door the joyful cries of children filled the evening air, playing kick the can and hide-and-seek with the neighbor kids. Even Alfonso was limping after them.

Her massage stirred faint desire. Martin took her hand and led her into the house. Even in that godforsaken village with so much poverty and hard work, desire awakened under the juniper tree.

———

K, I'm slow. I suddenly realized I've been writing stories. Or something like stories wrapped in letters. I wrote too, you know. Not as well as Fonso, but I wrote. Never published. I used to show my stuff to Fonso. He encouraged me. But no, he was the writer . . . So here goes, more stories. Bet they never get published. Ha!

Rafaelita had an intuitive knowledge of the body. Did it come from her close tie to the earth where she was born? Her adherence to the moon?

She knew how to massage sore knots out of Martin's shoulders, and soothe the muscles where a steer had kicked his leg. Bones she knew, her babies she knew. A gentle massage made a constipated child's bowels move and empty; being rocked on her knees while she sang lullabies sent them to heavenly sleep.

Every woman is a curandera, a healer. The magic in a woman's hands can wipe away a tear, or chase away a sorrow.

So daily she massaged Alfonso, and his hand improved, though he couldn't open and close it; the weak fingers were simply not responding. Would he go through life with a nearly useless hand?

He learned to walk with the pair of crutches the doctor had given him, his left leg dragging a little. It would improve slowly, so by the time he entered high school one could barely tell that he limped.

Agapita came often to crack his spine and set it as straight as she could. The village children gathered at the door to watch until one or another whispered, "witch," then they ran away in a flutter. Curious birds sensed that this was no longer the Fonso they had once known. Was he awakening? Was he new? He walked funny; had he been born again?

A new life was beginning, that's for sure, for him and the family. Alfonso's mother decided they should move to Santa Rosa de Lima. She needed to leave the village that had caused her so much pain. She blamed herself. What if I hadn't let him go play with the boys that day? What if I had kept him by my side? Those thoughts tormented her.

Alfonso understood. Women truly know sorrow, he told me once. There is no greater pain for a mother than to see serious injury befall her child. What if he had died? Some mothers did cut themselves off from the world when death took a child. That bond between mother and child was as strong as the gravity between sun and earth, earth and moon.

What did leaving the village mean to Alfonso's father? War had been declared, and suddenly those faraway horizons curved around the earth and touched the people of the llano. Ranch boys enlisted and went overseas. The village emptied of its youth.

As it had been for his generation, as it would be for the world without end, amen.

His sons had signed up; in a few months they would be on foreign fields, Salomon sailing the Pacific to Iwo Jima and other foreign islands, Laute and Martinito in the army. He had raised them tough, they would survive. He knew they weren't cut out for ranch life. They didn't have his love for horses. That's it in a nutshell: a love for horses. He felt that passion the first time he mounted the pony his father had given him.

Maybe there stirred in him the blood of the old Spanish conquistadores who once rode into New Mexico. Men on horses, suited in iron, trampling everything in their path for gold and the Holy Cross. ·

The people of the llano didn't read their history in books. Perhaps the ricos had a few books and a Bible in their homes, but for the mass of Nuevo Mexicanos there was little education and few books. The history they knew had been passed down by word of mouth, from one generation to the next, until they carried history in their blood, in the collective memory beneath the conscious memory. Their history was a path to a higher consciousness, and the path was illuminated by the stories they told.

"Learn," they implored their children. "Learn! There is a goal in life as your ancestors taught you. Learn everything there is to learn." That path described Alfonso's trajectory, his life. He wasn't a saint, as Agapita said, he was common. But even a common man could strive for that connection to universal consciousness.

K, I'm reminded there are hundreds of New Mexico folktales, the cuentos of the people. Stories full of magic, humor, farmers, tricksters, pícaros; even Cinderella appears in one of the cuentos. Juan del Oso and Pedro de Ordimalas, characters who taught valuable lessons. But I haven't found a folktale about the Spanish conquistadores. Not even Oñate appears in the cuentos. Why didn't the oral tradition of the Nuevo Mexicanos include cuentos about the conquistadores?

Was it because of Oñate's original sin? He had the feet cut off the Acoma Indians he had taken prisoner. He enslaved some of the women.

Villagrá had written *Historia de la Nueva México*, an epic of sorts, but there were only one or two copies of the tome in New Mexico. Poor people couldn't afford such a book.

The people knew their history. They told stories. When the men gathered on Saturday afternoons to drink the delicious yeasty home-brewed beer that Martin made, bottles stored in the cold water of the well were pulled up. A fiddle and a guitar were then sure to appear, and the men would sing ballads, the corridos everyone knew by heart. The songs would be gathered by the wind and spread across the land, competing with the songs of the owls as dusk fell over the llano.

Those hardy, work-worn people honored their ancestors. They praised their abuelos y abuelitas. They kept no written genealogies, but they knew the names of their grandparents and great-grandparents. They knew where they came from: the village, the rancho, the river, or the hills that described each particular community. That was enough. They were people of the earth, workers, not ricos. They owned no riches, only the houses they built with their labor. Strong arms and hands molded the adobes.

And family. They prized familia. A man took care of his family, lived fully in the day, and at night the comfort of his wife's thighs eased away the day's work and brought restful sleep.

Life on the llano was difficult, Martin knew. His older sons were gone. And Alfonso? The crippled son would never ride beside him in the open air, never throw a rope on a steer, never cut a steer from the herd. A thousand other things this son could not do.

He accepted his wife's wishes: best move to town.

He rode out into the llano and rested there where Moises used to brew bootleg whiskey. Mula, because it was like the kick of a mule. He drank and said his goodbyes to the llano, the land he loved. So many things coming to an end.

He sold everything and packed his truck with beds, kitchen stuff, his wife's plaster saints, clothes. They had seen the Dust Bowl Okies en route to California, and they had often fed Mexican workers walking north in search of work. Now he would move his family a few miles up the road to town.

I never thought it would come to this, he thought. We are the new Okies. Only a few miles, and it seems I'm leaving a lifetime behind. Entering the unknown. He could work in town, construction or hauling garbage or pumping gas and cleaning gas station toilets. Anything to provide for his family. But deep in his heart, he knew the hands of a vaquero were not meant for such work. His hands were callused from work on the range, grit worn into the pores; the sweet smell of horse sweat burst loose when he washed his hands. Too much history was written into his hands. Would they accept a new history?

He looked at his hands, then at Alfonso's timid hand. What could the boy do? What kind of life could his son compose? A man needed strong hands to make a living, to have a wife and children, to create his history on earth, to fulfill his destiny.

What could Fonso do? He could barely open the hand; his fingers didn't respond. The hand had lost its memory, nerves and muscles were damaged. He would help his son, but in the same thought he cursed God. Why did the Almighty allow this? And the foot? It was just beginning to look like a foot again. It curled inward. No shoe would fit, so it was wrapped in cloth for the time being. Later he would cut slits in a leather shoe so he could slip it on.

He looked at his own rough hands. Fingers broken with hard work, but the bones had fused together. Wrap them and go on working. Throw a rope or tighten a saddle cinch, and the pain reminded him of the time and place where the accident happened. A bone in his leg was broken and the muscles were bruised, but he recovered from the hardships. There was hope. Maybe Alfonso's injuries would heal with time.

He thought of his compadre Santiago. When he was young, a horse smashed his foot beyond repair. Now he wore a boot with a three-inch-thick sole. Santiago Bonney, brother of his wife's first husband, was one of the best vaqueros on the llano in his day. Now he rode a truck. He came by to visit often; he loved to tell stories. All the Bonneys were great storytellers, and some could cuss like the devil.

A local judge had once accused Martin of rustling one of his steers. He had written the accusation in a notepad he pulled from his pocket. "I've got the facts," he said. Martin didn't scare. He pulled out his own notepad. "Well, lookee here. My notes say you've been visiting a married woman in Vaughn. Doña Luisa."

Santiago stood at Martin's side. "Bet her husband would like to know," he said. "And your wife"—case dismissed.

They laughed when they told the story, and many stories, and Fonso sat in the shade of the water tank, listening, the fan of the windmill softly turning, water flowing, his mother calling them to lunch, her apron swept by the gentle breeze, the aromas of food pouring from the kitchen: beans, tortillas, fried potatoes, fried slices of the large roast Santiago had brought, smells of home wafting in the cool summer breeze. These sounds and fragrances were the home music that added meaning to the story being told by the windmill, Martin's laughter, tío Santiago's imitation of the judge, their words leaping across the llano where the eagle soared, leaping into Alfonso's imagination. He could see, feel, and smell the story unfolding.

Such was the homespun creativity of the people in that fortuitous time. Alfonso breathed deep. Such moments would stay with him forever.

The father turned and looked at his son. Would Alfonso limp like his tío Santiago? Why was life so hard?

My niece, who is my caregiver, is reading these letters. She takes each one to the post office, and she asks why I don't date the letters. Why date them? One day folds into the next, until the end. I write on the calendar the days I have doctors' appointments. That's all.

Dear K, I've been gone a few weeks. Had some heart problems. I didn't bother the family with this. I didn't call you. I don't use the phone anymore. Why? I'm fine, fine as wine. So here goes. You want to know about Agapita.

Who was Agapita? Was she just another name from those blessed names of long ago?. Was she just another curandera? In that fortuitous time, every village depended on someone who could minister to the people, healers who used common remedies, delivered babies, and were always ready to battle evil. The Anglo newcomers called them medicine women.

You know Ultima's story. Fonso's little book became quite well known. So I'm just trying to fill out the story, give it flesh as they say.

Today's health stores, with their stocks of vitamins, herbs, oils, organic produce, etc., are descendants of the healing traditions from folk medicine. People have always known green is good, and green comes from the earth.

There's always been a portion of magic in the healing arts. Call it miracle or faith. You must believe. By laying her hands on her sick child, a mother can bring welcome relief from a common cold, from a fall, from an earache or stomach upset. A mother's song can soothe the soul.

Agapita came to see them off. She wanted to bless the boy who had provided her with rabbits. Now she would have to find a new boy in the village, and the cycle would begin again, ad infinitum. Alfonso, her apprentice, was leaving. What had he learned? What knowledge of birds, beasts, and the people of the village would he take with him?

She looked around. It had once been a thriving village of thirty families; now only a handful were left. Struggling. Village life on the llano was ending. The big ranchers were fencing off the land. She cursed the man who had invented barbwire.

Cuando llegó el alambre, llegó el hambre, the people said. When wire came, hunger came. The Homestead Act brought the English language to the land where once only Indian, Spanish, and the gossip of owls were heard.

The llano was bought and privatized, encircled, closed off to common grazing; animals were branded. The old families moved into town, where freedom-loving, hardworking men had to take menial jobs working at gas stations, their wives cleaning motel rooms.

Highway 66 was roaring with activity. Buses stopped at the Club Cafe, where tourists and servicemen chowed down on the best New Mexican food west of the Mississippi. Town boys, and this would later include Alfonso, hung around outside the bus station with homemade shoeshine boxes looking for shoes to shine. The doughboys gave good tips.

Trains had arrived in 1880. The cattle and sheep industries thrived. Ranchers gathered daily at the Moise warehouse to buy supplies, visit, and exchange news. When Martin slaughtered a sheep for meat, he gave the pelt to Alfonso. He nailed it on the roof of the chicken coop, and when it was dry he took it to Moise and sold it for a dollar.

"Hijo," Agapita said, leaning close, her clothes smelling of wood smoke, her breath tinged with marijuana, the stigma of sweat permeating her long black dress, a dress given to her long ago by a witch a man had shot on the Piedra Lumbre ranch. Either he was a bad shot or she had some kind of protection, because she lived long enough to curse the man. He died within the week, thrown by the horse the woman had touched.

"Bendición," Agapita said, making the sign of the cross on Alfonso's forehead. "Que Diós te cuide."

Nuevo Mexicano Catholics give a blessing at every turn. Get up in the morning, Bendito sea Diós. Eat breakfast, another blessing. Kids go to school, bendición. A man comes to lie by his wife, and she makes the sign of the cross and utters a blessing as she receives him.

A blessing for every aspect of life! They even bless God! ¡Bendito sea Diós!

How can you bless God? He doesn't need a blessing! He's God!

"No matter, hijito," they answer calmly. Blessed be God.

A faith instilled in them long ago, from the time the friars journeyed up la Jornada del Muerto from México. Those friars converted every native on the road, from Las Cruces to Santa Fe. The Catholic faith of Spain arrived in New Mexico in 1598. The colonists were mostly Mexicans born of Spanish parents in México plus a few Mexican Indian families. Cleofes Vigil used to say that when the Spanish arrived in New Mexico, they didn't bring many women. The men found beautiful inditas, and so a rainbow of colors evolved, from blonde to dark brown, a mestizo nation.

K, my mother was like Alfonso's mother, Catholic to the core. I identify with Alfonso; we had the same upbringing. As I write these letters, I become Alfonso. I am Alfonso. Our mothers' faith was the same, it took root in our blood. Jesus died for our sins, we were told as we dragged through catechism classes, carrying the weight of original sin in our hearts. A faith that had driven the Moors and Jews out of Spain.

I'm feeling a little queasy. It happens some days. I can't find the right word to use, and then a minute later it pops into my mind. I feel a flutter in my heart, my bones ache, I feel like going back to bed.

Faith. Alfonso was drenched in faith. His mother poured the power of God and the saints into him, by word and in the milk from her breasts.

Maybe that's where faith begins . . . in mothers' milk.

Alfonso's religion later plagued him. During his university years, he began to discard some of the beliefs that as a child he had thought were so true. As he began to give up dogma and look for his own answers, he felt a vacuum in his soul. Our university years were a time of liberation, also years spent in turmoil. We were questioning everything. Is there a God? Who is the God of my ancestors? Is there a heaven where my ancestors rest? So many doubts, and Fonso's faith came tumbling down.

What did Agapita believe? She sat in the cemetery during Sunday mass. God was in the decomposing bones buried in the dry earth.

She could hear the dead grieving for those inside the church. The dead gathered around clubfoot Jesus, and he taught them songs to sing for the living.

That's what she knew. She knelt before a tombstone, the one inscribed with the names of Rafaelita's twins, Teresa Candelaria and Juana Clorinda. They died shortly after they were born, in 1932. Agapita communed with them. Niñas santas. The innocent babies had become saints.

She went on mumbling, talking to old friends who had passed from this life to the next. The dead had gone to a place where Jesus taught them prayers and songs to bless the living.

Alfonso looked at her hands: The long, slender, bony fingers covered with a thin layer of skin. The white knobs of knuckles strong as flint. Arms of sinewy muscle and tendons, brown skin covered with liver spots, the stains of old age.

"I am centuries old," she said. "I came with my owl up the road that passes through the village. Long ago. I was looking for a lost boy; like La Llorona I came looking for my child. I crossed the river at Chamisal, now called Juárez, El Paso. Four centuries ago, when the españoles came to settle this land, they held a feast of Thanksgiving at that river crossing. Those are memories, hijo. History is a memory. Smart men try to write it down—phoo! ¿Qué saben? Nada. It's the people who know suffering and sorrow. The españoles came north looking for gold; I came looking for a lost boy.

"You!" She poked Alfonso. "I found you! I pulled you from your mother's womb. With these hands, I took many children away from La Muerte. In those days many children died at childbirth. The mothers called me when they were due. ¡Voy a dar a Luz! ¡Ven Agapita! Deliver my baby! Don't let him die! In those days we had no doctors. We delivered life on the llano. I delivered their babies; they loved me then. Gave me slices of sweet mutton to eat, served me tortillas and coffee with sugar. When the birthing was done, they sent me away. Back to my casita by the arroyo. But I found you, my lost boy! I beat La Llorona!"

She poked him again, and Alfonso laughed. He had heard the story a hundred times.

She loved Alfonso. She taught him how to call coyotes. He got so good, his loud, piercing yip-yap brought coyotes down from the mesas above the village, there where now are installed dozens of tall steel turbines that convert wind into electricity. The owls are dying.

At night he could call owls down from the juniper trees. He was of their blood. He fed them the skin and bones of dead rabbits. He could imitate every bird on the llano, from the roadrunner to the lowly crow.

She taught him the constellations—not all eighty-eight, just the ones she cared to point out. The night sky above the llano shimmered with stars. The village homes were lit with kerosene lamps, no electric lights to compete with the brilliance of the stars.

"See that wide band of stars stretching across the sky?" she said as she and Fonso sat near the juniper tree. "That's the Milk River. You know how it got there? My comadre Eloisa was milking her cow. The bucket was full when the cow kicked my comadre so hard, she jumped and threw the bucket up in the air. The milk splashed all over the sky, and each drop of milk became a star. The Americanos call it the Milky Way, but no, it's the milk from my comadre's cow."

Some nights she would say the stars were a road to heaven. The path is long, but there's milk to drink. Also ice cream.

They sat on a cedar stump eating dry kernels of corn she had roasted with rabbit fat and a little salt. Around them the llano grass shimmered with starlight. Slight shadows moved. All was alive.

"Listen, you can hear the stars singing." He stopped crunching corn and listened. "Stars make music," she said. "The first star was God made of music. From that star came all the others."

It was true; Fonso could hear the symphony.

"See the seven stars." She pointed at the Pleiades. Yes, he could see their trembling light and hear their song.

"They were seven sisters who lived over there by the Gonzales ranch. They loved to dance, but their father was very strict. In those days there were only strict fathers. One night the sisters sneaked away and went to the Ortega dance hall. They danced and danced and got very drunk. When their father found them, he kicked them home. But he kicked them too hard, because they landed up there in the sky. Seven sisters."

Alfonso was learning the night sky according to Agapita. The story of the Pleiades was a story he would remember.

"See over there." She pointed at the immense sky, her fingertips almost touching the stars. "That's Christ carrying the cross."

"But last night you said it was Juan del Oso," Alfonso reminded her.

"Oh, sí, I forgot. Those stars are Juan del Oso. Once there was a beautiful young woman. One day she was taking care of her father's cornfield, and a big bear kidnapped her. He took her to his cave. He never let her out. A few months later she had a baby, Juan del Oso. John of the Bear. The baby grew ten feet tall in one month. He was very strong. In order for him and his mother to escape from the cave, Juan del Oso hit Bear with a giant tree he had torn from the ground. Juan was afraid Bear wasn't dead, so he and his mother ran away. They ran so fast they climbed to the sky and became the Juan del Oso stars. Look closely. There is Bear chasing Juan. When the stars go to bed, Bear cannot see. He cannot catch them."

The story of the seven sisters swirled in Alfonso's imagination. Imagine, those sisters from a rancho in the llano becoming stars. Everything was possible.

"Tell me more," he said. "Tell me more."

"See over there. That's San José taking care of the baby Jesús. He was a good father."

"But the other night you said it's Pedro de Ordimalas."

"Oh yes, I forgot. It is Pedro de Ordimalas. He is a pícaro. Always getting in trouble. See the stars, how they move. Pedro is up to no good. When he dies, he will go to hell. The devils were to have a feast, so the Chief Devil told Pedro to get the chairs ready.

"Pedro put tar on the chairs, and when the devils sat down, they got stuck to the chairs. Then Pedro began to shout the Holy Names. ¡Virgen María! ¡Jesucristo! ¡San José! The devils do not like to hear the Holy Names, so they jumped up to escape, but they were stuck to the chairs. Pedro went on singing, 'Jesús, María y José, bless our home!' It made the devils crazy. They jumped out windows with chairs stuck to their nalgas."

Alfonso laughed so hard, the coyotes answered him. "Then what happened?"

"The Chief Devil went to St. Peter and begged him to take Pedro. That's how Pedro got to heaven."

"Does he get in trouble in heaven?"

"Oh yes. A pícaro gets in trouble anywhere. Don't be a pícaro, hijito."

"I promise not to be a pícaro," Alfonso whispered.

"The stars." She pointed. "See that group there? That's La Llorona walking along the Milk River. La Llorona is crying for her lost children. She threw them in the Pecos River and they drowned. Children sometimes drown in the river. La Llorona carries a bag. If she finds a naughty child, she throws him in the bag and takes him away."

"Where?"

"To her home. She feeds them atole with milk and honey. The children are happy, but they can never return home."

How sad, Alfonso thought. But all wasn't lost. Last night the same stars had been Santo Niño de Atocha holding a little basket. He guessed the constellations could be whatever Agapita named them.

"See the star that moves? That's el Cucuy. El Coco, the Coco Man. He grabs bad children. Some say he is the son of La Llorona. Be good so el Coco won't get you."

Fonso trembled and drew close to Agapita. "I'll be good."

"Stars guide our destiny. See the big star? It is always there. If you get lost at night, you follow the star and get home safe. Stars show us the way. When you grow up, you will find a woman with a good star and marry. She will shine on you. If a woman does not have the right star, she will be cross all the time."

Alfonso looked puzzled. He couldn't conceive of marriage, but he would remember what Agapita said that night. You know, he often said he had married the most heavenly star. She was a woman who paid attention to the cycles of the sun and moon. Cosmic.

Agapita lit one of the marijuana cigaros she carried in her bag. The flare of the match shone like a star on earth, illuminating her owl eyes.

That's how he learned the names of the northern constellations, and each one told a story from the folktales of the people. Canis Major and Canis Minor were village dogs who chased horses and cows and got in trouble. Cinderella Martinez was a girl who almost burned the house down while baking tortillas. Round tortillas appeared all over the night sky, so real they made Alfonso hungry just to look at them.

"The girl's slippers? Over there," Agapita pointed. "See."

Yes, he saw, and the magical stories woven into the stars stirred his imagination.

"We call the planetas stars. They are also very important. Planetas can tell if a man will be happy or sad, make money or lose his wealth, love or not love. It is the same for a woman. The planetas pull us like the moon pulls the ocean. The Moon, Mujer de la Luna, is in love with Brother Ocean. I should say King Ocean. We are made of water; we belong to the Ocean as much as la Tierra. The farmer plants corn or the ranchero castrates bulls only when the moon is in a certain place. Lady Luna is very powerful. The most powerful is el Sol. The first born, he is el Abuelo. Grandfather Sun. He is old and hot as a goat in heat. That is why he can give us life. Bless el Abuelo every day and thank him. He makes clouds rise and rain fall. But he can also make the land dry and brittle. Remember that."

Alfonso nodded. The blazing summer sun that baked the llano dry now had a name: el Abuelo. Family existed beyond the limits of his home. Family existed in the stars and planets.

"There is a small planeta. I call him el Mocoso because he is small and runs around el Sol very fast. The Americanos call him Mercury.

He is always spreading gossip. He steals the girls' cherry. One day you will know what that means. Next is la Dama del Amor, la Luna. She brings love. But be careful, she brings every kind of love. Some is as gentle as a breeze, or it can be murder. I pray la Dama del Amor will someday give you a good wife, hijito.

"We live on Madre Tierra. She gives us everything we need. Corn, fish, birds, all the creatures and insects. I don't know why she gave us cockroaches and mosquitos, but she did. We learn to live with all her creatures. Love Madre Tierra, hijito, and take care of her. Around her goes Lady Luna. She is for lovers, but also she can make people crazy. Lady Luna pulls at Madre Tierra and the ocean goes in and out, like a man and wife in love. In and out. Diós mío. A beautiful dance.

"A long time ago, the Aztecas lived in México. They had many gods. One of those got mad and threw a rabbit at the moon. You can still see the shadow of the rabbit on the face of the moon. See?"

"Yes, I see."

"Why that god didn't throw a noble wolf or a fierce jaguar, I don't know. He threw a lowly rabbit. We are the rabbit people; we praise the rabbit on the moon because it is a great mystery. Rabbits are fast and wise."

"If they're so fast and wise, why can coyotes catch them?"

"It's like this, hijito. Life is a chain. Every creature has to eat or die. The rabbit gives himself so coyotes can live. And the coyote becomes fast and wise when he eats the rabbit. Bless the rabbits. You, too, must thank brother rabbit when you eat his meat, and thank fish from the river. Those creatures are your brothers, they give their flesh to you. Someday I'll tell you the story.

"The next planeta is always fighting. His name is Guerillero. The Americanos call him Mars. He brings war, over there where men kill men. Maybe we should not blame el planeta Guerillero. Maybe war is in man's heart. Always fighting. Drop a nickel, and boys run to fight over it. A pretty woman enters a room, and each man wants to own her. Even babies cry, mine, mine! Your father's name, Martin, comes from that planeta. But your father fights with himself only when he gets drunk. Then watch out. I pity your mamá."

On and on the stories went. Those summer nights when his father was busy and didn't make a campfire under the juniper tree, Alfonso went to sit with Agapita and listen to stories about the constellations and how they got their names.

When Alfonso was in school, he happened to find a horoscope chart with the signs and names of the zodiac. One of those that propose to tell events and fortunes for people born under a particular sign. He was shocked.

"This is not true," he blurted out. "These are not Agapita's names." Spurred to find out why the zodiac didn't use Agapita's names, he looked in an encyclopedia for a map of the constellations. Sure enough, the star clusters all had Greek or Roman names. How could it be? At first he was confused. The ancient Greeks had named the constellations, and each one told the story of a Greek hero or god.

Had the Greeks come before Agapita?

He began to read the Greek myths and was fascinated by the stories. He read other mythologies and understood that other cultures had named the constellations, each according to the folk stories and heroes of the culture. Agapita had named the stars according to the stories of the Nuevo Mexicanos. The stories described their history. His history.

The constellations could have many names, and he could honor all of them. But he never forgot the names Agapita had given the stars those summer nights when they sat together and she pointed at the sky. The stars are guides, she had said, but keep your feet on Madre Tierra.

K, I want to share with you the story Agapita told about Fonso's birth.

"He came in the bag that had held him prisoner those nine months," she said. "Drowning, yes, he was drowning in that sac. I unwrapped the cord from around his neck, sucked mocos out of his nostrils, blew deep into his mouth, saw his lungs rise and fall. I placed him at his mother's breast. He sucked the hot juice of life as it poured from her nipples. 'Alfonso,' I said, 'you will be a lover.'"

But a lover after what? Agapita didn't say. Truth, beauty, the art of love . . . Ah, yes, a lover.

She went on and on, describing how her work as a midwife connected her to Alfonso.

Damn! I'm beginning to dislike her—but this is not my story.

"I held the baby by his feet with one hand, in the other hand I held the placenta, and I went outside to the tree that lightning had struck the night the giant comet lit up the llano. There the owls waited. They were crying, 'We're hungry, we're hungry.' I threw the placenta and the umbilical cord on the ground, and the owls swooped down to feast on the bloody mess."

In another story she told, and there were many versions, Agapita buried the afterbirth in Rafaelita's garden. Alfonso's mother came from farming stock, and each summer she struggled against the hot winds of the llano to raise corn, chile, and squash in her small garden. Alfonso brought cow dung from the corrals to fertilize the stingy earth. He carried buckets of water from the windmill tank, there where the boy had drowned, his image still floating on the film of gently rocking water, restless.

Together, mother and son nurtured that bit of green, a garden defying the dry yellow horizon of land, the endless llano of brittle grass begging for rain. Rains were a blessing on the land.

Which story do we believe?

The old woman buried the afterbirth in the mother's garden, or she fed it to the owls. "Only I will know your destiny," she said, adding, "I stole you from your mother so you will live many seasons on this earth. You will know summer and winter; each comes with its blessing. You will have a great awakening."

But damn, she didn't tell him about the train! For every reason, there is a season.

Agapita told Fonso this story: "Hijo, long before you were born, Summer was a lovely woman who came every year with her daughter Spring prancing before her. They came from Aztec México, from the south they came. One day Summer ate six kernels of corn that were sacred to the Sun. His name was Tonatiuh. El Sol got mad. He told the Devil to take Summer down to hell to punish her. The Devil stole Summer and took her to his home in hell. Without Summer, the earth got cold and froze over. The people were freezing. Summer's daughter, Eternal Spring, went to the Devil. 'I will lie with you for three months,' she told the Devil, 'if you release my mother for a season.' Sweet corn pollen covered Spring's thighs, the perfume of lilacs blooming wafted from her hair, her nipples soft green buds. How could the Devil refuse a young thing like Spring?

"A woman's thighs will make both man and devil dizzy."

She had taken Demeter's and Persephone's story and made it fit the world of the llano. Instead of pomegranate juice, Mexican corn pollen colored Spring's hair and ran down her legs.

It wasn't Jesus at Easter time bringing summer to the land so crops might grow and Earth might green again; no, it was the sacrifice of Spring. A daughter giving of herself so her mother might bloom again. But this is the truth of all cycles: Spring is destined to die when Summer returns.

She screwed up the Greek myth. So what, it made for a story that entranced Fonso. What this tells me is that Agapita wasn't just a country girl; no, she knew stories from other cultures. Where she learned them, I don't know.

Anyway, let's say she buried Alfonso's bloody afterbirth in the garden and the corn grew ten feet tall, each stalk producing ten big ears of the sweetest corn ever tasted by the tongue of man.

That's the story to tell children. Don't tell them about the Devil's conquest of Spring.

"The owls ate your blood and your soul," she told Alfonso one day when they were out gathering llano herbs and sweet roots, camotes and wild onions.

The boy believed her, he believed her stories.

"Yes, your soul was attached to your mother's blood, but flesh and soul came out the night I pulled you from her womb. Part of that cord was wrapped around your neck; you didn't want to leave your mother. I had a hell of a time untying you from her."

She laughed and blew smoke in Fonso's face.

"You're going to be a mamá's boy," she gurgled, spitting out bits of marijuana. Alfonso nodded. She was telling him his history. How else was he to know?

"You gave everything to the owls?" he asked.

"Yes. They were hungry for a baby's soul. All righty, all righty. The owls ate your soul."

"But I can make a new soul," he said.

"Yes!" she cried. "As I taught you! Bright boy!"

Alfonso beamed. He knew the story. He knew he had been about making his soul since she first told him the story.

"You have your mother's blood and your father's sperm," she said. "But separation from the womb is a sorrowful beginning. Mothers tell their children not to cry. Your soul came from heaven, they say. See how it shines. ¡Mierda! I know better. You came from your mother's soul, eternal, as she came from her mother. Look around you. See the earth, grass, trees, coyotes, antelopes, cicadas chirping, clouds, rain, lightning, thunder, aromas of nature: everything is born from a womb. All of this makes your soul."

"Is there more?" Alfonso asked.

"Yes. You will live by a river. You will walk in your grandfather's orchard, taste the apples after first frost, meet friends, fall in love, feel your cosita in a woman, feel the film of love in your mouth after you kiss her. Your love is that eventual woman who waits for you after you're done with your sorrow. She will kiss you and bring you joy."

"And no more sorrow?" Alfonso asked.

"The world is full of sorrow. There are different kinds. Even in love, sorrow can come to test the lovers. That's part of love, so don't give up."

"I won't," he said.

She paused, then said, "Ay, cabroncito, there will be many women in your life. The path is not straight. You will go to school, maybe to the great university in Alburquerque. You will read books that will make your mind tingle. Never forget the inheritance of your ancestors, their memory is in you. Oh, you will see and do many things before you die. That, too, is a sorrow. Parting from earth is a great sorrow."

"Will I be happy?" Alfonso asked.

"Yes," Agapita said sadly. "There is some joy for my little crippled boy. Fill your soul with joy. There is a word—"

I think the word she was searching for was ecstasy.

"Yes! That's it. Find God in all you do! Make your soul one with God's creation! God is the llano and smell of earth, the crunch of grass beneath your feet, the taste of crunchy apples, juices that make you smack your lips—like when you kiss a woman! Yes! Taste her every nook and cranny, her breasts! Feel the texture of her skin, her sweat! By God! You're going to make it, Fonso!"

She went on and on, and Alfonso was enraptured by what she said. Everything went into the making of soul. Mother and church were teaching him something different, some static version of the essence within. There was very little in his catechism about growing soul; it was just there. But for Agapita, soul had to be made one brick at a time, nature's stepping stones.

No wonder visions spurted before his eyes. There was joy to be experienced. The old woman gave him clues. He loved her.

And she loved him. That's why she taught him to experience life. See, taste, feel, hear, smell, create. Joy and sorrow come into everyone's life. "Get used to it," she was fond of telling him.

"But I will be a cripple," he said. Already, he knew that reality was beckoning.

"Bah! That's only the outside skin," she scolded. "Your smelly self! Vanity of vanities! That's in the Bible. The important thing is what you have inside, the soul in your blood. You will be strong enough to face all the sorrows life throws at you."

"How many sorrows are there?" he asked.

"Seven. From birth to death, seven."

"Will I be happy?"

"Each day is a joy," she answered, puffing on her cigaro. "Nature is full of joy for you to find."

"What do you mean?"

"Go live in the world! Haven't I told you?"

Alfonso nodded. She had taught him, but she had also said that men are thick-skinned. They find little joy in God's creation; instead, they surrender to greed, rage, envy, jealousy, and all the other destructive emotions.

"Don't let money be your goal, hijito. You have the magic touch. Money will come to you, but you must not desire it."

Alfonso listened closely to the bits of wisdom Agapita offered.

The family moved into town, where his father constructed, with the help of his three older sons, an adobe home a stone's throw from the river. Alfonso remembered them making the adobes, the pit where portions of earth and straw were mixed with water until the mud was ready to be shoveled into wood forms. As soon as the mud set, the form was lifted, and there sat two adobes ready to be sundried. These earth bricks were a poor man's building material. Anyone could mix clay with a little straw and make adobes with which to build a house.

Alfonso wondered at his father's ingenuity and the strength of his brothers, who worked all day making adobes. He could do little except carry water buckets and go to the lumber yard on errands. He felt close to the men who could raise a house they would call home.

Across the river lay the town of Santa Rosa de Lima. The Catholic church's tower and the town's water tank rose above the smattering of homes.

Cleanliness is next to godliness, his mother liked to say. She was meticulous about keeping her home and family clean. Come the first sunny spring day, she would wheel the washing machine out under the elm tree. Edwina and Angie helped her carry mattresses, blankets, and sheets outside, where she opened the winter-worn mattresses and thoroughly washed the ticking and the wool contents. Alfonso helped hang the clean mattress covers on the clothesline and spread the wool on sheets to dry in the sun. The washing and drying took all day, sometimes two or three days. When the clean mattresses were reconstituted, everyone slept in the clean aroma of spring.

Of course they prayed a rosary before going to bed, and so cleanliness was next to godliness.

Years later, Alfonso marveled at the stamina his mother possessed. The same was true of his wife. Those two women gave their strength to him. They made him a man, not only from their sense of responsibility, but with their love and affection.

He learned that a woman can make the man, but it is difficult for a man to make a woman. Men just don't have the intuitive spirit that constructs life.

Mockingbird Hill, the kids called their rocky half-acre. It was much like the Pastura del Llano with its wild grasses, yuccas, mesquite bushes, birds, lizards, cicadas, and all the other insects that made summer days buzz with life. From here the llano rolled south, flatter and flatter, hotter and hotter.

Ultima's owl sang in the juniper tree near the house. Alfonso's destiny would be revealed.

Fonso and the Chavez boys, Ron, J. D., Charlie, and Jerry, raced to the river; sometimes Edwina, Angie, Dolly, and Ida ran with them. They dove into the muddy water and floated south with the current, then swam back against the flow. Swimming in the river strengthened Alfonso's battered limbs. Some days they made the trek to town to swim in Park Lake or Blue Hole.

In those days there were no scuba divers exploring the depths of Blue Hole, that natural cenote that gushed with cool, pristine water. In its depths Alfonso discovered the large golden carp, a mythical fish that he had first seen in the river's deep pools. Were the waters of the river connected to those that for hundreds of years had flowed out of Blue Hole? Were all the underground waters of the Pecos River watershed connected? If so, the golden carp of legend could be everywhere. The stuff of myth swam in his imagination.

In the water, Fonso was equal to the other boys; he could swim as strongly and as fast as they could. In the water he was not a cripple, and although his broken hand could hardly cup water, his arms grew stronger. The river helped more than the doctors.

K, it's midnight, and I pause. I hear a crow scratching at my window. Or the owl? When I started these letters, the owl came to sit in the tree. Am I writing my own biography? Who is the spirit that appeared one night and told me to put her in my story?

Ultima.

The river was magical, Fonso told me often, describing how he dove into the depths to swim with the golden carp. He was composing myth. All children create myth. The baby's growing brain goes through the same steps humanity has experienced in its evolution from original ape to present primate. Babies in the womb first live in the jungle, then they walk upright in the savannah, and finally they enter caves just as our early ancestors once gathered to make fire and tell stories. Creating stories while saber-toothed tigers roared outside was *Homo sapiens'* first step toward civilization.

I will guard my cave against all others, was his second impulse. We haven't lost that destructive instinct. Look around you.

If only we had access to children's minds, if only they could write their passage from heaven to the migrations out of Africa, what a plethora of legends we would learn. We do have parts of mankind's original mythology, writ in bones and ancient writings that archaeologists dig up. But instead of listening to children's stories, we hurry to teach them the alphabet, thus early on erasing primitive memory and the remnants of original stories. We resort to books instead of listening to the child. The gods and heroes of our past are clouded by time.

Fonso's mother had expected more help from the doctor in Santa Fe, but there was little he could do. Besides, Alfonso was getting stronger, thanks to her home remedies and massage. Mothers were the healers in that fortuitous time, as it has always been. She massaged Alfonso's foot and hand with Mentholatum and Vicks Vapo-Rub, the common unguents she bought at the drugstore.

Alfonso often disappeared, quietly slipping out of the house and down to the river. There, in the dark green forest, he listened to the river's song, a mournful sound of wind and flowing water. He heard the prayers of the dead, as Agapita had said. He heard hordes of ancestors grieving, and the sweet voices of his mother's twin babies who had died shortly after they were born. The grieving did not frighten him; it filled him with serenity.

He fished and took fat catfish to his mother. He gutted and skinned them, and she covered them with cornmeal and fried them. She was proud of her elusive son. So quiet. He spent time with her, but did she know him? Was he an old soul, as Agapita said? She prayed that he would recover and be strong and healthy. Whatever happened was God's will. Faith ran in her as deep and profound as the water of the river that flowed south.

Alfonso attended school. He learned that the world spoke English and not Spanish. He loved the children's books the teacher put in his hands. The children in the picture books didn't look like him. He was brown; they were a pasty color. Where are they from? Do they live far away? Would the blonde-haired, blue-eyed children like to visit the llano and the village? Could they help their fathers butcher a sheep like he did? Slash the throat and save the blood in a pan? His mother would knead the blood, throw out the impurities, and fry the pure blood with bits of onions and liver.

There were few kitchen aids, certainly no blenders; everything was done by hand. She kneaded the dough for tortillas in a bowl, then with a rolling pin she rolled each ball of masa round and flat and tossed it on the hot comal. She flipped each tortilla over so both sides cooked toasty, and the stack grew high, filling the kitchen with the essence of home.

Remember home-cooked tortillas?

Pinto beans were a staple, so every day she placed a pile of beans on the kitchen table, and he helped separate the good beans from the dirt and old beans. She cooked the beans in a large pot for hours. The pressure cooker came later, dangerous as hell because if one was careless, explosions were known to occur.

Next she removed the stems and seeds from red chile pods, and in that famous bowl that bore her signature, she crushed the dry chiles in water and pressed them with her hand until the sauce was ready to cook. Her hand turned red and burned from the hot chile, but she took no notice; she was preparing the daily meals for her family. That's the way it was in those days, food prepared by strong, loving hands.

She prepared a guiso, flour added to bacon fat and browned in an iron skillet on the stove. She poured the chile into the skillet and it thickened, filling the small kitchen with a mouthwatering aroma. Chile colorado is a typical New Mexican dish. Tortillas, chile and beans, fried potatoes, a slice of mutton or hamburger meat cooked with the chile: soul food. Soul grew from those simple but delicious dishes.

Alfonso helped whenever his father butchered a sheep. He knew the organs of the sheep were the same as his. He knew the animal's spine and ribs. Someday he would be able to butcher a sheep just like his father. Already he could kill and clean the chickens that his mother needed for Sunday meals.

He knew the llano, its animals and weather; he kept true to Agapita's lessons. At school he learned letters and math. He wondered if children from the East knew how to butcher sheep and chickens. He looked for clues in the picture books the teacher offered, but found none.

"Dick and Jane live in the East," the teacher explained. "Where do we live?"

"New Mexico," the students answered.

"Where is the East?" Alfonso asked.

"Far away."

"As far as the moon?"

Hundreds of kids flocked to school, not the few he had known in the village schoolhouse. The children took little notice of his slight limp. Some asked him what had happened. He hated to explain. What could he say? "Agapita said it's my destiny to be who I am."

"Wher'ju come from?"

"There." He pointed to the llano that opened up beyond the mesas that encircled the sunken Santa Rosa de Lima.

"Can he play baseball?"

"Yeah, if he kinda stuffs his hand in the glove."

"Ha, ha. Can he run?"

"Out at first. Let's go!"

In his nightmares he saw the world ending. A train had delivered the burning light seen around the world, the atomic bomb. The kids whispered, the world was ending.

June of the blue eyes. Agnes, who drowned. Mary Lou. Lydia, his cousin. Sadie he had kissed in the supply closet. Lloyd he always beat at marbles. Horse and Bones, who were so rough with him. Kiko, his fishing buddy. Bobby, Tony, Manuel, Chris, Abel, Red, Ernie, Ramon . . .

They made up stories and tried to understand what atomic meant. Los Alamos. Where in the hell was that? Alamogordo desert. Trinity. Mushroom cloud.

Teacher said to look it up. The tattered encyclopedia in the library didn't help much.

Some parents whispered, "It's a thing of the devil. Cosas del diablo." The people prayed a lot.

Agapita told him everything ends, like the seasons. They come and disappear. Men think they will live forever. Their lives are shorter than the sputtering candles on the church altar. Poof. Se apagó.

"Is it true?" he had asked.

"Oh yes." She chewed on her gums and licked the pieces of weed that stuck to her teeth. "The old need remedios for their pain. Your father and his friends drink on weekends to ease the fatigue of work. The women need the marijuana I grow, so I sell them some. Especially las viejitas; the old grandmas have smoking parties when the men are gone. Shh, don't tell. Sí, my comadres love to puff on yerba buena. For arthritis, they say." She laughed.

"The bomb that exploded?" he asked, tugging at her sleeve.

"Ay Diós," she moaned. The children are frightened. It will get worse. The train burns the fresh air of the llano, the cars and trucks leave black smoke that chokes. What will become of our llano? More monsters appear on the horizon, wires and telephones. Can we save the children?

The older boys spurred him on, threw him a football, then tackled him. Coach Lemon gave him a big glove, which fit over his hand. He could catch and throw, and he was getting better at running the bases.

One day after school, Agnes took his hand. She held his hand and smiled. He wanted to pull away at first. No one but his mother and Agapita had touched his crippled hand. But she held tight, saying nothing. They walked to her home, where she said goodbye. He waved. He would see her often.

"Your hand has memory," his mother said as she massaged it. "It will remember how it was before the accident. You used to wrestle and play with your brothers. We pray that the Virgin will protect them. You brought me water from the well, helped with the garden, took Agapita rabbits for her meals—you could do many things. Your hand remembers. It will get strong again."

There was much goodness in Alfonso's life. He loved school and his playmates, fishing and wandering along the river, and visits from his uncles and aunts who came from Puerto de Luna. He loved his abuelo Liborio, the old mustachioed man who brought apples, fresh corn and chile, ripe tomatoes and cucumbers.

The love of nature he had known in the village, even though the village was now a memory, was rekindled in the town's environment.

Busy Highway 66 brought tourists to the gas station where he went to put air in his bike tires. He was there the day a car pulled up, and a man got out and asked the attendant for directions. There was something rotten on the road to Tucumcari, he said.

"Road kill," the attendant said. The man shrugged.

Alfonso stared at the boy and girl in the car. He had seen them somewhere before. Where? In picture books at school! Yes!

"It's Dick and Jane!" he shouted, and waved. The blonde, blue-eyed kids waved back.

"Hi! This is New Mexico. I live here. Are you from the East?"

The boy and girl nodded and giggled.

"Where's your dog?" he asked, and a small dog appeared at the window, barking and wagging its tail. "Spot!"

It was true! Dick and Jane. See Spot! See Spot run! Then the car pulled away. "Bye!" he waved.

He hadn't told them his name.

"I'm Alfonso," he whispered. "Agapita said I would have seven sorrows!"

K, there is good news.

His hand was getting stronger, and the shoe his father had cut and sewed to fit his foot worked well.

He wondered what kind of shoes clubfoot Jesus wore. Would an angel bring him a pair of sandals? Or was there a saint in charge of shoes? There seemed to be a saint for every need, so why not one that brought good-fitting shoes? Santo Zapatos.

If your shoe doesn't fit well, especially if you have corns or flat feet, you pray to Santo Zapatos for relief.

Then there was Agnes. Late afternoons he played hide-and-seek with her and her brothers and sisters. The first time they hid behind the outhouse, Agnes held him close and kissed him. Her soft lips pressed against his, her tongue slid into his mouth. It was warm, a sensation he had never felt before. It only lasted a moment, but for him it created a world of dizzying time he did not want to disappear.

The kiss left a thin film on his lips, her sweet saliva, the membranous covering of her tongue. He came to believe that everything in life came wrapped in a membrane of one sort or other, holding life together, like the smooth, sticky, almost invisible film that had lubricated his first kiss. All the liquids that come when making love are silky, aromatic, tasty, he said. The juices of lovers that erupt during love's passion are the essence of love; they slide lovers into the absolute moment. God.

Everything in nature was connected with these films of love, even the rocks that lay at the bottom of the river. When he walked barefoot, he felt the slippery green algae and moss that coated the rocks. The water's gift, a sensuous touch.

He helped his father butcher sheep in the corral by the windmill. He cut through the sticky thin membranes, blood-veined fabrics that held the organs and intestines in place. Everything came enveloped in a wet sheath—the brain, the heart, even, he guessed, the fetus in the womb. Membranes were, he thought, what held the universe together.

The dark matter of the universe was the membrane that held galaxies in place. Were it not for the elasticity of that organic energy, the tremendous pull of gravity would destroy everything. Was dark matter a membrane analogous to the one he felt from Agnes's kiss? Were he and Agnes connected to the universe, that miracle of miracles that Agapita called the Great Mystery?

Was the Big Bang a universal kiss? A single-cell kiss that blew the universe into existence? Whose kiss had created the galaxies and the membrane that spread across expanding space?

Her kiss was a blessing for shy Alfonso. She, in her innocence, had offered something that no one else could give. Her lips and hot breath pressed into him, and he kissed her back. His first childhood kiss, the thrill, the unexpected feelings, his heart pumping, hormones rushing, Mother Nature at work.

I know Fonso had enjoyed some flirtations during high school, and when we were students we hung out with the pizzeria girls. Those young women were far more experienced than we were. He slept with one, but I guess her kisses couldn't hold him; the membrane of love snapped. Perhaps he never forgot that first kiss from sweaty, dusty little Agnes.

He remembered Agnes pressing against him, her small breasts rubbing against his chest. Her summer blouse slipped down, and he saw, in the dusk of evening, her pink nipples. A moment of revelation, an emotion so keen he closed his eyes.

He had known other sensations. One day while walking on the llano, a bald eagle buzzed him, swooping down on him so close its claws scraped the top of his head. The cries of the eagle were a message. Passion in nature. He was too young to understand the fuller meaning of passion. He just felt blessed.

He gutted rabbits for Sunday dinners, their blood ripe-red on his hands, slippery like the mucus on the catfish he caught. Was everything like this? A blessing. The membranes tearing apart and exposing throbbing life.

Agnes was a creature of nature, as he was, a blessing. Her touch was the touch of passion. Agapita had taught him to respect everything that lived in the natural world. He would respect Agnes. Like the eagle that had left its message imprinted in his heart, Agnes's warm lips and saliva filled him with a burst of illumination, a new delight. How could this be? How could a simple kiss hold so much excitement?

Puppy love? Yes or no, what difference does it make? They were innocent children drawn together, as Adam and Eve must have touched each other in the Garden. You know Eve couldn't reach the apple high on the tree, so Adam wrapped his arms around her thighs and held her up. What fragrances unrolled as he held her steady, she reaching for that fateful apple, becoming the woman who would be his wife, the aroma of the apples wafting throughout the garden, the animals crying hosanna, liberation! Juices imagined bursting from that first bite. Who took the first bite? Was it he who desired the apple? When he let her down, was it he who took the first bite? Did desire thrive in the garden?

Do you remember your first kiss? Let every kiss be like the first. I don't know what else to say.

The river, ah, the river. There is no Alfonso without the river, the tranquil Pecos, a beautiful stream gurgling down the flank of the Sangre de Cristo Mountains, flowing past Indian pueblos and Hispano villages: Cochiti; Kewa, which used to be Santo Domingo; Anton Chico; Santa Rosa de Lima; Puerto de Luna—the names are music, the poetry of the natives who settled along the river. Hard-flint people who struggled to make a living from fields of corn irrigated by the river. They built churches and attended mass on Sundays . . . a spiritual people who drew inspiration from their connection to earth and sky.

The elements of nature flowed through the Nuevo Mexicanos.

Nature gave and nature took away; they bowed their heads and thanked God. There was meaning and purpose in their lives. God commanded, they obeyed.

Even death could not destroy their faith. The people gathered in a capilla built by a family who had the means to construct the small chapel and dedicate it to the family's patron saint. La Virgen, San Miguel, San José, San Martín: the Catholic religion has no shortage of saints. Perhaps one of them had performed a miracle, maybe cured a sick family member, and a vow had been made to honor that saint. A capilla was built and the statue of the saint placed inside.

Those small towns and wayward ranches most often had no attending priest. Penitentes existed in some towns, the brotherhood of the Nazarene devoted to Jesus. The men were active in community affairs, attending to funerals when a priest was not available, helping a poor widow in her time of need. They carried the burden of the Lenten season, re-enacting the Passion. In the dark of the morada, their prayers shook the walls, alabados for the Nazarene who watched over them.

Alfonso remembered the cries of mourning women, funerals, young and old, passages.

Agnes loved the river as much as Alfonso. In those days the summer floods were torrents that swept the river channel clean, leaving behind sand beaches, playas where Alfonso and his friends played. That's where Alfonso and Agnes loitered that summer afternoon. The town kids splashed and swam by the bridge—the one where Lupito was killed by the men from the town. He had murdered the sheriff, then ran to hide under the bridge. Fonso saw it all. Our innocent two sought a quiet place downriver, a playa full of sunshine yet protected by the giant cottonwoods.

They talked and threw pebbles in the water, and slowly but surely the emotions of the river lulled them into the time of the river, a time of sharing. They kissed, as they had done when playing hide-and-seek, and even at that age a bond was formed. Fonso felt that Agnes had entered his body. He felt her inside, as she felt him.

The day was hot. The sun beat brilliant on her pale skin, his dark brown from days on the llano. For both, the emotion of the moment was unexpected. Laughing, they took off their clothes and ran into the river, splashing, chasing each other, then running back to roll in the warm sand. Their bodies covered with sand, they dove back into the water and washed each other clean. Then quickly they dressed, and hand in hand they walked home.

I revel in their joy. I am happy for my Alfonso who was to know sorrow. Their days together make my story worthwhile. But what if she had spoiled him forever? Would he expect every woman he knew thereafter to possess the magic he had known with Agnes? Was it her soul that slid into his body? Did her soul now live in him?

I would call that true love, even if it came to two so young. Have you known that emotion? That delight? Does one know only one true love in life?

Will there ever again be a love like your first love? If you find that second love, then you're lucky. If not, are you destined to remain a seeker, always searching for the bliss you once felt to the roots of your soul?

"The Great Deceiver lurks by the roadside," the priest said. He was trying to explain budding sexuality to the children. "You are becoming young men and women"—he paused. "Your bodies are changing." The young priest who had problems of his own didn't quite know how to explain sex to the eager boys and girls.

What? their eyes asked. Tell us.

They understood. A change was coming. No, it was already here. Most of them had practiced kissing. Some were into touching. It all felt good and strange and brought dreams at night, dreams they couldn't understand.

"The devil will tempt you," the priest said. There it was, temptation and sin. The things they did with their bodies during this time of awakening led to sin. Do not touch. It's a sin, and if you die with mortal sin on your soul, you go straight to hell.

That sense of guilt has plagued many a good Catholic. It was a constraint Alfonso had to reconcile or break if he was ever to know happiness.

Alfonso glanced at Agnes. She looked at him from where she sat with the girls, huddled together in fear. Had they sinned? The small pleasures they found in each other seemed more like being in God than being in sin. Should they believe the priest and break the bond of love they felt?

What followed was the agony of Saturday afternoon confession.

The children practiced, laughing, joking, making lists of sins, comparing their lists, who had the most and biggest sins, who would get the biggest penance. Then doom set in. The practice was over. It was Saturday afternoon. The church now felt like a huge, dark dungeon. The sweet aroma of candle wax was gone, leaving in its stead a musty smell. The silence was deafening. Then the priest's footsteps sounded on the weathered, wooden floor. He looked at the children in line, nodded, and entered the confessional.

It took all the courage each child could muster to enter, make the sign of the cross, and whisper, *Forgive me, father, for I have sinned.* It didn't end there for Fonso. Even penance and absolution could not erase the seed of guilt the priest had planted.

Ah, Catholic guilt, K. You haven't been plagued by it like Fonso.

Doubt crept into Alfonso's mind. Doubt made good Catholic boys and girls think twice. Budding flesh could not be trusted. This was long before people talked about hormones, but the message was clear. Maybe it was best to wait. But give Agnes up? She who held his hand and walked beside him. She who had kissed him deeply and formed a gold bond between her heart and his.

Her breath was his, his hers.

Now he held back. They talked, but it wasn't like before. Even the tone of their voices changed. The love they had found was now tinged with the fear of sin. Their young, inexplicable longing for each other was now curtailed. The priest had won, the church had won. The body was no longer innocent; it came tainted with original sin.

Why is there original sin? he asked himself. Who told us so? Who placed it in my soul?

Why so many rules that contradicted his growing sense of self? Why was he disbelieving? The commandments of the church had been his moral foundation, built block by block, each block a teaching he had taken to heart. Now, as he questioned the rules, the foundation began to crumble, dust sifted through the cracks.

Could he find new, kinder rules? Where?

Winter came, and the river grew sluggish. They covered their bodies with thick coats and jackets. Brown, decaying cottonwood leaves covered the sandy beaches of summer. Hand in hand, Alfonso and Agnes walked across the bridge. His friend, the Vitamin Kid, came running and challenged him to race, but Alfonso didn't respond.

He and Agnes walked in silence, over the river and away from the town, Santa Rosa de Lima.

How did the small town on the eastern llano of New Mexico get its name? Alfonso told me this story. Long ago there lived a young woman in Lima, Perú. Rosa was a votary of the Virgin Mary, and she spent long hours helping the poor and homeless on the streets of the city.

As the Virgin Mary ascended to heaven, according to Alfonso's story, she cast a shadow on earth. The sun shone on her as she rose, and her shadow fell across a certain longitude. The Virgin's shadow lingered on the land, and those who stepped on it were blessed. They could perform miracles. One day on her way to help the homeless, Rosa stepped on the Virgin's shadow. A voice from the sky whispered, *Hence you will be known as Santa Rosa de Lima.*

That's how Rosa became a saint. A lovely story—

Wait, there's another story. La Virgen de Guadalupe had appeared in México in 1531, according to church records. She gave Juan Diego a bunch of rosas de Castilla, which he bundled in his tilma, the cloak that later held the image of the Virgin. Roses became the spiritual flower for Mexican Catholics. In 1598 the españoles and Indians who colonized New Mexico brought with them rosas de Castilla, lovely bushes that bloom with delicate roses. Thus the trinity that intrigued Alfonso: Juan Diego, Santa Rosa de Lima, and the roses from Castile.

Saints can turn earthly matter into sacred essence. These happenings are called miracles, and Catholics have a saint for every purpose. You lose your wallet, pray to St. Wallet and it will be returned. Your car breaks down, blame St. La Cucaracha Ya No Puede Caminar. You lose your girlfriend, Santa Amor didn't answer your prayers. Need a job, pray to Santo Jale. And on and on.

Alfonso believed in the saints and their powers. His mother had taught her children to pray to the saints of the church. Because she believed, Alfonso believed.

Santa Rosa de Lima's specialty was curing cripples. On the streets of Lima she prayed over cripples, and when she was done, the lame threw away their crutches. Her specialty was clubfeet. She could work miracles on deformed feet. Now she was the patron saint of the town of Santa Rosa de Lima, Alfonso's home.

I don't know what to make of that connection. Did it mean that

Alfonso would someday walk without a limp? He did, you know, but it took years of dogged determination.

Or was it the saint from Perú who cured him?

Alfonso's mother had led him on the path of the saints.

The shadow of the Blessed Mother still lay on the earth. Where it fell, miracles were bound to occur. Did the Virgin's shadow fall over New Mexico? Spirituality runs deep in the land. This is a sacred place, the natives say. The Pueblo Indians believe they emerged from the world beneath this world through the sipapu. The earth is our mother, they say. Then along came the españoles from México. We came to settle this land through the intervention of Jesucristo, the Catholic Hispanos say. Either way, there's a covenant with the earth, la sagrada tierra.

But why is there so much poverty in this spiritual place? Why so little arable land to cultivate? Why do people have to work so hard to make a living? Are we being tested? Is our struggle a blessing or a curse?

What about Pastura del Llano, Pastura of the Holy Child? The village was becoming a memory. Fonso could still smell the llano earth after a summer rain, hear the wind rustle dry grasses, hear the shrill song of cicadas. Nature would always be in him.

And Agapita?

He loved the old woman. The midwife whose hands were the first to touch him had been like a mother to him. She had passed her wisdom into him; she had taught him the way of the creatures in that wide and windy plain.

Now he lived and breathed the air of Santa Rosa de Lima. He swam in the river and walked in the hills. The town was situated in a large depression, and the legend was that sometime in the future it would sink. Did the story mean really sink, or was sinking a metaphor? Interstate 40 was destined to replace old Route 66. As fewer tourists stopped in town, a downward economic spiral began. Across the country, towns bypassed by the interstate began a slow death. They sank.

Alfonso and his friends hung out at the gas stations and looked at the tourists. The families who stopped for gas were from another world. A gas station attendant gave Fonso an old map that a tourist had left behind. He studied the map and learned there were fascinating cities beyond the town's horizon. Early on, he got the urge to see those cities. Years later, he and his wife would visit many foreign cities. Once in Machu Picchu in the Peruvian mountains, he walked among the mysterious and intriguing ruins, sensed the ghosts of the worshippers who had built the city, wondered if the Virgin's shadow had fallen on that place.

After leaving Santa Rosa de Lima, tourists driving west would climb a long slope up to the timberline, juniper, piñon, and pine. Antelope herds grazed peacefully on either side of the road. Overhead, vultures and hawks dotted the clear blue sky. Beyond Alburquerque they would arrive at the Continental Divide, and from there coast down to California.

Driving east, the land flattened as the road entered West Texas and the Great Plains beyond. The year he was fired by the rancher, Alfonso's father loaded the truck with family and supplies and drove to West Texas to pick cotton. Times were difficult in the years after the Great Depression. War had exploded, and many of their neighbors moved to California to work in the shipyards and agriculture. Alfonso's father didn't want to leave. The llano was still his home. He would work for a season in the cotton fields and return home.

Neighbors from nearby villages and ranches joined the trek into the Texas cotton fields. They worked alongside blacks and learned their ways. After a day's work, the children played together. At dusk, after supper, neighbors gathered to talk and listen to songs. Life was difficult, but singing eased the pain.

The experience opened Alfonso's eyes to a new world. He never forgot what he learned that singular season in those fields. He never forgot the nobility of hard work. The poorest family shared what they had with neighbors. Fonso's mother fed her family, but there was always enough to share with others. If there was a sick neighbor unable to work that day, Alfonso would deliver a bowl of his mother's soup and a sweet potato pie. Everyone helped each other. A life's lesson learned.

It was survival. The majority of people from that area were poor. Hispanics had been in the state over four hundred years, but except for a few rich families who owned land, the majority remained rural poor. Most had little or no education. Alfonso's mother stressed education to her children. The village school taught only the first few grades. In town, Alfonso and his sisters could graduate from high school. But work was not easy to come by, especially for their parents, who had only a second-grade education.

He remembered following his mother into town, where for a while she worked cleaning motel rooms. "Thank God for Highway 66," he told me. "It not only provided work at motels and gas stations, it was an education."

"How?"

"Tourists," he answered. "I loved tourists. We would hang out at the gas stations. We always needed air for the bike tires. Tourists were like ants, traveling west, some east. They weren't like us. Tourists were Americanos, we were Mexicanos. In school the teachers said we were Spanish Americans. Later we became Mexican Americans, then Hispanic. In the sixties we called ourselves Chicanos. Then Latinos."

He told me that he helped pick cotton. Not with the long sacks the grownups pulled down the rows, but using a small sack his mother had made for him. He remembered the day a dry devil's claw pierced his leg. He cried as his mother pulled it out. Perhaps the devil's claw was the symbol of the hard work in the hundred-degree sun, the heavy sacks that had to be dragged to the weighing station, women working alongside their men and still having to get dinner to feed the family. Bone tired.

The fields were full of devil's claw vines. Workers wore two pairs of pants for protection. If you brushed against a vine, a claw might sink its barbs into your flesh. Grown men cursed when they pulled out a claw, wiped the bloody wound with rotgut whiskey or kerosene oil, and hoped it wouldn't get infected. That would mean days lost from work.

Fonso got strong with work. He returned home having lived through an experience that most of his friends would never know. He had seen a world that robbed the sweat and strength of men and women for a few cents.

K. The river; oh, the river. So much happened at the river. He wrote about death at the river. Remember Lupito? And Agnes? He would never get over Agnes.

He spent summers at the river, fishing, playing with J. D., Charlie, and Ida, summers of green joy. Huckleberry Finn had his Mississippi, Alfonso had the Pecos. Every kid should have a river. Water was a theme in his life. His mother's maiden name was Mares, from mar, the sea, the embracing sea. His father was Martin, more akin to the Roman god of war because he could be a terror when he went on a drinking binge.

Perhaps there's some destiny written in our names.

It was in one of the creeks that emptied into the Pecos that Fonso saw the golden carp for the first time. An epiphany, a river god swimming in the clear, pristine water of El Rito. He returned often to sit in awe on the bank of the stream as the golden carp swam by. Fonso was entering the world of myth and legend.

So many spirits lived along the river: the Crying Woman, the Coco Man, witches. When night fell, shadows from dreams screamed at the boy lost in the web of river willows, lorded over by the gigantic cottonwoods with their fierce dark branches. The darkness was green, green men and women reaching out to take the boy.

The river could be as labyrinthine as his nightmares.

Alfonso wrote the encounter with the golden carp as legend, the making of a myth that was to persist, as all myths persist in the dark subconscious of man. The carp swam from the Blue Hole down El Rito and into the Pecos. Water everywhere. No need to retell that story.

Tramping up and down the river made him strong. He knew the river and its seasons. "The river is in me," he said. I didn't quite understand what he meant. "The llano is in me," he said. "The people are in me." La gente. His soul was made from those things. He made soul from nature and people.

Maybe his story is about the making of soul. You know about the train accident, but did you know he went through an out-of-body experience? In spite of all the doubts he was later to have about religion, he believed in soul, the inner essence that for a few minutes left his body that day.

The train had flipped him down the embankment. He fractured a vertebra in his neck. He couldn't move, so he lay face down, breathing dust, waiting for someone to come. But his frightened friends had run away.

He waited, he said, for an eternity, hardly breathing. Then he felt the shadow of death hovering over him, beckoning. As he was about to take death's hand, his soul began to rise into the blue sky, his soul separating from his body. In a cylinder of light, his soul rose and looked down at the body lying on the ground. Soul saw the train disappearing in the distance, the grass bathed in a golden light, Fonso's friends running toward the village. His body remained face down on the ground, but his soul had risen. Soul and flesh had come down his mother's birth canal, and now soul was separating from flesh. Going where? To eternity if soul did not return to flesh. Instead of panic, he told me he felt very calm. He smiled. He was dying, but there was no fear of death.

Many have described out-of-body experiences, the sense of soul leaving the body. Such accounts make believers out of us skeptics. I trembled when I heard Alfonso's account of those precious moments. Finally, Agapita picked him up. She saved his life, because I suppose a minute more and his soul would have gone up into the clouds, beyond retrieving. Breathing dust, he would have died.

That's the way it happens: soul leaves the body and we die. That year his body would be weak, but not his soul. Life-changing events like that build inner strength. Trauma kills us or makes us stronger. I think that's why he became a writer, to tell with each story the making of soul.

The land and the people were in him. He wasn't part of nature, he was *in* nature. He was *in* the people.

Alfonso, Alfonso, if only I could take away the sorrow of that day and the many days to come. So much sorrow caused by the accidents of life. To love is to know sorrow. I can only imagine the sorrow his mother felt, but how can I, a mere shaman of words, probe the emotions of her heart?

I did love him. Loved him more than my brothers. Yet when I tell his story, I realize there's so much I didn't know. We shared a lot when we were at the university, times spent talking about art and literature, reading the Beat poets of the fifties, weekends spent fishing the Pecos and Jemez Rivers. So much is now only contained in the thin and fragile membrane that is memory.

One can never completely know a person. Not even in the deepest love. There are many rooms in every person's heart, rooms filled with experiences, thoughts, memories. A distant primitive memory lives in the blood, images from our past, our inheritance from the cave. Perhaps that's why there's so much violence in this world. We are creatures molded long ago in the ancient caves. We do great things, we love, we help others, we have evolved. Our species has written the stories of heroes and gods. Great religions have sprouted from our spiritual yearnings. And yet.

Can that dark inheritance be overcome with love?

Maybe that's what Alfonso's story is all about. Love. How many different kinds of love are there? Love of father, mother, siblings, ancestors, place, country, God, and on and on. Or is it all the same? What do we want or need when we seek love?

Alfonso spoke of primitive love, a love deeper than romantic love, not love as Hollywood movies portray it. Love should be natural, uncompromised, love in nature like Adam and Eve must have enjoyed before the apple fell—but even the Fall couldn't end their love. They stuck together, went out into the wild, had children, became the metaphor by which we judge ourselves. How many can say they have loved naked under the apple trees, like Adam and Eve, or like Alfonso and Agnes at the river on a summer day?

His favorite poets those university years were the English

Romantics. He read widely in world literature, but Wordsworth, Keats, Shelley, Coleridge inspired him. He found a music room in the Student Union Building where he could listen to recordings of classical music. He spent hours listening to Tchaikovsky's piano concertos, Rachmaninoff's 5th Symphony, his gloomy composition full of grief when Tchaikovsky died. Everything he heard stirred his soul, and from that grounding he would compose his early poetry and stories. Lost now.

The Romantic poets loved nature in all its aspects, and they believed in freedom from the drudgery of meaningless existence. They intuited that the world was becoming too much for us, the age of the machine was exploding and there was no stopping it. Unchain mankind, cried Rousseau, and the capitalists went to Africa and enslaved its natives. Men and women became property to be bought, sold, and traded.

Is love an attempt to save oneself? Can the person we love save us?

Is love a complete ecstatic surrendering, a commingling of body and soul? Does God partake in the ecstasy? Or is it that we as nature's creatures create God in the image of our love?

How often was Alfonso to be disappointed in love? Until he met the woman he married. But that book is already written, and I don't want to get ahead of the story.

He told me about the summer his family went to work in the West Texas cotton fields. In the forties, families throughout the state were still suffering from the Depression. Entire families packed up and either moved to California or went to work in Texas, Colorado, or Wyoming. Many never returned to their native villages. The culture of the Nuevo Mexicanos began to dissipate; the children were forgetting the language of their ancestors.

Laute and Salomon, his older brothers, bought pints of cheap whiskey and stashed the loot under the truck's floorboard. The Texas counties were dry, so they had no trouble selling the contraband. Every penny went into their mother's jar. She was the banker of the hard-earned money.

They lived in a shack for a month. The rancher's wife was kind, he remembered. But there existed deep racial prejudices in Texas. Mexicans and blacks were in the same boat; they couldn't use white facilities. Pick cotton, then go home was the rule. The era of Jim Crow was alive.

Some of those prejudices spread into the eastern part of New Mexico, often called Little Texas. He remembered the day they stopped to gas the truck, but couldn't use the bathrooms. NO MEXICANS ALLOWED, read the sign. What does that do to a child?

Nuevo Mexicanos whose ancestors had colonized the Territory of New Mexico in the late sixteenth century were held in contempt by southern whites who had migrated into the state. Two of his brothers who had just returned from military service were not allowed to eat lunch in a Clovis restaurant. They told the story around the kitchen table. Too many infuriating stories to tell.

School was in session when the family returned home. Alfonso and his sisters were late. Hispanic families taught their children to feel shame if they did something wrong. Ten vergüenza, they admonished. If you disgrace your family, you must feel shame. Years later his sister Edwina told him of the shame she had felt being held back a grade because she had missed a month of school. Her schoolmates knew she had been working in the cotton fields.

Poverty teaches survival, but it can also create feelings of shame. The kids whose parents had regular jobs in town didn't have to pick cotton. The poor did. Did feelings of shame create feelings of inferiority? Alfonso felt it, but having home and the love and unity of family provided a circle of strength.

We compare ourselves to others, and when we fall short of the norm, the feelings can lead to a kind of sadness. He didn't have the things his friends had. Grade-school friends shared candy he couldn't buy. He didn't have money to buy marbles, so by borrowing a few and becoming an expert at the game, he beat the other boys and soon had a jarful. The bike his mother got him was bought on credit, and the payments were gorged with interest.

The divide between the rich and the poor grows and grows. The world will crash.

The family returned with hard-earned money in their mother's jar. Alfonso got a bike to pedal to school and to his favorite fishing spots. His Uncle Pablo's family moved to Alburquerque and left their dog. Sporty moved in with Alfonso and became a faithful constant companion.

Alfonso's sisters got new clothes. School seemed to slowly erase the time they had spent in the cotton fields. On the surface things returned to normal. But shame never goes away. It's like grief: a person can move on, but the memory remains.

Are feelings of shame a kind of sorrow? Is that what Alfonso felt? Life in the small town was molding him as much as life at home. But that doesn't explain why some of his experiences were unique.

Late one afternoon while he was walking along a river path, a huge white owl came swooping down on him. Its wings were spread out like the picture of the Holy Spirit he had seen at church. In the picture the Holy Spirit is portrayed as a dove with wings outspread, the spirit of God's love.

The white owl flew over his head, illuminated briefly by shards of light from the setting sun. "The Holy Spirit!" he cried. The spirit of the river had touched him.

Why did that magnificent bird appear? Remember, Agapita had fed his blood to the owls. He was of that family. Maybe that's why the white owl came screeching down on him, fanning him with its huge wings, as the owls at his birth had fanned the breath of life into his lungs. The owl's bright eyes pierced him with a look of recognition. It flew so close, he heard its scream. "Truth and goodness," it cried, then lifted away, over his head, its wings blessing him as a priest might bless a child by passing his hand over the little one's head. The owl turned toward the dark hills, where a jagged thunderbolt hit the earth and exploded.

The white owl and the dove were the Holy Spirit. The white owl had been real; the dove he saw only in pictures. He could honor both because they were one and the same. The dove appeared in pictures; the owl was the living spirit of the land. The owl had blessed him as the Holy Spirit blesses all. The owl had given him a message: He could be good. All was good. Goodness prevailed. The image of the owl and its message never left him.

The next time he went to church, he looked at the picture of the Holy Spirit, and there, superimposed on the dove, was the image of the white owl. He rubbed his eyes. Owl and Holy Spirit were one.

With time he learned that images from the cultures of the world could be laid over his cultural images, and thus they gained extra power. A Tibetan mandala lay beneath the New Mexico Zia sun symbol: the two were one and the same. He learned that folktales, images, and symbols he had thought were particular really weren't. Everything had been on earth before his time, his dreams had already been dreamt. He was part of all that had been in the mind of humanity and the earth.

He was unique for his time, but universal because he was attached to history's umbilical cord.

K, everything was changing in a changing world. His three older brothers had returned from the service, stayed awhile, then moved on. Alburquerque and Santa Fe held excitement and work. They came and went.

Would they become a memory?

Alfonso vaguely remembered each brother's characteristics. Martinito liked to gather his brothers and sisters in a small bedroom, turn off the lone bulb, and frighten them with spooky stories. He teased the girls to the point of exasperation. Ranch work with their father wasn't for him. Sometime during those years, he attended classes at Highlands with the help of the GI Bill. He stayed in Las Vegas and started a family.

Fonso looked up to his older brothers, admired them, prayed for them when they were away, but he was too young to be part of the trio. His first novel described them as giants. He remembered events, jackrabbit hunting. They were experts with the .22 rifle. They hunted birds along the river and fed them to the pig. Once they took off his pants, and laughed as they beat on his chest with their knuckles, calling him an Indian because he was the dark one in the family. Then they ran off to town.

Did they love him? Yes, but later he realized he was never that close to them, he really didn't know them. They remained vague images in his dreams.

Laute would stay on in Santa Rosa de Lima for a few years, work at a local grocery store, finish high school, start a family. He gave Alfonso a first-base glove, and they played catch. The town kids formed a baseball team, the Comets. A wonderful summer, he remembered. He was growing stronger each day.

Laute moved to the Barelas barrio in Alburquerque, and in 1952 Alfonso's family followed. He described the move and the barrio in his second novel. Laute was athletic; he loved to play whatever sport was in season with the barrio kids, teaching them the finer points of baseball or football. They admired him for that.

Salomon was an enigma, the oldest, a good worker. Alfonso remembered his brothers coming home from work, their backs red and peeling from the sun. The story was that years earlier, Salomon had fallen from the railroad water tank in Pastura del Llano. The three liked to climb the steel rungs of the ladder and sit at the top. From there they had a 360-degree view of the endless llano. Nothing but cattle grazing and the ubiquitous vultures circling overhead. Miles away lay the escarpment of the mesa, the tabletop hills where deer ran.

The brothers saw an empty landscape. Maybe that's why they left as soon as they could. Agapita had taught Alfonso the beauty of the land and its seasons; they only felt monotony. Either that or the sight and sound of trains receding into the horizon, going west to California. The mournful wail of the outward-bound called them, a restless loneliness settled in their souls, and they had to move on.

Alfonso's first novel described his childhood friends, his older brothers, his sisters Edwina, Angie, Dolores, and Loretta. The girls seemed to live in their own world. He played jacks with them, watched them cut out Sears catalog models and spend endless hours playing paper dolls. They listened to the radio, distant stations from Oklahoma and Texas, cowboy songs, pop tunes, Mexican ballads. Alfonso listened and learned the songs, but he didn't quite belong to the circle the sisters created for themselves. With their mother's permission, Edwina and Angie talked on the crank telephone with school friends in town.

Those were the days when you lifted the receiver, turned the crank, and waited for the operator to say, "Number, please." She then connected you with the party you were calling. Party lines abounded, so you could listen in on your neighbors.

Compare those phones to the ones today, and you get an idea of time past. Of time and the llano, all only vague memories now.

Fonso's mother assigned him to accompany his sisters to Saturday afternoon movies. The path into town and the town itself were safe, but the old Hispanic tradition of a man always walking with the women clung on, and it took a strange twist in this case. The small boy walking his sisters to the movies was hardly a bodyguard.

The girls didn't like the idea of needing a chaperone, especially their kid brother, so they made him sit apart from them in the theater. From there, every Saturday afternoon, Alfonso watched the unfolding worlds of Gene Autry, Roy Rogers, Tarzan, Frankenstein, Abbot and Costello, Mexican movies like the ever-popular Cantinflas, and the serial stories with their weekly chapters. He was fascinated by the to-be-continued plots that left the hero in distress, hanging in suspense, a time that suspended disbelief. He looked forward to the next Saturday to see how Tarzan would escape from the lion's den. The Pecos Theater was a godsend for a thriving imagination. Thank his mother for scraping up enough change to send him to the movies.

The world delivered by the Movietone News taught contemporary events and foreign history to an impressionable Alfonso.

He sat alone in the dark movie house, nursing a Payday candy bar so it would last, one of the few treats his mother's piggy bank could afford. Movies stirred his imagination. A movie was a story he could figure out even if it was in English; in fact, being at the movies became a language-learning experience. The movies weren't like the stories his father or Agapita told. Their stories reflected life around him. Sitting next to Agapita he felt close to her, and he believed in the reality of the folklore characters he knew by heart.

"La Llorona drowned her children and ran crying along the river," Agapita intoned, and Alfonso could see the Crying Woman running through the river forest he knew so well. Pedro de Ordimalas, Juan del Oso, el Cucuy, the song of Delgadina, all characters living in the stories. Sitting next to Agapita, he participated intimately in the story as she at times changed her tone, inflections, and facial expressions, and with each telling she created new surprises. Sometimes she changed subtle passages from the last telling, creating a new twist in the story. One had to listen closely.

She couldn't change the Ave María or the Lord's Prayer, but she could work wonders with slight changes as she told the cuentos, making them come alive night after night. The children never tired of those folktales, even though they knew them by heart. Absorbed in the time of the story, they became part of the narrative.

The movie stories lay flat on the screen, far away from where he sat in the dark theater, and those stories belonged to everyone sitting in that dark theater, not just him. Still, they were stories. His world began to be made of story.

Alfonso stayed close to his mother. As soon as their home was constructed on that rocky hill by the river—the hill they called Mockingbird Hill because of the abundance of the birds—he and his mother dug out rocks from a large plot by the side of the house. Martin brought loads of cow manure and tilled it into the soil. The following summer they had a thriving garden irrigated by water from the well. Their garden produced enough green chile for home use, and extra for Alfonso to sell. He pedaled into town and went door to door selling chile. Twenty-five cents was the most he could ask for a bote de diez, as the can was called. A morning's work for a dollar.

Sometimes he ran into classmates in town. "Fonso's selling chile!" they laughed. It seemed to Alfonso that the town kids didn't have to work. They always seemed to have money for candy, nice school clothes, new pencils, erasers, brand-new tops to spin during top season, loads of marbles to put in the ring in the schoolyard before and after school.

They were small things, but those small things made a lasting impression on Alfonso. In his world, there were those who had and those who didn't. Many of the neighbors and family friends who came to visit were poor. They belonged to that broad stream of the poor who had weathered the Depression, for whom the process of recovery would take generations. For some, recovery never came;

the downward spiral of poverty would continue, especially for those without an education. It was difficult for Nuevo Mexicanos to get a good education beyond high school. Alfonso knew the struggle first-hand. He knew the stories of those denied.

Home held the family together. Alfonso's father, with the help of his older sons, had built their home near the river. They were poor, but having a home and a piece of land made a difference. Making their own adobes, they constructed the house with the sun-dried mud bricks. The family had a roof over their heads, and a windmill to run cold, clear water into the house. A cistern collected rain for drinking water. Martin and his sons had dug a large hole for the cistern, lined it with concrete, then installed gutters to channel rain from the roof into the tank. Fonso, the child observing the work, admired his father's ingenuity. Was this the same man who on some weekends drank too much and became a terrible storm?

They excavated for a well, using dynamite to blow up the conglomerate, then went down into the hole, filling buckets with sand and gravel and hauling them to the top. No machines, all done by muscle and sweat. And the scary day when a package of dynamite sticks didn't go off. The men waited and waited. What had gone wrong? Why hadn't it exploded? They wiped the sweat from their brows, knowing one of them would have to go down. Wisps of smoke rose from the hole. The string had burned, but it hadn't set off the dynamite. Finally, Salomon made the sign of the cross, tied a rope around his waist, and slid down the dark shaft. After several anxious minutes, he called out that everything was okay. They slipped the ladder down and he came up, sweating profusely but smiling. Pats on the back and homemade beer were the reward.

They had only half an acre, but it was enough to keep a few animals. A pig, chickens, a cow with calf, rabbits. Alfonso's job was to care for the animals that were used for food. When his father wasn't doing odd jobs in town, he worked on the ranches. He always returned with a fat sheep, which he slaughtered in the small corral behind the house. Mutton for chile stews, ribs browned in the stove's butane gas oven.

Martin liked to tease his children. Although the head of a sheep had little meat, he would place it in a large pan and bake it in the oven. After dinner, Alfonso and his sisters sat around the table picking at the bits of meat and the brain. Alfonso recalled it as one of his fondest memories. There was lots of laughter as his squeamish sisters picked at the skull. The family was together.

The sheep's stomach and tripe were thoroughly washed and used to make menudo, a stew sometimes flavored with posole, a common New Mexican dish. His mother's New Mexican dishes were delicious, tasty, satisfying soul food. Later in life, Fonso would seek out restaurants that served menudo, posole, and red chile stews accompanied with homemade tortillas, always searching for a flavor that would match his mother's. The food was nourishing, but most of all it held his mother's love and her tenacious devotion to her children. She was food and love, care, prayers, soul.

There are too many events in the life of a man, some joyful, others so full of sorrow they can kill. What doesn't kill re-creates the person. The old personality slips away and a new one emerges. Personality is the exterior coat we wear; the essential soul remains, and soul retains memories.

Is soul memory? If soul is eternal, so is memory. A metaphysical question he needed to answer.

Does the universe have a memory of its beginning and evolution? The universe is conscious, he wrote, and therefore it must have memory. If the universe is God, then it must have memory. Do we live in that memory? Are we merely repeating a life that has been lived before in other forms? In other places?

Being born anew is not easy. So it went with Alfonso.

K, we were sitting at Okie Joe's, a bar near the university, having a beer and talking, smoking. Those days we smoked, thought we were grown up, spent hours talking philosophy. Both of us worked part-time so we could afford Saturday night beers.

Around us swirled city workers, nurses from the Presbyterian Hospital, university jocks, secretaries, bar regulars, and old farts from the neighborhood. It was a typical 1960s bar near the university, with 1950s music blaring from the jukebox. A sexy waitress who was interested in Alfonso always had a smile for him. He attracted women.

What was her name?

After beers we usually headed over to the Casa Luna pizzeria, where the gals we were dating worked. Free pizza, late parties, more beer, and sometimes we spent the night with them. I look back now and think they were wasted nights, but not at the time. We were young, and sex was consensual. Face it, I really enjoyed those years. Everyone seemed to understand, no commitments.

We had just seen a Bergman movie at the Guild, a local arts theater, and we were discussing the magical world of *The Seventh Seal* when Alfonso brought up the subject of witchcraft. Bergman, he said, could have made a movie about the llano and its people. Agapita did more magic than the characters in the movie. "I believe she could fly," he whispered. "How else could she appear so quickly when I lay splattered by the tracks?"

His father told a story about an old man, the camp cook for a group of vaqueros working on the llano. He was cleaning up after supper while the vaqueros got ready to ride to a dance hall that was miles away. "Let's go," they told the old man. "You go on," he replied. "I'll finish cleaning the camp." The vaqueros rode hard, and when they got to the dance hall, the old man was sitting by the door waiting for them.

"How?" I asked Alfonso.

"I don't know," he replied. "I only know how to fly in my imagination. But that man could appear wherever he wanted."

Bilocation?

María de Agreda (1602–1665) was a nun living in a convent in a small village in Spain. They say her body remained in a convent in Spain but also appeared among the Jumanos, Tejas Indians living in West Texas. She may also have appeared as far west as the Abo area on the east side of the Manzano Mountains of New Mexico. Anyway, she taught the life of Jesus to the natives in their own language, then returned in body to the convent across the sea. That happened over four hundred years ago.

When Spanish friars arrived in the area, the natives told them that a lady in blue had come often to teach them gospel stories. The lady in blue was María de Agreda. The natives recognized her blue cape.

Is bilocation possible? Can the same body be in two places at the same time? Or did she go into a cataleptic trance, a kind of deep dream? And what of Fonso's out-of-body experience? Can soul move around, in dream or in reality? Can the body? Questions for the spiritual and metaphysical mind.

By the way, the body of María de Agreda rests in a glass coffin in her convent. The body has not decomposed.

The old people used to tell stories about witches who turned into coyotes or owls to travel. That belief is probably as old as mankind.

What do I know about witches? I thought they were evil men and women who could put a curse on you and make you sick. Like Alfonso, I grew up in a Catholic world that honored the saints. But you can't have saints without witches. Some old folktales were witch stories, but the elders also told about real events that happened in the village. A woman made little rag and wax dolls and stuck pins in them. The people represented by the dolls got sick.

Today, everyone in the movies can fly, and the witches are often beautiful and spectacular. Hollywood has created false mythologies to make money. The more fantastic the witches and vampires, the more money is pulled in at the box office. Nothing is sacred anymore.

Alfonso's childhood taught the difference between good and evil, God and the devil. There existed a constant battle for the souls of sinners.

Rafaelita was his guide. She taught him the prayers that had come down from her parents, and before that from her grandparents. A line of unbroken prayers that came in the migrations from México and stretched back to the Iberian Peninsula. A chain of prayers. Alabados, rosaries, novenas, all recited daily in a Spanish that rang with ancient faith.

Now the prayers are being forgotten. This generation doesn't pray like we did. We spent hours on our knees. We had plenty to pray for. The war had taken the village boys; the Depression came, and with it the dust storms of the Dust Bowl. The way of living was changing from Spanish to English. There were new bosses and only menial work for the Mexicanos. The town banker spoke only English. Try getting a loan.

These young kids don't know anything. They're attached to the Internet, the worldwide ombligo. Puppets dangled by forces beyond their control, and those few who do control the net are making lots of money. Phones provide invisible umbilical cords to the brave new world. Prayer has become a quick text message. Soon they will have sex on the Internet, real sex. Bilocation. Everything and everyone is for sale in our new phantasma.

Catholicism from Spain evolved into New Mexico Catholicism. The Inquisition was always around the corner; heretics had been burned in Spain. The Moors and Jews were kicked out in 1492. Convert or face the gallows.

New Mexico became a Catholic country. Alfonso grew up in that old-time religion. First Communion and the sacraments. He knelt by his mother as she intoned the rosary every night. The family followed her to church on Sundays. And Lent? Oh God, forty days of suffering.

The Stations of the Cross every Friday, spring wind howling in torment. Nails driven into Jesus were felt by the very faithful and very sensitive—my Alfonso. He had felt other nails, all right: The train. His fall. Maybe that's why he left the church, stopped attending. He felt the pain too deeply.

A sensitive soul? Why are some born to feel more? That's a sorrow.

Faith in God and the church, his inheritance. Faith was belief. If you believe the world is one way, then later you learn it's not that way, there will be turmoil. A crisis of faith. That's what we went through during our university years. The ideas we were exposed to didn't mesh with our Catholic upbringing. There couldn't be two truths.

I wasn't as deep into needing to know the truth as Fonso was. His mother had instilled faith in the boy. It wasn't just his mother, it was the family and the community, Catholic history and faith embedded in their lives. Their ancestors had brought the Holy Cross to these lands. Tierras de Adentro, la Nueva México. They subdued the Pueblo Indians with cross and sword. Not a pretty history for those who claimed to be driven by the charity of Christ.

One's view of the world is a foundation until it conflicts with other beliefs. World wars have been fought by one faith against another. Still, a culture's beliefs must be taken as its moral foundation. What Alfonso's community believed had sustained them in the face of great adversities over four hundred years in la Nueva México. If you believed in the New Testament, if you believed that Jesus spoke and performed miracles, there was life everlasting.

Demons exist. Or are the demons in the heart? There are demons with powers to influence the affairs of men and women. Since the beginning of time, every cultural group has told stories of devils that set out to destroy a person or the group. And the devil often comes in the form of a person who has acquired great power.

Every group has its witches, or they invent them. The Pilgrims had their Salem witches, New Mexico Catholics had their brujas. Stretch history back, and you find the eternal battle, good versus evil. Lots of crucifixions and tormented punishments line that route.

What happens when you begin to question the beliefs that have been your foundation? If you begin to doubt what you were taught? There's the rub. Could Fonso find a new faith? Damn, it's not easy. The bottom fell out from under him. He found himself wandering in an abyss, looking for answers, trying to keep his soul intact.

Dear K,

The more I write, the more I'm absorbed with Alfonso's story. Call it an obsession. I was writing a novel (my last novel) when you called and asked me to tell you what I knew about my dear friend. I put my novel aside to write you these letters. The novel I was working on is about a boy's rites of passage, the story of my growing-up years. Don't we write our own lives? That's what Alfonso did. His stories reveal the plot of his life, a trajectory from childhood to the old philosopher—he always dealt with basic human issues, but as he got older he went deeper and deeper. His struggle with God and the knowledge of God, I call it. Don't we all want to know the truth? Especially when the years close in.

For him, in the end, the universe was God, not the kind old patriarch as depicted on the ceiling of the Sistine Chapel, just the Great Mystery of the expanding, organic universe. There's the crisis: Isn't it better to have a kind old man as God than a mystery? Can we pray to the universe and feel satisfaction?

Anyway, I put my novel aside and began writing about those years when Alfonso and I were close friends. I know I'm writing memories. Do my memories become a memoir? Am I writing his biography? How much is factual if we can never completely know a person? I write not only what I remember, what we shared during our university years, what he told me about his life, but I also write what other people said about him. And I write his ideas. Am I mixing his ideas with mine? I've read all his works, of course, so I know his thoughts on many subjects, and much of what I write you already know. He appears here in his own voice—no, that's not true. What I write is filtered through my thoughts, the angle from where I now see his life.

Damn! Is my novel mixed in with these letters? How much of my novel is becoming Alfonso's story? How much of Alfonso is becoming the character in my story? It would be nice if I could keep things separate, clear-cut, each subject in a different box. You understand what I mean. But I can't. A story is more than the sum of its parts. Everything goes into the hopper. Alfonso and his sorrows were more than can be contained in my letters to you.

Did I slip and go back to writing the novel I had put aside? Will my letters reveal Alfonso or my fictional character, who really isn't completely fictional because he is me? But I gave the character a new name, so he's not me. As if changing the name could change the soul—a rose by any other name . . .

I guess I've opened Pandora's box, or Alfonso's box, meaning his life is now pouring into my memoir/novel/biography/whatever you wish to call it. How will you decide? How might a future reader of these letters decide? The secret wish of writers is that their works will be read in the future, long after they're gone.

Alfonso said everything is story, because everything said or written comes from a person, and mere humans cannot know absolute truth. We are doomed to write fictions, allusions of reality, approximations. Not doomed, liberated. Story liberates us from the petty days of our lives. We write the mundane and thus change it, and by making story from daily toil, we liberate ourselves, we set free all of life. Imagination trumps reality.

From the time we discovered language, we became storytellers and story gatherers. What stories tell about us and our relationship to the earth and the universe makes us human. Stories free us from the literal confines of reality. Our feet may be stuck in mud, but our soul flies when we tell stories.

I feel better having said this. I can go on with Alfonso's story, which is the story of every person, living or dead. Stories create freedom. Each story is my story, your story. Like the poet said, I am involved in mankind, and if I cannot be there in person, I can be there in story. Thank God.

K, a group can't be completely overrun by evil, because there will always be good people who stand against evil.

From the beginning of time, groups have developed ways to counter the effects of evil: gods, priests, prayers, symbols, liturgy, chants, Stonehenge gatherings, places to honor the light of the sun, Machu Picchu, great cathedrals, the Siberian shaman—ah, the shaman. One who casts out demons, or as I came to understand, one who reestablishes harmony in the soul of a possessed person.

Spells and curses can hurt a person, but there's help. A priest or shaman can reveal the person's soul, usually during a community ceremony, and thus help the person return to the wellness circle, which is the community. Counseling, therapy, dancing and chanting, hallucinogenic drugs—remember LSD? The man was a shaman in his own right, stirring the brain with drugs and observing the results. Attempts to view soul.

Because of Agapita, Alfonso saw the shaman acting in more organic ways, closer to nature and its remedies, closer to the power vested in prayer. The people of the llano and the river believed in the efficacy of prayer, so a wise healer used the people's faith to effect a cure. The shaman/priest has always played a role in his or her community. In New Mexico the shaman is a curandera, or curandero if the healer is a man. So said Alfonso. The role of these healers goes all the way back in history. Blind Tiresias.

Jesus as shaman. He came from a line of prophets, old men who fasted in the hot Galilean desert and saw visions. The word of God shook their emaciated bodies. Their visions became the stories they told, Old Testament tales that pack powerful punches.

So there was help when an evildoer cursed the tribe. The word of God was more powerful than all the evil spread across the world.

Isn't that what our counselors and psychiatrists do? Work at casting out the inner voices that haunt the psychotic. Help lead the neurotic out of their fears. Good shamans are still with us. There are people with positive energies who practice helping people.

Our New Mexican curanderas were our first spiritual feminists, daring to step out of their traditional roles to help the community. They used remedies as old as the culture itself, herbs and prayers.

They could heal the possessed because they knew the ways of soul. They cast out demons, the source of the curse, and reestablished harmony.

Alfonso was still a young man when he wrote Ultima's story. What did he know? Remember, he came from Agapita's world. That old woman had traveled in the underworld of the soul many times. She knew the subconscious, and she had delivered him into the world. Her hands had pulled him from the womb, he had inhaled her breath, her marijuana-laced spittle had burned his tender skin. Perhaps the shock was a way for him to acknowledge that he was among the living and no longer a soul in search of home.

Everyone has those positive/negative energies. It all depends on how they're used.

We were sitting at Jack's Bar discussing the magic of movies and the characters who played out their emotions as shadows on the screen when Alfonso told me about his mother. She had a spell put on her by a family member.

Why? I wanted to know. He had never revealed this before.

Hate. Fear. Revenge. Envy. Greed. Wrongful desire.

I leaned over the beer-stained table and strained to hear above the hubbub of the bar.

Rafaelita took sick. Couldn't sleep, kept vomiting bile, kept seeing the face of the woman who had brought her the food she had eaten, the food with the curse hidden within. Martin recognized the signs, but he didn't want to believe that a curse had made his wife sick. He and the daughters did what they could to make her comfortable. Alfonso sat at her bedside in the dark room and prayed.

Alfonso's father did what was normal under the circumstances. First he called the doctor, but nothing he prescribed helped. Then he called the parish priest. A wise man, the priest. He brought the Holy Eucharist. He placed a purple sash around his shoulders, which he first kissed, then prayed. Alfonso listened. Like a penitente in a dark morada, he prayed. Strange noises filled the room, the tinieblas announcing the death of Christ, those high-pitched songs sung the last three days of Holy Week.

Was she dying? Nothing helped.

"Go for Agapita," she said. Martin brought the old woman. Agapita arrived. She leaned over Rafaelita and spoke in whispers. Finally she said, "Your sister-in-law says you stole something."

Alfonso's mother shook her head. "I only helped my brother."

"Her envy makes her do evil. She made a doll. It is here in the room." She looked around, then reached under the bed and pulled out a small rag doll, its tiny face contorted in pain. "Look closely," she told Alfonso as she placed the doll on the small altar that held the Virgin's statue. "La Virgen will help us," she said. "I will teach you the prayers that bind us to the Eternal. We will cast out the devil. Here, place your hand on her stomach. Pray."

Pay attention to what Agapita said. A ceremony was starting.

She was going to teach him her prayers.

Alfonso was surprised. How did she know? Or was it, he thought many years later, that there had been no doll under the bed? Agapita had brought it with her. A visual symbol to help effect the cure.

"The saints are strong," Agapita said. "We pray to the Holy Family. Come, take out envidia."

Alfonso stayed in the room that night. He saw what happened. He heard the prayers. He saw how Agapita wrestled with the shadow in the room, finally subduing it. His mother coughed out whatever it was that had sickened her. When Agapita had cleaned up the mess and finally sat back smoking a cigaro, Fonso asked her, "Why?"

"People do good or evil."

"Everyone?" Alfonso asked.

"Yes," Agapita answered. "If you believe the evil person has power over you, her evil thoughts will make you sick. Have faith in yourself and the saints. Have faith in your ancestors who watch over you and protect you. They are the true santos. Isn't that true, Rafaelita?"

Fonso's mother nodded. Her faith in the Virgin Mary was profound.

Hadn't the Virgin taken care of her sons while they were in the service? Had her faith wavered? Is that why the sickness took root?

So that was Agapita's magic formula. It didn't seem like much. But think. That's been the power of faith for centuries. Believe in yourself. You can cast out your demons.

Agapita winked. She burned piñon and juniper sap in a dish, the incense of the New Mexican healers. The room smelled as sweet as the hills after a rain. She had Rafaelita drink a tea brewed from herbs she had collected in the llano and along the river. Simple remedies taken from nature held healing powers.

She held the statue of la Virgen de Guadalupe near. Rafaelita kissed her guardian. "That Indian woman can cure anything," Agapita chuckled. Alfonso's mother smiled—her first smile in weeks.

"Place your hand on your mother's stomach," Agapita told Alfonso.

Alfonso did as he was told. His mother's stomach rose and fell with her breathing. Agapita prayed to the Virgin, prayers Alfonso had never heard, but he repeated the words. He remembered praying until he fell asleep. By morning Rafaelita had improved. Agapita opened the windows and let in fresh air and light. She rolled a marijuana cigaro and turned to Alfonso. "Did you see?"

"Yes." He had seen a dark vapor pass out of the room. He had felt the life his mother had once given him pass through his hands into his heart. Prayers, his touch, and faith.

He looked for the doll. It had disappeared.

By evening his mother was able to sit up and eat her first meal in weeks. The family ate and celebrated. Relief had returned.

"Ya me voy," Agapita said, and later everyone swore she had flown away because Martin had offered to drive her home, but she waved him off. "I have things to do," she said, whispering to Alfonso, "Always burn the evil things, always burn your hair when you cut it."

Back to her hut on the llano. Such things happened in those innocent days when faith could cure.

Tragedy was always around the corner. Agnes drowned. Summer rains had filled the river—or maybe the golden fish had pulled her under and taken her to his watery depths—as Demogorgon had taken Demeter to Hades, the Greek underworld. She had eaten six pomegranate seeds, so six months of winter came upon the land. But she would return and spring would blossom; that was the agreement. Six months of summer in which to grow wheat, grapevines, and olive trees.

You see, we are not yet done making myths. We know the myths from long ago, but it doesn't end there. We are still telling stories that help us understand life and death. Why are we here? Who brought us here? Do we return to the arms of God? Or are we destined to walk the paths of the underworld with Demeter?

Soul doesn't end, but we don't know its destiny.

Dear K, sometimes the truth hurts. Is this a sorrow? Agnes drowned. She was swept downriver. Her body was found six days later.

"Why? Why? Why?" Alfonso cried the night he told me the story. "We used to dive into the currents of summer and swim across the river. Were we testing ourselves? Is all of youth a test? A sorrow? We loved the water, we were strong swimmers."

When the big summer floods arrived, people gathered at the bridge. It was quite a spectacle, watching the raging muddy waters four to five feet higher than the normally placid river. That was long before the Santa Rosa Dam was built upriver to control flooding. Floods didn't cause damage to the town, but downriver at Puerto de Luna the flood destroyed the entarque, a dam made of earth and rocks that turned river water into the acequia madre, the mother ditch used to irrigate fields and orchards. The farmers cursed, but as soon as the river subsided, they were back at work rebuilding the dam. They needed the precious water. Water was survival.

Agnes was a strong swimmer, but the current carried huge logs. Or she might have been slammed against a boulder.

Ancient deities plied the river banks. Alfonso knew. He had heard the cries and seen the shadow of La Llorona, the frightful Crying Woman who stole children. Once he had been chased through the dark, thick river brush by the Coco Man, el Cucuy. Now Agnes had become spirit, a mermaid, a Persephone of the historic Pecos River that flowed past Santa Rosa de Lima.

"What do you mean?" I asked Alfonso.

"The river is everything," he said. "It is life. History flows in the water. Comanches and other tribes knew the river long before my ancestors came to farm in its valley. The españoles wrote their history, and therefore the history of the river."

I had studied the entradas of the first European colonists, the so-called conquistadores of New Mexico. They thought another Aztec empire lay to the north of México, so parties were organized, men recruited, wives and children, animals. One such party came up the Pecos River in 1590.

The Castaño de Sosa expedition had left Almaden, México, and traveled up the Pecos River to its headwaters in the magnificent Sangre de Cristo Mountains of northern New Mexico. Following the river north, they were the first Europeans to camp at sites that would much later become the villages of Puerto de Luna, Santa Rosa de Lima, Anton Chico, Pecos, and finally Yuque Yunque, an Indian pueblo. Crossing Glorieta Pass into the Rio Grande Valley, Castaño explored as far south as present-day Alburquerque and the Bernalillo area.

Those hardy people explored the valley that Fonso's grandfather would farm centuries later. Day after day, they wrestled land away from the nomadic Comanches. Intrepid explorers. They knew New Mexico and its rivers centuries before the American mountain men came west.

But the Castaño expedition was an illegal entrada into New Mexico, or Tierra Nueva as it was known then. He didn't have official authorization. In 1591 the Viceroy in México City sent a party led by Juan de Morlete to New Mexico to arrest Castaño. The entire expedition was led back to Spanish jurisdiction at Santa Bárbara, México.

Well-known history.

Yes, those Spaniards kept meticulous records.

Some say we speak the Spanish spoken by Cervantes. Ah, we're a very proud people—poor but proud.

"So those españoles who followed the Pecos and camped on its banks were illegal?"

"Yes. Illegal. Who isn't?"

"Illegal immigrants. After all, the Comanches were on the llano first. Later came the illegal Americans."

We laughed, finished our beer, and went off to get a pizza.

He didn't want to talk about Agnes that night. Later he told me about the sorrow he felt. It drove him to the river, and that's where he saw her. He was sitting on the banks, grieving, when he saw her spirit rising from the depths, dressed in the river's white foam.

Her spirit, he said. Her ghost. Why? She held out her hands, palms toward him. She smiled. "I will always be here," she said. "Don't grieve for me. I am safe in the arms of God."

Where were the arms of God? Where was God? Why had He allowed the river to take Agnes? Was the river God? Yes, of course. God was everywhere! Those were the scriptures his mother and the church had taught him. God was in nature; he had learned that on the llano when he walked with Agapita. He had walked with God, he swam in the river with God, and when he lay with Agnes and tasted her sweet, warm lips, he tasted God.

Agapita had told him, "The dead grieve for us. Why? Because they are released from the flesh and rest in the arms of God."

"Don't grieve for me. I will always be with you." Agnes's spirit appeared, standing on the water and offering condolence and love, the innocent love of their brief childhood together. For Alfonso it would always be thus when he sought love, a meeting and a parting. Isn't it like that for everyone? Moving through life is like a dream, a continuous dream, and the dreamer has to find meaning in the dream. Find love.

Was Alfonso too young to understand this? It was a beginning. A gift from Agnes, gifts from everyone he would meet in his dream of life. It was true: La vida es un sueño. Life is a dream. The young don't understand, but when they grow old, the truth hits them like a ton of bricks. Too late.

Around that time, the family decided to pull up stakes and move to Alburquerque. They moved into the Barelas barrio, where he met new friends, all from good, hardworking families.

He spent the ninth grade at Washington Junior High, then went on to Albuquerque High School. An exciting new life, but he couldn't forget Agnes.

We were always philosophizing; that's what young university students do, especially if they're reading books that lead them to new ideas, new ways of thinking. Is God everywhere? That was a question that haunted Fonso. God had drowned Agnes.

Seeking answers became Alfonso's passion. He spent long hours in the library, reading, taking notes, ingesting everything. The new knowledge often conflicted with what family and church had taught him. Conflict burned in his soul. What to believe? His faith in the solid world he had once known was shaken. Oh, Lord, there's nothing worse than questioning your faith. Nothing worse than losing it. What could replace the innocent beliefs of childhood?

We questioned, we argued, and with each doubt we fell deeper into a crisis of faith. It drove Alfonso into his dark night of the soul, a term we became familiar with, an apt description for what he was going through. I feared he might contemplate suicide. He never mentioned that, but he was searching desperately for a kind of moral certitude he had once known. Do you know what it's like to lose the truths you once believed?

"God is everywhere," he whispered. If He is everywhere, why do bad things happen? Why is there evil in the world? Did God make evil? The angel Lucifer, angel of light, had revolted. Fonso, too, was revolting.

I was questioning, too, but I wasn't as deep as Alfonso. He argued with God, went right to the source. He didn't know he couldn't win. Or could he?

We were drunk, the table sloppy with spilled beer, thick cigarette smoke, a loud jukebox blaring in the background, arguing with a bunch of friends, when someone asked, "How many angels can sit on the head of a pin?" Everyone guessed: one, two, five, a million!

It wasn't a serious question for Fonso. "Bullshit!" he lashed out. "Ask, do angels exist? Who made them? Where are they? Why?" Always why. Those questions drove us nuts, and we talked until Okie Joe's closed, then wandered drunkenly down an almost deserted Central Avenue to the pizza place.

P.S. We were always tossing around ideas about the nature of God and the universe. Fonso said everything on earth comes wrapped in a sac, you know, a sheath, case, or pouch. Fetus in a sac of water, brain covered by neural tissue, organs of the body kept in place by thin membranes. Peas in a pod. You get it. So, Fonso reasoned, the universe must be encased in a pouch. Millions of light years from one end to the other, but every sun and galaxy in a pouch.

God picks up the pouch and puts it in His pocket. The stars are His coins. Is He going shopping? Is He going to use the immense power of all the stars to create a new Big Bang? A parallel universe? Is He so big that he can put the universe in His pocket? He goes off whistling, leaving the Virgin Mary to fold up the empty sky/space.

The elders had taught Fonso adivinanzas, riddles, and each one needed an answer. A kind of foretelling that sparked Fonso's imagination. Raised on divining led him to create his own riddles. This one about God's pouch. But deep inside we felt angst; the Great Mystery had no answer.

Dear K,

When he told me what had happened, he cried in anger. "God was at the river! God is the river! The arms of God drowned Agnes! Pulled her down. Why? Why? Why?"

It's true, the arms of God are everywhere: they embrace the motorcyclist dying at a bloody accident, those dying of cancer, incurable diseases, AIDs, the Ebola virus, drug overdoses, sadness, those dying of hunger, dying in war—He takes them home. Where? Was there no promise? No resurrection?

Alfonso suffered. I wish I could have read his mind. There was a universe there. Cada cabeza es un mundo, every mind a world. Each of us carries a world between the ears, brain cells fired by electricity, neurons sparking. Yahoo! I think, therefore I am! And the world entrusted to mind becomes a memory. There is nothing real but what's stored in the brain/mind. It will flame out, like shining from shook foil.

Deleted, the new code word for gone.

Was this one of the sorrows of his life?

He was standing on the river bank when he saw Agnes rise from the water, her body covered in foam, the frothy stuff churned up by the ferocious current.

"Agnes!" Alfonso called to her. He was ready to rush to her when a warm, gentle breeze blew the foam away from her body—oh Lord!

What did Alfonso see? A mermaid! Agnes had become a mermaid!

Half of her was still the lovely creature she had been in the days they had lain together on the warm sand; now half was mermaid, her glistening fish tail swaying in the water, her shiny scales reflecting the rainbow. It was the loveliest thing he had ever seen. He called her again. She blessed him and disappeared into the water, destined to become a legend in Santa Rosa de Lima. Another legend in the many stories told there.

Later, others from the town swore they had seen her. Jimmy Chavez, who had been fishing late one evening, stopped by Joe V's Bar near the Club Cafe, where he started drinking, acting strange. Finally he slurred out a confession: "I saw her! I saw the mermaid!" The barflies nodded, yeah, sure. Jimmy's been drinking again. He fishes after work, in the dark, thinks he's going to catch the big bass in El Rito. One of these days he might fall in the river and drown. Or the mermaid might take him. Raucous laughter filled the bar.

Alfonso didn't write Agnes's story; he couldn't. A manuscript soaked in tears. Instead he wrote about a wondrous golden fish the kids saw in the lakes and streams around the town. The golden carp.

"If I'd written Agnes's story," he told me once, "I would have called her Melusina." He knew the legend of a water spirit named Melusina who appeared as a mermaid. So many legends, and Alfonso had read dozens. In the myths and legends of world cultures, he believed he could feel the true essence of the group's wisdom, those truths they passed on to the future. In myths he could touch the soul, the mythopoetic that described any particular culture.

"We are a storytelling species," he said. "Story is all we have."

From Buddha's quest to the Old Testament to a poem being written today, we are storytellers. Whether we write the story down and record it or just tell it in daily conversation—there it is, a story. The most enduring stories record our relationships to God, the gods, nature. Our eternal quest, seeking to understand why we are on earth, why we tell stories. The mythology of the world.

We are still writing those relationships today, in present time, and some of those stories become contemporary legends. Nature inspires us; our protagonists and antagonists are drawn from people we know, family, the town.

It was his relationship to God that troubled him in those early years. Less and less he accepted the common dogma. He began to read holy scriptures and legends that recorded the lives of heroes. He found the myth of eternal return everywhere, our wish for a dead hero to return to guide us. Adonais did not die, he lives! We want

César Chávez to lead the farmworkers again, Martin Luther King to finish the unfinished work, strike down racial prejudice forever. Jesus Christ Superhero! He didn't die!

Melusina. What a lovely name, a lovely sound, like a cool breeze or gentle, flowing water. If I had a daughter, I would name her Melusina. She would always be there, a mermaid spirit blessing the water. Fonso gave Melusina to Santa Rosa de Lima, and to this day lovers and fishermen say they have heard her singing by owl light at Hidden Lake, Twin Lakes, at the river. Dusk is the time of spirits.

Alburquerque was a rangy, coming-into-its-own town in the early fifties. Big compared to Santa Rosa de Lima. Its economy was tied to the air force base. But this isn't a story about economics, unless it's important to say that even federal money couldn't erase poverty in the state. Things haven't changed much.

The family's first house was on Pacific Avenue in the Barelas barrio. Nuevo Mexicano families who moved to Alburquerque during those years lived in the barrios: Martínez Town, Plaza Vieja, Duranes, San José, Five Points, the South Valley. The city was split along ethnic lines. Anglos lived up in the Heights area, and Hispanos in the valley. Public places weren't segregated, it only seemed so. Anglo kids up in the Heights had a public swimming pool; the barrio kids had Tingley Beach. The small lake had once been the pride of the city, but by the fifties it had become a dirty pond infested with the polio virus.

Fonso's brother Laute lived next door with his wife and their kids. He remembered the family gathering to watch television, the first TV set he ever saw. *I Love Lucy, Ozzie and Harriet, Leave It to Beaver.* Hollywood producers wanted everyone to believe that every American family was like Beaver's family. It wasn't true for the poor. Working-class Hispanos weren't like the Cleavers. Too many cultural differences. English/Spanish, Catholic/Protestant, white skin/brown skin, money in the bank/poor as hell. Good jobs/backbreaking low-wage jobs.

Images can be deceiving. Hollywood was presenting stories that resonated with white America, not with ethnic communities of color. Vicarious assimilation took place as Chicanitos identified with Beaver.

A revolution was needed. That came with the black civil rights movement in the sixties, followed by Mexican American demands for equal justice. The Chicano movement exploded into action and began to change the course of history for Mexican Americans. In the early seventies, Alfonso was part of that struggle.

I'm getting ahead of the story. Protected? Yes, I think that's true. Fonso's brothers were gone, and his sisters lived in their own world, busy with friends and school. His mother's love loomed over Fonso, caring for him. What mother wouldn't care for a son so crippled?

We don't use that word anymore. Today it's handicapped or disabled. We have nice words to describe infirmities. I'll go along with that. I won't call him a cripple anymore. But what did Alfonso feel inside?

High school was difficult. From the barrio to Albuquerque High was a long walk. Friends with cars often picked him up, but most often he walked. Schoolwork wasn't difficult. He was smart, read all the books, was always prepared. He was bored with studies that were too simple, except math. He struggled with algebra. "The quadratic equation did me in," he told me once.

The world can hurt a too sensitive soul. Bummed out, the kids say. A disabled person lives with constant challenges. Alfonso wasn't afraid. By walking everywhere, his legs grew strong, and he learned to live with his disabled hand, still so weak it could barely hold a book. He learned to hide it from others, even from his family.

Small tasks like cutting his fingernails were difficult. Like other handicapped persons, he was learning to live in a world that was no longer normal. Cope, adapt, survive. Destiny was churning in his heart.

Most of the kids in school were doing all the things normal kids do. Classes, student council, sports, letter sweaters, jocks, cheerleaders, sock hops, Saturday night dates, the guys bragging about going all the way, marijuana and beer parties. There was a lot to do in the life of the normal.

Fonso knew he would never be normal again. He would never run and play baseball or football like he used to. Was there some consolation in Agapita's warning? If the baseball glove doesn't fit, play chess.

What was he to do?

K,

Do you believe in karma? That's a word we often toss around, usually without fully understanding its meaning. The adage goes something like this: What you sow, you reap. That's it. If you lead a good life, you get your reward. Where? Heaven? Nirvana? Eternal rest in a lotus blossom? What is a good life? A life lived in moderation, said the ancient Greeks. Most of our species has never lived in moderation. Might as well live in a monastery, and even that's not moderation if the monk spends most of his time praying. Excessive prayer can't be moderate.

What does moderation mean, anyway? You can have one ice cream cone, but not two. Is moderation a diet? Only one glass of wine, one chocolate candy, one big laugh, moderate sex, don't get carried away. Wait a minute! Society isn't like that. The American system is built on competition, not moderation. Me, me, me! Go Get It, Last One In Is a Rotten Egg, Nice Guys Finish Last, When the Going Gets Tough, the Tough Get Going.

All that competition creates disparity in wealth accumulation. That's what we have now, one at the top, nine at the bottom. In Spanish the saying goes like this: "La gallina de arriba se caga en la gallina de abajo." Bet you learned that one from Fonso. He fed them, made sure they had water, collected the eggs, cleaned the coop, knew how they roosted.

Anyway, back to karma. Is the eventual goal of karma and the Christian heaven the same? Are the Muslim or Jewish heavens different? What was the ancient Egyptians' heaven like? Bliss in the arms of the sun god. Did Neanderthals have a heaven? Stonehenge people? Does heaven reflect the culture? It did in Dante's *Divine Comedy*. One book describes those suffering in hell. They got their karma. Or the consequences thereof.

Alfonso described his own heaven in that beautiful book he wrote after his wife died. The main character, the old man, wants to know where his wife's soul went after her death. He finally encounters her on a beautiful New Mexico summer cloud. He climbs up to her, and together they circle the globe, happy as larks, conversing and enjoying all their earth memories. Heaven is being with those you love; the grieving is over.

What happens when you don't lead a good life? Who or what punishes you? Does one go to hell, Dante's Inferno, or wherever hell exists, or does one keep reincarnating, the soul traveling from body to body until it finally, and this could take thousands of years, gets it right? Soul finds a body whose karma is full of charity, good deeds, righteous living, and soul can finally rest.

Beatitude. Reap the benefits of good living. Soul can rest in nirvana. No desire for things in external reality, no more thoughts from the busy brain. Oblivion. We're back to that.

What was Alfonso to do?

Limp through life, trust in the love he had at home. His mother massaged and wrapped his hand those winter nights, straightening out the fingers, trying to awaken their memory so they would work the way they used to, but . . . it was not to be.

The memory in the nerves had died and would no longer move the fingers. Atrophy.

Does all memory eventually die? What's left?

"You ask too many questions," an irritated Agapita scolded Fonso. "There is a law in nature. Sooner or later everything falls apart and cannot be put together again. Like the song you learned in school. The egg that fell off the wall."

"Humpty Dumpty," he said.

"Sí, the broken egg. No one can put a broken egg back together."

"God can," he said.

"¡Anda! ¡Véte!" She scowled and rapped him on the head. He ran home smiling. She, too, smiled. He had learned.

He massaged his injured hand, hoping . . .

What was it about the high school years he remembered? These are the events I gleaned from our conversations. One day he had started up the stairs of the Albuquerque High School Main Building, struggling with his load of books, when a fellow student also began the climb. The other boy, who had muscular dystrophy, was a lot worse off than Alfonso. He wore leg braces. They were almost at the top when the boy's books slipped out of his hands and went tumbling down the stairs. For a moment the two looked at each other, cripples meeting on the mountain. Like Sisyphus walking down the hill for the boulder, the boy would have to go down the stairs and start over.

It wasn't fair. The punishment of Sisyphus wasn't fair. The gods weren't fair!

Just then the you're-late-for-class bell rang their doom. The normal kids were already seated, the teacher taking roll. Fonso and his fellow cripple were struggling on the stairs, for an eternity it seemed. Why this punishment?

Meeting the boy on the stairs was a revelation. There were other kids who had it worse than he. Why complain? Lesson learned. But, as has been eternally true and ever will be till the end of time as we know it, the weight one carries is personal. Only he who carries the sack knows how much it weighs. Walk in the other man's shoes, then you know his troubles.

He wasn't as bad off as the boy with muscular dystrophy, and there were other handicapped kids scattered around him, each encased in a world that others couldn't penetrate. From an upstairs window, Alfonso looked down on the main patio. A girl on crutches struggled across the courtyard. He looked closer. Those with broken bodies were obvious; the ones with their minds on fire weren't.

Johnny, get your gun. The arming of America was beginning.

He didn't attend football games. The normal kids were rowdy, loud, always pushing. He stayed home. Books became his refuge.

Today the handicapped are out in public. Prosthetic devices work wonders, specialized medical treatments, physical therapies, severed spinal cords connected with implanted wires and batteries allow the paraplegic to walk again, the joy of handicapped children involved in Special Olympics. Back in the fifties the disabled were mostly invisible. There were no handicapped ramps or parking places. It was sink or swim.

Why did you ask about girls? Are you writing his biography? Is this why you want my notes? Okay, here's something that happened.

The Heights Community Center held Saturday night dances for the high school kids. Fifties be-bop, slow waltzes so each guy got to hold his girl close, smell her perfume and bubblegum breath, make small talk face to face so all sorts of dreams and desires broke loose. If the embrace got too hot and heavy, the couple might be tempted to dash out to the car and jump in the back seat.

Those be-bop Saturday night dances led to some shotgun weddings. Back-seat fondling led to unplanned pregnancies. Still does.

Alfonso was a dreamer. He should have kept a journal. His thousand and one nights were full of dreams, nightmares, apparitions, his mind constantly conjuring up dream after dream. He said they came from the primitive part of his brain, and he thanked God. Too many dreams to write down. Journals full of dreams would reach to heaven.

Do dreams come from heaven? If they do, why do monsters, demons, and the most murderous events occur in dreams? Surely God doesn't send frightful nightmares to disturb our nights. Is the primitive part of our brain always at work? Are dreams the soul's language? If so, what do they tell us? It gets complicated.

Dreams are born in that mass of neurons enclosed in our skulls, and dreams don't reflect only on the day's events; they have a past, a primitive past like Fonso said. Strange images, shadow characters, and symbols we don't understand haunt the corners of our dreams. Dark creatures and indecipherable messages are the content of some dreams. A warning! What if those dream creatures break free from sleep and appear in full daylight? What if those nightmarish voices begin to speak to the dreamer? Oh, brother!

Is there no rest? No cure? Where's the help? A talented psychiatrist? A plethora of medications? Anything to quiet the voices and make the creatures retreat. Retreat where? Everything exists in the brain. And if the wonders of medical science fail, the demons seek another way out. They become so strong, they leave the nightmarish world and appear in the world of light. The dreamer begins to speak to the shadow/creatures, they begin to take over. Madness! Insanity!

Is it true? The world is full of sorrow. Did Agapita mean we're doomed? Is there no cure? Where are the angels? Where, oh where are the angels?

It's not all negative. There's beauty in dreams! Revelations that make prophets speak. The first musical notes of a great symphony may sound in a dream. Picasso's art! Poems and the architecture of buildings can began in dreams! Love also flourishes in dreams!

"Did Ultima come to you in a dream?" I asked.

"No," he said, "she appeared in person." He was writing his childhood story, and there she was, standing at the door. "Put me in the story," she told him. Was she an archetypal character from the cultural memory of his people? No, he insisted. She was real! Was she the curandera his mother had consulted? No, the old woman who appeared wasn't Agapita. It was Ultima!

(I began to suspect the two are one and the same.)

"I am Ultima," she said. "Put me in the story you're writing." An owl came with her, a protective spirit. Remember, the owls came when Agapita called; they ate his afterbirth.

(See what I mean.)

The owls ate rabbit carcasses. The owl would die. "No, you cannot kill the spirit of the land," she said. "The body dies, the spirit lives on."

"I will appear in many guises," she said. "I cured the sick from those villages you once knew as a child, and I have come to guide you. The near-drowning accident not only broke your body, it damaged your soul. I will keep reappearing in your stories to guide and care for you."

(Near-drowning? Wait a minute. Has she changed the train accident to a near-drowning accident? Fonso wrote in one of his novels about what happened when he dove into an irrigation ditch and hit the bottom. He was paralyzed at first, but he recovered enough to spend months at Carrie Tingley Hospital, encased in a body cast. That's where he earned his nickname, Tortuga. That's what really happened. You know.)

Ultima became the central character. He obeyed the vision. He searched his memory and remembered that Agapita did not walk alone. Always there was a shadow at her side, the shadow of a healer, a man who could fly like an owl. Many healers existed in that time, getting ready for Armageddon, the final battle with evil. That's why they kept coming into his stories. He was preparing his soul for the never-ending struggle. Do we still struggle against evil in heaven?

Ultima was only the most recent reincarnation of a past laden with people of power. Those miracle workers represented the cultural soul of the people in Alfonso's childhood. Ultima knew the art of healing. She embodied the history of the people, their collective history. Goodness would overcome evil.

Fonso swore she was real. He saw her in his room while he was immersed in writing, caught in the web of story, the power of creativity and imagination. She stepped out of his imagination and reincarnated long enough to step into the story. If you see the movie, you see a physical image of her. The image on the screen is one more step toward becoming real.

(But can that really happen? Reincarnation of the spirit of the people. Didn't I just say that some subconscious visions leave the darkness and step into the light?)

Let it be.

Many asked him, "Did you name her Ultima to tell us that our Nuevo Mexicano culture is dying?" Ultima, ultimate, means the last one. Are we the last? So many young Hispanics no longer speak Spanish, they don't know their history. Does all history eventually pass away? At least Alfonso captured his time in the Ultima novel. Story can stop the flow of time. Story is as powerful as meditation or sexual consummation. Those moments stop time.

Death also stops time. Perhaps for the flesh, but soul is made of light, the purest energy in the universe. It will not be denied.

"But why did you name her Ultima?" The question persisted.

"Ultima she was, and Ultima she will remain," he responded.

"And why are there so many other healers in your novels? You say they are guides. Your main characters usually enter the underworld, the subconscious, but they need a guide. The first was Ultima, then don Eliseo, Jalamanta, Lorenza, even Salomon the boy in the iron lung is a healer. Unica is the guide for Randy Lopez, now Agapita. Why so many healers, curanderas, shamans in your stories? Where did they come from? Why?"

He wasn't perturbed by the questions. He had written a novel for every stage of his life, and in each new plane of being he needed a healer to guide him through the tempest called life. He prayed the Ave María in Spanish; the Virgin was there to help him. Doctors who had helped him throughout his life also appeared in his dreams, as did the wise and helpful professors of his university years. Grandparents appeared, and they blessed his path, his recovery of soul. He, in turn, blessed them, and as he fell asleep, he said the prayers his mother had taught him.

But, and here's the terrible question, was it all in his mind?

He honored the vision, he honored the history of the people. That's all a storyteller can do. Why expect so much of my hero, my poor crippled Alfonso.

Which brings me to the Saturday night dances at the community center. The DJ played vinyl records, 45s, the music and technology of the time. Fats Domino, Bill Haley, Little Richard, Bo Diddley, the Platters. The movies of that generation: *Blackboard Jungle* (remember daddy-o?), *East of Eden*, *Giant*, *Shane*, *On the Waterfront*. The first 3-D movie played at the State Theater.

An innocent time? Not really, but they were sixteen, cruising Central with friends, and everybody chipped in, so Arthur, who looked older than his age, stopped at the liquor store on Coal, where the clerk sold him two quarts of beer, which were passed around and chugged down, so by the time they got to the dance, everyone was feeling good. The place was packed, the music blaring. What could go wrong?

Even Alfonso felt a little buzzed, and young men who are feeling the booze get cocky. Fonso stuck close to Eliseo and Arthur, but they quickly found dance partners, girls they knew from Martínez Town, Sanjo, and Tortilla Flats. Fonso sought a dark corner. From there he studied the dancers and the others like him who weren't dancing. He was being cautious, like a wolf coming up on new surroundings. This was his first time at the center. His friends had dragged him out, and he had agreed. But could he dance? He had practiced with his sisters, but it didn't go well. Angie and Edwina were good dancers.

They had been jitterbugging from the time they could turn a radio knob to rock-and-roll and Mexican rancheras.

Could he be-bop? Did he belong in be-bopper heaven with the dark-haired beauty wearing a St. Mary's sweater? He had been watching her, hanging with her friends, all attractive girls, their hair teased up, lips brilliant with red lipstick, and alluring eyes peering out from under eyelashes dark with mascara. Young women with dark secrets. All great dancers.

"Go dance," Eliseo said. Easy for him, athletic and fun-loving, but not so easy for my Alfonso.

"Who?"

"That one, María. She was looking at you."

"María." He heard Melusina.

Finally he made his move. She had smiled at him when the last dance ended, and he had smiled back. She had danced every dance, each with a different partner, so she didn't have a date. That's what every young man needed, a date. That's what Alfonso secretly wished for, but things were complicated. He was handsome enough: curly black hair, brown eyes, reserved, polite, not loud like the others who hung out in gangs. He didn't need a gang, no tough guy poses. Was he aloof?

They didn't know he was frightened.

When you're young, life is always lived on the edge. He held back.

_____

137

I don't blame him. He was wondering, Can I do it? Will some laugh?

Bullies laughed at those who were different. High on beer and pot, they were the ones who usually started fights.

Alfonso had friends he could count on, but he wanted to prove himself. On his own terms. He didn't want to be an object of ridicule or pity. He had learned to hide his hand; like a turtle he had built a shell, always ready to withdraw for safety.

There are a thousand and one ways a person can be hurt. Words injure. Tell a girl she is ugly, and she will begin to feel ugly. If enough around her repeat the curse, she will begin to believe she is ugly. Same with boys, especially when they're going through the pimple stage. Fonso had gone through the curse. He scrubbed and used acne ointments, but the red bumps returned. The more they were popped, the more they spread. Arthur had found a doctor at Medical Arts who administered low-level x-rays to the face while protecting the eyes with lead covers. The treatments worked; lots of kids lined up.

Oh, the sorrow of youth, pimples!

He finally got the courage to approach the girl. His friends encouraged him, teasing, "Come on, get out there, dance. She's looking at you. ¡Andale! Ask her!"

María. Melusina. Agnes.

Why did the names rush over him? Agnes, Ida, June, Mary Lou, Gloria, Sadie, Rita, Lydia, Dorothy, the Santa Rosa de Lima girls. They had been with him through the elementary grades and First Communion, and they were with him now. Why at that juncture of his life? Asking a girl to dance was simple, for crying out loud!

Was my Alfonso lost? He was a romantic at heart, in the poetic sense. He started writing poetry during our university years. Thank God we lived during a poetic era. It wasn't just the Beats he read; he read all sorts of poetry. Poetry changes the soul, enlarges the soul, and the stuff changed him. Poetic stirrings awakened.

I still think the llano landscape and its people were the original inspiration. The river, the people and their stories, the spirituality of the place, it all came together. His destiny? I think so. The poetry he read confirmed his path. "I, too, can write," he said. Small beginnings.

To every man there comes a time when he opens his eyes and recognizes his destiny. A moment of complete awareness, an epiphany. He lives in that ecstatic moment completely alive, a superman, all-knowing, if only for a moment. He recognizes not only the joy in the world, but also its suffering. The young feel sorrow most keenly, simply because they're young. They know they live in a not-too-friendly world. Some of the most heartfelt poetry comes from that sense of alienation.

He moved toward her just as the Platters song "Earth Angel" filled the dance hall. She waited for him. He took her hand and asked her to dance. Yes, she smiled. A slow waltz, a melody of romance, couples swaying on clouds made in heaven. Arms of the men and arms of the women, embracing, all lost in longing, shadows in search of love. True love.

He knew he had to make small talk. What school? What grade? What did you do this summer? You got a boyfriend? Kid stuff.

In every life there is a Before and After. Some say it's only the elderly who look back longingly at their youth. Their past is their constant lament. Before my body began to fall apart, I could do everything. You should have seen me before time and its atrocities got hold of me. Before my heart problem, before cancer, arthritis, bone fractures, Alzheimer's, forgetting, depression. I could make love all night—Before.

The Before time becomes the After time, and for a split second the Present sits in the middle of the two. Best to live in the Present, psychologists tell us. Do they know the Present is only a memory? Everything gone into memory. The old ache to live in Before time, when they could do everything; the young want to hurry time into the future, usually missing out on the Present.

Before time exists only in memory. Everything that happened in Before time becomes memory. The split second you just experienced has already become memory. Memory is all there is. We live our lives in memory, the pleasant and not so pleasant. Everything is stored in memory. So what we call time is just memory, and both time and memory disappear really fast. Sooner or later we forget those moments we once called real. External reality becomes an illusion. Ask anyone who's dying. Life is difficult either in the Before time or in the Present.

Present time exists only for a second, giving way to the illusion of the future. There is no future. The only reality is the split second we call being alive. Senses receiving the external world, breathing, nerves firing, brain computing, life.

La vida es un sueño, the poet wrote. Life is a dream. A dream stored in memory.

So what's real? we poor mortals ask. Let God decide. Or scientists, those who break atoms apart and tell us that the resulting subatomic particles are the only reality we know. We're composed of particles, molecules, atoms, quarks, energy. Scientists at the Hadron Collider finally found the Higgs boson, how a particle acquires mass. Something like that. I love the science programs on PBS. And the shows on nature. You can get an education watching those.

Anyway, the particle began to be called the God particle. As if God is a particle. I think God is bigger than that. God created the universe, so God *is* the universe, expanding galaxies, a dance and song so wondrous it can kill just to contemplate it.

That's what the old prophets meant when they said it's certain death to look at the face of God. Sheer ecstasy kills, or leads to madness. The mind was not meant to contemplate such beauty. On a dark night we look at the stars and say God made them. But we don't spend night after night staring at the heavens. Not even the wisest mystic spends every night looking at the stars. No, it's best to look within. The wise look at the present moment, which is the soul. That's where you'll find God and discover the hardest truth: human bondage is time bondage.

Know thyself, the ancient Greeks taught. A wise rule. God is within. You are God because your soul is from God. All is God. Can we really know ourselves? Our self? You can know your personality, the outer skin that's reflected in the mirror. But where's the mirror that reflects the soul? Soul must be the reflection of the Great Mystery that is the universe.

Is there no joy? Yes, look around you. You live on the most wondrous planet in the universe. There is no other like it. You are here; now, breathe, live the moment, go out and do something positive for your fellow human beings, for the earth and its creatures. Create. That's what Alfonso did.

Store as much joy in memory as you can. You'll need it.

K, I feel I'm walking in Fonso's shoes. I am his doppelgänger. I move through his experiences and emotions. Is this the relationship of author to character?

On Christmas Eve, friends and I drove to Taos Pueblo to attend midnight mass. When we came out, the luminarias, which had been set up from the front of the church to the plaza, were blazing and smoking. Bright sparks were floating up from those four-foot-high stacks of piñon logs into the dark sky, slowly dissolving as they rose, perhaps wishing they could join the stars in the firmament. Visitors huddled in the cold; all had been awaiting the lighting of the bonfires.

Alfonso's old friend Cruz Trujillo took my hand, and we formed a line of joyous participants, dancing and weaving around the luminarias, stepping to the music of the spheres. The piñon smoke nestled throughout the pueblo, an aroma that is the quintessence of winter in New Mexico.

What joy! If there is communion in Christ's season, then we were filled with it as we laughed and shouted, "Merry Christmas! ¡Feliz Navidad!"

On Christmas Eve, luminarias are often lit in front of Catholic churches in northern New Mexico villages. Luminar, to illuminate the road to Bethlehem. Such bonfires were probably burning outside the stable where Jesus was born that cold night. Shepherds warmed themselves by the fires and stared at the star whose bright light announced an earth change.

The star was light, the Child was Light.

Alfonso visited the stable in Bethlehem, remembering it as a kind of grotto. Once inside, he was surprised to feel a strong spiritual presence in the enclosure. He would also feel that spirit at Machu Picchu, Stonehenge, the Giza pyramids. Consecrated spaces. It is true, the earth has spirit. Or perhaps we imbue earth with spirit when we celebrate the spirituality in ourselves.

The llano and the river also held familiar energies. The earth was imbued with God.

One Christmas night, Alfonso was working in Trampas with a couple of gals from Hollywood who were filming the folk play *Los Pastores* inside the small church. When the play was over, both actors and audience went out into the midnight cold to enjoy the luminarias, burning bright, lighting the way, the warmth of Christmas.

That short VHS film exists somewhere in his files, as do others. Now everything is digital. What next? Holograms that allow the recipient to walk into the projected image and become one with the message? Maybe a wormhole so we can travel through time/space, be there and here at the same time? Wormholes are the coming thing. Not just for travel from one galaxy to another, but also to go visit grandma.

Exhausted, shouting goodbyes, we ran to our car and drove out of the pueblo into the starry night that held all the wonder Christmas can hold. Fusion of religions, syncretism. The Pueblos accepted some Catholic ways, while holding on to the way of their ancestors. If all the cultures of the world participated more often in each other's religious ceremonies, we might have fewer wars.

You asked about Cruz. He's an old man now. Long ago he took Alfonso hunting up on Taos Mountain. That's when Norman and Rachel were still living in Taos Canyon. Alfonso followed the stocky man up and down ravines and deer trails, pausing to eat lunch under shimmering gold canopies of aspen. He told me about the time he got separated from Cruz.

Lost, he had started down the mountain when he came upon a doe. He knew he shouldn't have shot it—he was alone—but he did. Worst of luck, he only wounded it. He was tracking the deer's spoor, walking slowly, looking down at the tracks, when he smelled bear. He raised his head, and there in front of him were three brown bears, the parents and a large cub. The huge animals stood up, tall and massive, their attention focused on Alfonso.

He froze, contemplated climbing a tree, the bears so close their strong odor stung his nostrils. They were looking to hibernate when he came upon them. They growled loudly, opening their dark mouths with yellowed teeth, roars that shook Alfonso. He knew they would protect the cub. They measured him, the stranger on their mountain, snuffling, pawing the ground, innately sure of themselves. This was their home; the man posed danger.

Would they attack?

Finally, with a toss of their huge heads, they dismissed him and lumbered away. The mountain grew still and silent. A shaken Alfonso stood alone on the lonely slope, surrounded by tall, dark Ponderosa pines that seemed to look down on him in shame. He had wet his pants.

That night he dreamed he was in a courtroom being tried by the animals of the forest for having shot the doe. A bear was the judge; deer and other animals sat in the jury box. Was Fonso guilty of a transgression? The dream was laden with a message from the animal world.

Agapita had taught him to respect all the animals of the llano. So, too, the mountain animals. He put away his rifle and hunted no more. Years later, he gave the rifle to a nephew.

He lost touch with Cruz after Norman and Rachel sold their home and moved to Alburquerque. But he never lost touch with the Pueblo world. After he was married, he and his wife visited dozens of pueblo fiestas over the years. Patricia loved Pueblo and Navajo jewelry, squash blossom necklaces, bracelets inlaid with coral, dangling earrings. No New York gold for her; she loved turquoise and silver. And bowls. She bought bowls at the different pueblos—not as a collector, but for the love each bowl represented at the time. A story in each bowl.

When she died, he broke the bottom of a marriage bowl they had bought at Zia Pueblo. An ancient custom.

K, I'm back to writing my novel. These letters to you have become a novel of sorts, and I'm afraid the two projects overlap, run together.

Who cares. These e-mails are for you, not the public. What will you do with them? Show them to your grandkids? Think what I write will shed light on the sorrows of Alfonso? We pass away, everything passes away. It's a law of nature.

Christmas Eve. Good feelings permeated the air and enriched the Taos community with the essence of Christmas. A spirit of renewal filled the pueblo, and it would remain during Christmas Day activities, when the deer-men came down from the hills. Important traditions played out.

A river runs through the pueblo. There, early on the cold morning they were going hunting, Alfonso stepped out of the house and saw Cruz at the river, splashing freezing water on his face, arms, and chest. Ablution.

The man in communion with nature and Taos Mountain was the kind of thing Frank Waters could best describe. Frank lived next to Taos Pueblo for a long time. He knew the people. He was one of Fonso's favorite writers. Fonso and his wife were guests of Frank and Barbara many a time. When Frank came up from Tucson, those years when he wintered down there, he stayed with Fonso. He always drove his old jalopy, Fonso said. Once when he was backing out of the driveway, he tore down the mailbox post. What fun. Then he passed away, as we must all do, to the spirit world.

So Fonso began to understand a little of the pueblo way of life. It started with Cruz in Taos; later he got to know Joe Sando from Jemez Pueblo. They often ate together at the Indian Cultural Center. Joe told him a few things, witchcraft stories that Alfonso wouldn't tell me. Fonso knew witch stories told by Nuevo Mexicanos, the Hispanics of New Mexico, but what he learned about the Indian world he kept to himself.

Witches are people with strong negative energies that can hurt others. They have existed in all cultures since the beginning of time. Not mere hocus-pocus, but people who choose to do evil. They're still with us. For example, greedy capitalists whose only goal is to enrich themselves and in the process destroy thousands of lives—I call that evil. Tyrants, abusers of children, warmongers all qualify. You see, it depends on how you phrase the context.

Throughout the years, Fonso and Patricia attended dances at the different pueblos: Taos, Santo Domingo (now Kewa), Santa Clara, San Ildefonso, Jemez, Zia, Santa Ana, Isleta. The dances created a spiritual presence akin to that he felt in Pastura del Santo Niño during mass, the same strong aura he felt in the grotto at Bethlehem.

One time when they were at Jemez Pueblo, a group of Matachines dancers had just finished their performance and left the plaza. A friend nudged Fonso. "Walk on the ground where the dancers danced," he whispered. Fonso stepped forward. There it was, a subtle energy rising from the earth sanctified by the dancers, an energy connecting earth to community. Sacred space. The spiritual meaning of the dance realized.

Then he felt the sting of a whip across the back of his legs. He turned. One of the mayordomos in charge of the dancers had popped his legs with his whip. "Anda, muchacho," he said in Spanish falsetto. They knew, he knew.

There was more to the dance than the enjoyment of meeting friends, eating tamales and Indian bread, and drinking hot coffee on a cold December 12 morning, more than visiting the tables where Pueblo artisans sold their pottery and jewelry. The ancient story played out by the characters in the Matachines brought harmony to the pueblo. The history of the ancestors was renewed.

Fonso never went into a kiva. There was no reason why he should have. They kept their religion; he was struggling with his faith. He never went to kachina dances at Hopi, but as an old man he had Hopi friends who visited him. They sat and talked, revealing a few things, Fonso's cosmology completing itself. He even wrote a Kokopelli story, his attempt to reach out to those far-flung villages on the Arizona mesas.

Now we have conflicts in the Fertile Crescent, destruction of the World Trade Center, each sect claiming its priority to God. What nonsense! It's the children who suffer in religious wars. They cry in the streets of war-torn nations. Hunger, hate, and greed have become the deities of a world gone mad. Oil has become a god that war serves. We retreat to our families and communities and try to keep the faith. Perhaps in the sacred space we create lies the answer, faith in truth and beauty. We can overcome.

Christmas Eve, the joyous dance after mass was done, the pueblo fell quiet. Friends invited Fonso and Patricia for hot chocolate and empanadas. He remembered the empanadas his mother used to make, the true reward of Christmas. Maybe she had bought hard candy for their Christmas socks, and that was a treat, but for Fonso there was no better treat than Rafaelita's empanadas.

Piñon wood burned hot in the kiva fireplace, the aroma of smoke as sweet as any incense offered in church. The December stars were bright in the dark sky, and as we were leaving, one fell across the northern horizon. The star of the East, whether one believed the Bible story or not.

During our university years, Fonso went through an existential crisis, years of internal conflict, his faith sundered, but as he grew older, he drew closer to the Christmas story. He needed to believe in something.

Teach the children that many paths come to One, if only they remain true to self. Teach the simple joys. Joy in Christmas Eve at the pueblo, the procession of believers, the luminarias lighting the way, piñon smoke rising from pueblo home fireplaces, each home ready to receive guests. There was room at the inn.

Every year, he and Patricia were sure to be at the Matachines dance at Jemez Pueblo on December 12. It was one of his favorites.

The people of Pastura del Santo Niño also celebrated the holy days. A tattered calendar hanging on a wall recorded when the community came together for mass, singing, families gathering for the noonday meal, more family arriving, rocking each home with happiness. Each day was a holy day on the llano or at the river. Fonso was in tune with the spirits of those places.

His people were hardworking paisanos; most had little or no education and few resources. In work they were equal to anyone, but they were poor. Education was to be Fonso's way out of that trap, but it was a two-edged sword. It liberated him, while at the same time it cast doubt on his Catholic upbringing. Those despairing times were to be his greatest sorrow.

Dear K,

On summer days he and his friends swam in the river. They raced their bikes up and down the dusty streets all the way to Hidden Lake. He fished the Pecos River, the mythical river that was so important in his life. His brothers took him rabbit hunting on the llano; his sharp eyes could spot the prey. The large jackrabbits they killed were fed to the pig.

That October they butchered the pig. Early on a cold morning, the animal was shot, bled, and covered with burlap sacks that had been soaked in hot water laced with lye. The men used knives to scrape off the softened bristles. The fat was thrown into a large copper kettle over a blazing fire and rendered into lard and chicharrones, the tasty pork rinds everyone loved.

The meat was shared with neighbors—perhaps a widow struggling to survive or someone who had fallen on hard times. One day Alfonso delivered a food package to a needy neighbor. He asked his mother why they were sharing their food. "They're poor," she said.

"But we're poor, too," he answered, and received a rebuke.

"Sharing is our way," she told him.

He learned it was the Nuevo Mexicano way of life. Communities had survived because they shared what they had. The true workings of Christianity as his mother practiced it.

Baseball was his favorite sport. Alfonso and some friends organized a team, the Comets, and they played kids from Newkirk and Vaughn. When football season came, Ron Chavez organized the neighborhood games. They didn't have a football, so they stuffed rags in an old sock, and that's what they tossed around. George Gonzales had a basketball goal and a ball, so afternoons they gathered to play at his place.

One spring Alfonso accompanied his father and brothers to a nearby ranch. The lambing season was in full swing, and a cold blizzard was sweeping across the llano. In the bitter wind the men worked among the huge flock, gathering the just-born lambs and making sure the ewes accepted and suckled their offspring. El hijadero, they called it, a custom as old as the deserts of Nazareth.

Hijadero, from hija? Anyway, it means caring for the lambs, carrying lost lambs on their shoulders to the warm corrales, where they could be bottle-fed. The calls of the men and the bleating of the sheep filled the cold llano with promise. Kerosene lanterns pierced the dark night as the men spread out through the flock, saving the lambs.

In spring, shearing time meant more work, hard work for hard-muscled men, wages to support families, a profit for the rancher.

Some llaneros went to Wyoming to work el hijadero. They came back with money in their pockets and fabulous stories. Story was bred into their way of life.

Alfonso loved shearing season. It meant long days of work for his father and brothers, but it was also a festive event. Entire families showed up at the big ranches; every family member contributed to the work. Kids chasing each other around the cook's wagon, dogs barking, sheep bleating, clouds of dust swirling, coffee brewing, a large pot of beans simmering—so many to feed, the women making tortillas couldn't keep up. Martin had signed on as camp cook, and he made the best bread in an old sheepherder oven set over the fire. Mutton ribs roasted over the campfire, which blazed with the dripping grease.

Those were the years a sheep industry existed on the llano, a continuation of a way of life established centuries earlier when Basque families arrived and learned to live and work alongside the Mexicanos. Within a generation, Old World Basque melted into New Mexican Spanish; all became New Mexicans. But that way of life ended as friends and neighbors moved away and the village emptied. The llano breathed a sigh of relief and fell silent.

After a full morning's work, Alfonso sat with his brothers and opened the lunchbox his mother had prepared for him. A jar of beans, a slice of fried mutton wrapped in a tortilla, a slice of pie. "Never again did I taste pie as delicious as those my mother baked," he said one day when we were fishing the East Fork of the Jemez River. We sat at the edge of the stream eating baloney sandwiches and pie we had purchased at a Jemez Springs store. I sensed he was tasting his mother's pie again, and being again in that time, fully absorbed, like when he was writing and entered the timeless world of the story at hand.

Trancelike, bilocation, his body behind the computer, his soul in the world of the story. Some have trouble understanding the trance a writer goes into, but then, any true creative work sucks the artist into its being. Soul goes to soul.

Life was good in that Before time. One day his brothers caught the flock's ram, a carnero almost as big as a Shetland pony. The ram was in charge of the flock; he protected his ewes. He was mean and had been known to charge strangers. The brothers sat Alfonso on the ram, and he grabbed the huge curled horns and rode the spirited animal around the corral until it bucked him off. Clouds of dust and laughter filled the air.

They sat him in the shade of the ramada. He was satisfied. He had ridden the ram, and he hadn't cried when he fell. When the angry ram chased him, he climbed a fence. His brothers clapped and threw their cowboy hats in the air.

Above him the clear sky was dotted with a few circling vultures. Llano wind whispered around the dry, weathered posts of the corral. The wind told many stories, always the wind, la voz del llano, the voice of the llano, the blessing wind.

Summer came, and the grassland turned green. Fragrances in the breeze spoke volumes. The aroma of brilliant red cactus flowers foretold that there would be large, juicy prickly pears by midsummer. The boys would pick the plump purple pears, dust away the thorns, and suck the fruit's juices, spitting out the seeds.

Propagation by birds, prairie dogs, and boys.

Agapita was always nearby. He remembered the day she told him that one day he would write the story of the people of the llano.

"Me?"

"Yes, you. La voz del llano."

Damn! Don't cry for Alfonso! He had all that in Before time. Praise the precious time in your life. That's all there is!

Maybe I didn't want to get to this episode . . . I kept putting it off. Here's what happened:

He led the girl to the dance floor. So far they had just exchanged smiles. Yes, I can do it, he thought, trying to dispel his fear. He had chased the train and won the initiation of pain that would last a lifetime. Right then he wondered if he could dance. She was a good dancer; he had watched her. Why had she exchanged glances with him?

He held out his hand to take hers, but his fingers wouldn't quite open to cup her hand in his. The moment of truth hit him like sorrow. His stomach went queasy, his legs felt weak. If only he could explain, tell her he had chased a train and been initiated into a brotherhood of cripples. That's why his fingers were weak. The memory of what they used to do hadn't returned.

He looked into her eyes. He couldn't speak; and anyway, explaining what had happened when he touched the train would be a dumb thing to tell a girl he had just met. They stared at each other, pressed together by other couples dancing to the lyrics, Oh, yes, I'm the Great Pretender.

Was he a pretender?

He needed magic words! He needed Agapita's magic!

The girl reached out and touched his closed hand. Her fingers, aromatic with sweet lotion, softly wrapped around his, as if to say, it's okay.

But what did her eyes tell him? In the dark on the dance floor, he struggled to move his leaden foot. Around them, couples swayed to the music, the dancers praying that some chemistry would take place while they were in the arms of their dance partner, some sweet odor of love might erupt into unimagined ecstasy. Teenyboppers looking for love, hungry for love. The entire world looking for love, and Alfonso was caught in the web that his destiny was weaving.

For a moment he saw the flicker of a glance, her gut feeling expressed in her dark eyes. It seemed to last an eternity, he told me. She smiled when the dance ended, then thanked him and walked away. He remained standing in the middle of the dance floor, alone.

Don't blame her. The weekly dances were a courting game, as are wild, turbulent concerts today. Male looking for female, female looking for male, same-sex looking for same-sex, or for experiments after pot and booze, each with a subconscious list of things they want in the catch.

The lights were dimmed for the last dance, "Goodnite, Sweetheart, Goodnite," a slow waltz, almost erotic in the temptations it aroused in young couples. Then it was suddenly over; the lights came on, and everyone rushed out into the night, some looking for a ride home—hey, daddy-o, give me a ride, let's go to Lionel's for burgers, get some beer, one girl whispering as she passed by, "I'm not getting in the back seat with just anyone. If I do, it's going to be—"

That perilous night, the music ended. Would he try again? The dance at the community center was the place to be with his friends on Saturday nights. He wanted to belong. God, that wanting to belong is a basic human instinct, but if you don't fit, it can be a killer.

Would she keep his secret?

He didn't want others to know.

Outside, a group of boys were passing around a pint of whiskey. He looked up at the night sky, the stars eclipsed by bright streetlights.

He wished he were back in the llano, the village of his birth, the people, the wind carrying the fragrances of grass and blooming yucca.

Something had been shattered. He felt stupid. Why had he thought that he could join the crowd, the normal crowd? Never again, he swore. Never again.

Did he lose faith? Or was it just frustration? He had anticipated climbing out of his shell. What did he expect? Would every experience be like this? Wanting to indulge in normal activities, yet knowing his limitations?

Faith? What could he hold on to? "Your hand has memory," his mother had told him. "It will remember how it was before the accident." Faith ran as deep in her as the river. It was natural for her; she believed in God. God could cure any disease.

If Jesus made the lame walk and raised the dead, surely He could straighten her son's crippled hand. She believed, but Alfonso was beginning to question. What could he do in the future?

Was one's work in life ordained when the Big Bang exploded?

Was there an archetypal carpenter with hammer, nails, and saw constructing the universe? Or a universal electrician hired to wire the whole shebang, but instead the wires shorted and exploded, and the sparks became galaxies, flying into deep space? Or God's first musician instructed to create the music of the spheres. She strikes a musical note, only one note, harmonious unto itself, perfect in proportion, a sound bewitching in ecstasy. The note desires to express itself, so it explodes into a symphony. Galaxies go singing their way into space; the music of the spheres is born. The note's fantastic energy spreads out, and each speck of energy carries the memory of the first note. Music is energy.

Energy equals music times the speed of light squared. Energy and music, perfect mathematical proportions.

If the universe is a symphony, does it need a conductor? Does it need a master carpenter, a master electrician?

We laughed as we tossed ideas around. Those were some of my happiest times, talking ideas with Fonso. We wanted to know everything. What is real? What is the true essence of things? What did that first musical note sound like? Why did it explode into a symphony? Was it not content? Did it want to share its sound, its beauty? With whom? Did it know that billions upon billions of years later, there would be humans on earth listening to the music of the universe?

If a tree falls in the forest and there is no one there to hear it, does it make a sound?

So many questions, K. Did the first vibrating musical note have a need to express itself beyond the thin membrane that enclosed it? What was the substance of the sheathing that held the note in place? Was the note conscious? Was it the First Soul? Were note and membrane of the same substance, soul and body?

So many questions.

We come from that first note, children of the universe, our frail bodies enclosed in skin. How did soul come to be encased in flesh? Body is not only the temple of soul, it is alive with soul; soul is in the blood.

Need and desire drive us along the path of life.

The note exploded and the universe was born, spinning into its destiny. No one can know the destiny of the universe—maybe the conductor. We cannot know our destiny—maybe God.

At times we felt we had the answers; at other times we felt exhaustion, ennui. Maybe it was best to leave everything to God? That's the easy way out.

But like Sisyphus, we persisted. Was the musical note aware of itself? What melody? What duration? What pitch? If the Big Bang was the explosion of that note, was the birth aware of itself? That numinous note must have been the cell of Eventual Being, harmony unto itself, awareness unto itself. I am music, therefore I am. I vibrate, therefore I can be.

Alfonso came to believe that the universe is a conscious entity, far-flung and creating space/time as it expands. If the universe is aware of its beginning, it must have memory. Our function is to understand that memory.

If we go to where the tree fell in the forest, will we hear the universal symphony? In the beauty of the forest, we sense the work of the conductor. Trees vibrate with music, they *are* music.

We spent countless hours and beers tossing ideas around, arguing, discussing. Others joined us, young students, girls we met in art and literature classes, all looking for essential answers. Those were Beatnik days, sloughing off old ways of thinking, creating freedom with poetry, getting close to nature, saving the earth. We frequented the few coffee cafes in the city. We thought we were cool. We read the Beat poets, and we began to write.

Late at night, after many beers and endless speculation, Fonso, Jimmy, and I headed over to the Casa Luna for pizza. Pete was there; we had a crazy argument, and he and Jimmy left. We were as poor as proverbial church mice, so the pizzas our ladies served us were a godsend. When the pizzeria closed, we went with them down Central, winding our way to their apartment, where we sat around and talked, drank beer, and in the wee hours of the morning fell sluggish into their welcoming arms. Such were the wasted nights of our university years. Ideas, beer, pizza, and sex all seemed to come together.

Love flavored with peperoni pizzas, free love. Now that I think about it, maybe we were the first Chicano Beatniks. We were searching for answers beyond the boundaries of the barrio, beyond the religion of our forefathers. Awakening, agape, and trembling at the vast world we were finding in the world of books. Aghast might be the word.

Maybe it wasn't love we shared with our ladies, but comfort. Searching for love in the arms of women who understood our rite of passage.

Our ladies are old and wrinkled now, but often I wish I could see them again. One last time. Isn't that the way it is as we age? We want to gather all our friends in our arms one last time. Sorrowfully, we can't.

What did passage into manhood have to do with thoughts of a musical universe? Nothing. Everything. We pressed on.

Was the conductor aware of every galaxy speeding to the edges of a universe being created? Time was being created where before there was no time. Space created where there had been no space.

As the universe expanded, was it possible that the conductor lost sight of some galaxies? Suppose the Milky Way started to spin away, abandoning the symphony's leitmotif? Was there even a central theme in the unfolding musical drama? Suppose the conductor began to lose sight of the Milky Way, our eventual home? She took her eyes off the musical score for a moment and saw Planet Earth disappearing, a dot in the galaxy, a speck of energy in the galaxy. The symphony was gathering momentum, rushing to a crescendo, its destiny unfolding. Once music and light are set loose, they can't be contained. Could the conductor keep the symphony from disintegrating into chaos? Chaos would mean the death of music.

Then the music died. A folksong full of sorrow.

A violinist with a screeching violin played in the back row of the Milky Way concert hall. He wasn't keeping pace, playing a not-well-tuned violin, destroying the harmony. The conductor grew irritated; she got rid of the violinist, sent him off to play for Planet Earth. That's how we wound up with an incompetent violinist playing earth's evolution. Sometimes the melody is perfect, but most often it's way out of tune.

"So is our nature," Alfonso said sadly. "We create great symphonies, but also the horrors of a Holocaust."

Our late-night speculations had taken us down a road from which there was no return. The history of the universe was a chain that shackled us to a symphony we yearned to hear.

We sighed, wishing we could take back every time we had said, "I don't believe in God." We thought we were sure of ourselves, even as we denied the queasy feeling in our stomachs. Angst. We were treading on thin ice, and the only song on the jukebox was "Blowin' in the Wind."

A tremendous galactic wind was blowing the universe away, and us with it.

No wonder we sought refuge in the late-night arms of the pizzeria women. They were real. Only now do I give thanks, as Alfonso must have done, for those sex-strained nights. What was good for us was also good for the women. In their own right, they too were searching. We lived on the edge of survival, yet hardly noticed. We took care of each other.

———

K, it is the haunting time, dusk settling over our Rio Grande Valley, the city aglow with the last light of day, the Sandia Mountains a soft crimson. A covey of Gambel's quail scoot down the mesa. A flock of doves fly into the setting sun, becoming shiny globs of mercury as they turn in unison. The light is full of illusions.

Why was Alfonso haunted by sunsets? Why did he say that time of day was always nostalgic?

"A glowing sunset makes me feel I'm back in Santa Rosa de Lima," he said. "I see the haunted hills, the hidden lakes. I hear the cries of a lost woman at the river, a spirit woman."

Melusina.

La Llorona.

Agnes, always Agnes . . .

He described a brilliant summer sunset after an afternoon rain on the llano. The air was palpable with the sweet, clean smell of grasses, flowering white yucca, the aroma of wild mint and oregano growing by the roadside.

In the west the sun cast its light on billowing clouds, endowing them with fiery shades of red, hues of bright orange never seen before. Alfonso stood alone in God's grace, transfixed, transformed, watching the glory of the sun splashing its light on the heavenly clouds. He became one with the sunset and the music it evoked from the land. All was light and music, all was illusion.

That's what I understood. It wasn't just the beauty of the sunset he appreciated, like we might view a sunset and say "beautiful." We use that word so much it loses its significance.

Words signify. The sunset was full of words, the words of nature. Nature speaks, and we must learn her language. Enough of the apostles and empty prophecies! Let's use nature's language when we speak, write poems, make love!

Linger awhile, just as you are.

We are limited, we can only approximate, so we stand at the edge of the Grand Canyon, look into earth's womb, the sun splashing blood against sandstone cliffs, and we say "beautiful."

Sunsets were burned into his memory. Today we take instant photographs of sunsets with our smart electronic gadgets, and the scenes are burned into a chip. We can retrieve the images and share them with friends, but they remain static images. An instant of time enslaved for all time. Scenes from nature are alive when experienced in the moment. We only have a second before everything is swept away by the expanding universe, the setting sun.

Alfonso carried sunset images in his heart. He was forever caught in that time when he stood alone on the llano, shivering from the lingering coolness of the afternoon rain, looking into the fire of the setting sun, becoming one with fire, clouds, light, and color.

Perhaps those moments he learned to disappear, moving out of his body into the light.

Around him grasshoppers were chirping, a cacophony of life, including sounds from lizards, rabbits, hawks, shrill locusts, swallows darting down to the pond, hungry coyotes, sleeping owls, a cowbell echoing, the village church bell tolling, a woman weeping, horses racing, a vaquero calling—all of this became a time he could walk into and disappear.

Ah, my Alfonso. I pray for him. What did he feel when he entered God's sunset? Immortality? A child is immortal. Or did he feel insignificant? A small boy in a world so wide it has no end. The llano has no end. Sky and clouds have no end. Then brilliance dies as the sun drops below the horizon, and night encroaches with its own mystery.

The ancient brain fears the night, and we all retain remnants of that brain. The sunrise promises the renewal of life; sunsets remind us, if only symbolically, of the end. Maybe it's not symbolic—maybe we actually feel the death of the world at sunset, a knowledge ingrained in the blood.

Ancient humans huddled around a fire at day's end. The coming night was fearful, full of dangerous animals, full of ghosts the stories conjured up. Night was not only the end of day; in the minds of our first ancestors, it represented the end of life. What if the sun didn't return?

The seasons replicate the day, and thus the primal fear. Our ancestors from the cave knew that the winter solstice was the shortest day of the year. If on the morning after the solstice the sun didn't appear, then all was lost. Life on earth would end in darkness and ice.

Is this what Alfonso felt at sunset? At winter solstice? Did he share an ancient memory with those first humans who built fires to stave off the night? Of course he did. We all do. We have inherited that ancient brain. It connects us to the primal past. It makes us pay attention to the setting sun and enjoy not only its beauty, but the nostalgia that comes with it.

Ceremonies. Since the beginning, different communities around the world have gathered to sing, dance, and pray on the winter solstice. Pray that the sun returns. At Stonehenge, at Machu Picchu, at Chaco Canyon, at dozens of sites around the world, the shortest day of the year looms heavy. Yule logs are burned, green trees become Christmas trees, mistletoe is hung—celebrate the New Year, make music, drink last year's cup, it's all the same.

Solstice and we are reminded that the sun is at a precarious moment. We pray for its return and celebrate when it does.

Jesus, the son, is born. The faith of the fathers is renewed.

Becoming one with the sunset was rapture. The glory of God was in the sunset. The sunset was God.

Growing up on the llano and the banks of the Pecos River, he had experienced that oneness with nature. The natural world held the secret. One didn't have to die to feel rapture; the ecstatic moment occurred when man and nature were no longer subject/object, no longer separated into I/Thou. Becoming Oneness.

Do you remember that early essay he wrote describing man and nature as two magnetic poles, man and nature creating a field of energy? Walking on the llano, there were times when he and the earth created a magnetic axis, the axis mundi. The earth's magnetism realigned the energy field of body and soul.

Butterflies and migrating geese follow the earth's magnetic field. Locating and using the earth's energies has been practiced for ages. It's the secret of Tibetan monks who know how to align themselves as they chant. Aooomm is the sound of the energy field, the earth's harmony. Others knew the secret: the Ganges holy men, the ancient Mayas and Aztecs, and the worshippers at Stonehenge. Here in New Mexico, the ancient Chaco Canyon and Mesa Verde people aligned their buildings and kivas with the sun. The harmony of those lines was reflected in their way of life. When the energy field no longer held, they left their homes, left everything behind.

He told me about a sunset he once experienced on the beach at Mazatlán. He had traveled there with Ed and Sherry in 1965, a year before he married Patricia. He was standing on the beach one evening, the gentle surf lapping at his feet, a sky on fire spread out across the Sea of Cortez, reaching, it seemed, to the ends of the earth, reaching to China.

(See what I mean about alignment? It can happen anywhere one attunes oneself to the sacred in nature.)

The setting sun that day was as spectacular and glorious as any sunset on the llano. It enveloped earth and sea, and those walking on the beach. All became a vision of heaven, an illusion; the fire in the clouds was the fire of God. "I entered God's grandeur," Fonso wrote, "and blended into a greater world, not a spectator, my soul alive in the sun's light and the ocean's mystery. I felt like walking into the ocean and disappearing."

It made me think. We humans can only absorb so much beauty. People jump off the edge into the Grand Canyon; others jump off the Golden Gate Bridge. It's more than suicide; I think it's a way of *walking into the sunset and disappearing*. Agape. I wonder if that's the same feeling some get at the end of life. A feeling that you're intimately involved in the earth's consciousness, ready to let go of the body's love for the next day, ready for rapture.

Everyone can partake in that connection to nature. It's like being in love, melting into the person you love, becoming one, or as he said, the urge he felt to step into the endlessly rolling ocean, the life source.

The woman from the pizzeria was good to him, but the fit wasn't quite right. Was he in tune with his destiny calling to complete itself elsewhere? That's a difficult question to answer.

Does anyone know their destiny? I think we kind of stumble through life, aware of some things that seem to point to the eventual person we will become. But do we really know where life is taking us? I don't think so. We can look back and see the unrolling of our lives, but we can't peer into the future. It's too murky—

Or can we?

Once, in a dream, he was walking along a river path, and he came upon a dead body covered with leaves. He drew close, brushed away the leaves that covered the face, and saw that it was he himself who was lying there. A sadness filled him. Is seeing yourself dead in a dream one of the sorrows in life? Perhaps that's why we say that life is a dream. Look in the mirror! Are you awake or dreaming? Do we dream we are awake?

I asked him how he felt. Shocked? Afraid? Imagine seeing yourself dead.

"It felt real," he said. "I could hear the rustle of leaves in the trees, hear the river nearby, feel the sand beneath my feet. A great sadness filled my soul; I mourned for myself."

Most of us experience a death dream at one time or another. But usually it's someone else we see dead. A death wish? Who knows. Maybe that someone else in the coffin is a substitute because we're afraid to see ourselves dead. My dream mind is trying to protect me from the presence of death. I know I must die, but I don't want to face death.

We have many expressions that we use to scoff at death. When it's your time, it's your time. Same in Spanish: Cuando te toca, te toca. You can't dodge the bullet. The death bullet. His number was up, we say, as if there's a preordained number that will sooner or later come around. A lottery of death numbers. We brag and pretend we're brave. But are we?

There are a million poems written about death. Do not go gentle into that good night. La vida no vale nada . . . from a Mexican ballad.

"The dead grieve for us," Agapita told Alfonso. What an awful thing to tell a child. That's what I thought at first, but when he told me his dream, I realized she was preparing him for life. It made sense. We do grieve our death, and the death dream is a precursor. It tells us to live fully and not fear death.

He removed the leaves, those heart-shaped, glossy, pungent green cottonwood leaves. He said the story of a tree is written into the veins of each leaf. He was right. Each summer season is written into the leaf's arteries, creating the leaf's unique pattern. Come October, the leaves turn yellow and fall. Months later, all that remains is a spider web of veins on each brown leaf. You crumble dry leaves in your hand, and they become dust.

The leaf's DNA gone to dust. The tree survives to put out new foliage in the spring, but last year's leaves? Gone to dust, every one. So it is with us: each season is a chapter, and then we move on to the next.

Why the river, the river of his childhood? His older brothers taught him to fish as soon as he could hold a fishing rod. Alfonso, a fisherman after his soul. That's the way it had to be. In search of his soul, something eternal to hold on to.

What else can I say about Alfonso's high school years? A thousand and one incidents, a thousand and one dreams busted.

His friends stuck by him, but they had their own lives, part-time jobs, cars, dates on Saturday nights, Friday night football games. I think he realized that he slowed the gang down. Young men of high school age move fast. Alfonso limped.

One time when he was in line at a football game, a man pushed and told him to hurry.

"Move, gimp." Ugly words from an ugly man. The man's wife elbowed him. "Can't you see he's slow?"

"Oh, yeah. Sorry."

Too late—the damage was done. The embarrassment hurt. Those

nearby stared. Once again he was reminded of his handicap. He couldn't hurry like the others.

He closed himself off. Like a turtle that when poked and threatened withdraws into its shell, Alfonso began the long process of going within, shutting himself off. That meant staying home, finding solace in books. There were characters in books who had experienced the loneliness he felt. From them he could learn; he couldn't learn from the madding crowd.

There was loneliness in those high school years. How many kids are like Alfonso, staying home, not fitting in, not one of those who clamor to get to the top of the heap? Not everyone attended football games on Friday nights. The man's ugly words hurt to the core. Bullying isn't just pushing and shoving or a fight that breaks out; bullying can come from words meant to hurt. Words can injure.

Is loneliness a kind of sorrow? Does something in the soul die when you're lonely? It's not just self-esteem that is damaged when you're lonely. The soul hurts. You can cry all you want, but the pain won't go away.

Dear K,

As time went on, I began to appreciate Agapita. She had warned Alfonso it was best to be prepared . . .

Don't get me wrong, Fonso didn't go around saying he felt sorry for himself. He didn't show his loneliness; he kept his feelings hidden. His mother knew, but what could she do? There was little money. Her older sons were gone. Alfonso's sisters worked part-time at a small cafe in the barrio.

The time he felt most alone was during high school. Instead of eating lunch in the cafeteria, he usually headed to the back of the shop building, where an old man sold tamales out of a three-wheel wagon. Alfonso sat alone against the wall and ate his meal. A few other kids bought tamales and moved on. The cafeteria was just too much for him: the heavy trays, the cost, the rowdy energy of high-schoolers, the horseplay.

Eating alone is not good for the soul. One needs others to share the meal, companionship.

Later, during his years at the university, he and his best friend Dennis would hang out together, talking art and books, and always the lack of money. They partied with the pizzeria women, and whenever they could, they went fishing in the Jemez. From time to time he met with his friends from the barrio, but they were moving on, working, getting married. If a camera had followed Fonso around, it would have recorded a quiet young man. Thinking, chewing over the ideas that were opening up new worlds. Finding his way. A passage.

The family lived in the house at Pacific and Barelas for three years, then moved to Marble. K, you asked about Barelas. Just ten blocks south of downtown, the barrio was a friendly place. Fonso loved the barrio. The friends he met would last a lifetime. Vivian, Bobby, Jimmy, Pete, Arthur, Nick, Pat, Dickie, and Eliseo.

It was an exciting place, a great adventure for a boy who had been raised in a small town. Families visited; on summer afternoons people sat in their front porches, while kids played in the streets. Young men sauntered, a pachuco swing to their walk, cocky as hell, each thinking he was número uno. If one stopped in front of a girl's home, the parents knew that a dating game was starting.

Those were the Burque pachuco days of the fifties. Only a few young men from the barrios were pachucos, but the local papers usually blew up the numbers. Most of the boys were too busy working to join gangs, but the cops and the newspaper reporters at times profiled every brown-skinned Chicano as a pachuco. The stories sold papers in the Heights.

Barrio folks knew better. A protective father would question any young man who started to hang around his daughter. Who's your family? Where are they from? You have a job? If he was pachuco, the young suitor might be asked to move on.

Marijuana. How times have changed. In the fifties the weed was anathema to parents. "No daughter of mine is going to date a marijuano!" Ah, the traditional fathers of that bygone age. Bless them.

Sons usually followed in their fathers' line of work. A few were breaking the chain and aspiring to something different, college or a move to California for a better-paying job. Change was in the air in the barrios, but it came at a cost. Mainstream society had barriers, visible and invisible, and only a trickle could break through. Glass ceilings? Hell, that's nothing new. Study the history of minorities in this country.

The middle class wasn't a barrio issue. Maybe one or two families made enough money to qualify as middle class. Those who owned the barrio's grocery stores, cafes, gas stations, and furniture stores had money. Those who worked in the railroad shops made fair wages, owned a home and car—a working class that barely rose above the poverty line. Some Nuevo Mexicanos were starting trade businesses that didn't require higher education, and a few were entering professional fields, especially law. In New Mexico, attorneys and politics went hand in hand.

Would Hispanic attorneys who learned the law apply it to help their paisanos in the barrios? Some heroes had come out of the barrios and small towns. Senator Dennis Chavez, a real old-time progressive populist, comes to mind. La gente trusted the senator.

And Alfonso? Could he paint houses? Could he do the heavy work in the soot and grease of the railroad yard? What could he do? Limp from job to job? Don't misunderstand me, his loneliness was internal, something I can't quite describe. Maybe at times you've felt that emotion that wells up from deep inside, a sigh from the heart, a sense of aloneness, a lost soul, a feeling that you just can't go on—if so, you understand what he felt.

In Spanish we say "pobrecito": poor little one. The word describes anyone who's fallen on hard times. Joe Fulano was crushed to death in a horrific car wreck. The women crossed themselves and said, "Pobrecito." Pete Fulano lost the family's life savings at the casino. Pobrecito. Mary Coqueta got pregnant and the boy ran away to California. Pobrecita.

Relatives and friends visited Fonso's parents. "He looks thin," his uncle said. "And you say he can't move his arm up like this? Pobrecito. A terrible accident. Come here, open your hand. Like this. You can't? Pobrecito. Diós es muy grande. God is very big."

Alfonso wondered, is it true?

The railroad played a big role in the barrio's economy. When the yards were moved to Arizona, economic hard times hit. In the forties, Kirkland Air Force Base and Sandia Labs were established on the east side of the city, a boon to the city's economic base. The city was growing; the barrio struggled to retain its identity.

At the baseball stadium by the zoo, the hometown Dukes played visiting teams. During night games, Alfonso and his friends waited outside the stadium for foul balls hit over the fence. The pop of the bat told them when a ball was foul even before they saw it soaring over the wall. "Ooooo-over!" someone would cry. Shag! A recovered ball could be sold to the city league ball teams for a dollar. Years later, the stadium was demolished, and the shouts of kids chasing "overs" were no longer heard.

Alfonso's mother was the family's center of strength; she kept them together. Once his father had been the head, but more and more these days he took a back seat in family affairs. He missed the llano and his compadres; now he drank alone, which sometimes created conflicts.

Abuse happened. Fonso was six or seven, he didn't remember for sure, and he didn't know how the fight started. Their father was very drunk. It started with a loud argument, their father verbally abusing their mother, Alfonso and his sisters looked on, trembling, not sure this was the gentle father they knew. The verbal attacks reverberated in the kitchen. Martin's anger flared, his rage ready to become physical. What would have happened if Uncle Pedro hadn't stepped between the two?

The scene was etched into his memory. There was much good and strength in families, but in some there was also abuse, and often it was swept under the rug. Years later, he connected the dots. His father never got to the point of striking his wife, and he never laid a hand on his children, but Alfonso learned that other fathers were physically abusive. Friends told him they had been beaten.

The culture was going through a breakdown, losing the stability it had once enjoyed. Incidents of abuse were becoming more frequent. Booze unveiled the rage men felt when they lost their livelihoods, lost their ability to provide for their families. Years later, Alfonso wondered why it was the poor who suffered the most in that time of transition.

There's a history to all this, and it's not a pretty history. 1848: a year to burn into your mind. At the end of the U.S.–Mexican War, the once-settled Nuevo Mexicano communities had to cope with a new set of rules, a new language, a cash instead of barter economy, and a new set of laws. The new social pressures emasculated many Nuevo Mexicano men. The same thing happened among Indian families. The old traditional communities were breaking down. Life had never been idyllic; families worked hard to make a living. After

1848, the culture that had once been their refuge was slipping out of their hands.

"My husband beat me and the kids," a woman would whisper to her comadre. "He was drunk."

"I know, comadre, I know."

It was the worst of times, a time of social and economic transition. Culture clash!

Alcohol became a way to cope. A drunk man could be his own boss again; he could act macho with his drinking compadres, and when he got home, the frustration burning inside often made him strike out at those closest to him.

I won't go on. Those times have been documented by sociologists. Loss of a center affected many, and destructive behavior followed. It ruined families. It's not easy to expose abuse and the pain it causes. Is it because we don't want the world to know that our otherwise good fathers could turn into demons, and the wife was there to suffer his rage?

Rage fueled by cheap wine drove men to despair. Children sensed that there was something wrong. How can a child who knows a protective, loving father understand the same father full of rage and curses? What do children living in such a home tell their friends at school when they show up with bruises? What do they tell their teachers when they miss school?

K, the social breakdown that affected Nuevo Mexicanos is still with us. Read the papers or watch the evening news. Across the Southwest, Chicanos are the ones most often incarcerated, especially the young. So, too, blacks and Indians. It suits those in power to, consciously or unconsciously, nurture their racial prejudices.

We have a black president, a man who has tried to make things better for the country. Yet some who oppose him don't do it because of political differences: they still can't accept the fact that a black man is president. When will this ever change?

Life in the barrio was complex for Alfonso's father, and it wore him down. His age and the years of hard work caught up with him.

He took care of things around the house, helped when he could, but spent more time just sitting in the porch—an image Alfonso remembers from those days.

That's all we have, images from the past, and those years had not been kind to Alfonso's people. The trauma of cultural change that had begun in 1848 was cataclysmic for Spanish-speaking New Mexicans. As more and more Anglo Americans homesteaded in the state, they butted heads with established Nuevo Mexicanos. The Territory of New Mexico was now part of the union, and the rules and language of the Anglo American victors were the law of the land.

Culture shock affected Nuevo Mexicanos who refused to abandon their language and way of life. Those who could remained in the villages and ranchos their ancestors had settled centuries ago. They adapted, all the while keeping true to their traditions. Some of the newly arrived Anglos viewed mestizo Mexicans as subhuman. That view exists today in some corners of society. I write this to remind you of that chapter in history.

During the Chicano movement, instead of being ashamed of mestizaje, Chicanos celebrated it. La Raza. The people of the New World, a coming together of gene pools. A rainbow people born here in the Américas.

Language lay at the crux of the enormous change that came to New Mexico. The Spanish-speaking community had to learn English in order to survive, and that would take time. In the meantime, the transition was painful.

There was resistance, of course. Read the history of Las Gorras Blancas in San Miguel County or Elfego Baca's gunfight against a gang of Texas cowboys. Or study the Chicano movement of the seventies. Fonso had seen the culture of his ancestors displaced, and he knew firsthand the hardships suffered by Mexican Americans who resisted the new way of life. The Chicano movement accomplished a lot for our people. The struggle for equality wasn't easy, but it changed the course of history.

K, his chance at a university education was not yet on the horizon, so what could he do after high school?

Some of the barrio boys had joined the military. That was the tradition: Be a Marine. Mexican Americans had one of the best service records in the country. Fonso's father had served; so had his three older brothers. But for Alfonso, the military was out of the question. He visited the Selective Service office, filled out the paperwork, got a physical, and received his identity card: 4-F. You can't be a Marine if you're 4-F.

Identity? Is this what I'm getting at? How does an eighteen-year-old feel when his friends are working and he stays home? Endlessly walking around town looking for a job, checking the newspapers, applying here and there. "What can you do?" employers asked. Endless disappointments.

I'm getting maudlin, and I don't want to; that was never the purpose of my letters. You asked me to write what I knew of young Alfonso. After the swimming accident, he managed to complete the last two years of high school. The going is tough for the handicapped, and difficult for parents whose children need a lot of care. Autism, bipolar disorder, Down syndrome, diabetes, accidents.

How do parents feel if their child isn't normal?

By the time Fonso was in high school, his walking had improved. He couldn't run, didn't have the balance, but one would have to look closely to notice the slight limp. His hand was another story. It was never going to be normal; the fingers in his left hand were weak. Typing class? Out of the question.

There was little money, so he didn't see college in his future. High school teachers and counselors hadn't mentioned college; no seeds of possibility were planted. Even though the University of New Mexico was just a few miles up the hill from the barrio, the two were universes apart. He was smart enough, but the money question was always there. Even bright barrio kids who could have made it at the university often lacked family resources.

This is not fiction, but the reality Alfonso lived. High school hadn't prepared him for college. That spring day in 1956 when he and his classmates walked across the stage at Milne Stadium and received their diplomas was a time of celebration. Entire families attended, cheering for their graduates. A chain of despair seemed to have been broken. Barrio kids graduating in the numbers they did in the fifties was something to cheer about. Were things changing? When Alfonso's name was called to receive his diploma, his family cried with pride and joy. Our handicapped boy had graduated.

"I had no great expectations," he would tell his wife years later as they sat on the loveseat in the porch one afternoon, reminiscing. She nodded. She knew how difficult those early years had been for him. "No great expectations," she repeated. He had worked his way up from the bottom, and she was immensely proud of him.

K, maybe my letters should be called "No Great Expectations."

A pretty good title for every poor kid who's ever toughed it out, believing there was something better just ahead. At some point every broken child should be able to throw away the crutches that symbolize everything that's ever held him or her back: diseases, fractured bones, paralyzed limbs, skin color, poverty, dysfunctional families, nightmarish demons forever crying doom, the constant daily grind that wears down body and soul . . .

I had no great expectations, but I can create them, even if there's no savings account, no rich uncle.

What sorrows lie in the hearts of children who struggle to overcome difficult circumstances? There are a few who shine and stand out in the public's eyes, but what of the thousands in the shadows?

The morning after graduation, he asked himself, what now? His close friends were going their own way. Some had jobs; others were out looking for work, dealing with car expenses, dating and maybe thinking about marriage. The gang was splitting apart, each answering destiny's call. Alfonso had no car, no job, no girl, and he was 4-F.

Boys primarily went to work in family trades: construction, drywall, roofing, learning to repair cars, sacking groceries, gas stations, restaurants. Girls worked at the phone company or the credit bureau, or as receptionists somewhere; if they were lucky, they got hired at the air force base. Mostly it was menial work for menial wages. The Hispanic labor force was good for the city, but there was not much of a future for the workers.

Life was nothing like what was portrayed in the black-and-white television shows of the time. There were no *I Love Lucy* or *Leave It to Beaver* or *Ozzie and Harriet* families in the barrio. Life was difficult. I still look back in anger. So did Alfonso.

Maybe at the time we didn't know how bad things were. We were young. Whoever had a car picked up the others. We pooled our money to buy beer. We visited the girls in South Barelas, and we cruised up and down Central on Saturday nights, enjoying the brightly lit neon lights of Burque, meeting girls. And then there were those summer nights at the Sunset drive-in theater: sweaty nights, strange passions.

We swam in the irrigation ditches, played football and baseball in the park across from the Country Club and basketball at Eliseo's, a game for every season. The gang kept Fonso with them, but even then I had the feeling he was harboring deep, dark thoughts. The stay in the hospital during the summer of '54 had changed him. The accident and the paralysis he had to overcome would have changed anyone. He put all that in the books he wrote. You don't need my letters, K, you have his novels, the barrio story, the hospital story, everything recorded in his books. Fictions? You decide.

What was he to do? The Korean War had ended, and a few Mexican American vets would follow their World War II brothers and use the GI Bill. Some started their own businesses and became important resources for the city. World War II had changed the country. It also changed Nuevo Mexicanos. A coming of age.

So many dates in New Mexico history. Start with Clovis tribes wandering down the Rio Grande Valley fifteen thousand years ago.

Early ancestors on our land. Then 1598. 1680. 1921. 1848. WWI. WWII. Korea. Nam. Iraq.

Life in the barrios from LA to San Anton. Pachucos had come to the attention of the American public during the June 1943 Los Angeles riots. American servicemen ran through the streets of LA beating up Mexican American zoot-suiters. It was the U.S. Navy at its worst, acting out the racial prejudices that white America held against the Mexicano community. Riots broke out in many cities. Never mind that young Mexican Americans from across the country had enlisted and were serving their country.

The pachucos had taken on the role of cultural warriors. They dared to be different by openly identifying as zoot-suiters; they would become an important symbol in the Mexicano struggle for cultural survival. Pachucos looked sharp and cool in their baggy pegged pants, thick-soled shoes, and keychains. A new boogie-woogie sound filled the dance halls of the time.

Fonso had pachuco friends, and he learned caló, an idiom that mixed pachuco slang and rhythms into Spanish, creating a speech which drew that generation together in brotherhood and sisterhood.

Yes, sisterhood. Don't forget that a few of the young women in Barelas dressed as pachucas. Chicana beauties, stylish, their hair teased up like Afros, hanging out Sunday afternoons at the park, drinking beer with their homeboys, smoking pot, acting tough. I remember them well. They weren't like their traditional mothers; they were fed up with being treated like second-class citizens because they were brown and maybe spoke English with an accent. Those pachucas led a brown revolution long before the white feminist movement. And why not? The Adelitas, grandmothers of some of those Chicanas, had fought in the Mexican Civil War, marching alongside their husbands into battle, fighting for land reform and food for their families.

Pachucas broke with tradition. They flaunted their differences even as those differences called attention to their lifestyle. It was a time of revolution.

But what to do after graduation? The armed services were out of the question. He wasn't military material. He stuck the 4-F card in his wallet, a badge of sorrow. Carried it all those years until it faded. What the hell was he to do?

A few of his friends had joined the National Guard. That summer they went to boot camp for three weeks—an initiation Alfonso missed, as he was to miss many others. His friends returned with money in their pockets and adventures to talk about. Young women were the hot topic of discussion; they bragged about their adventures.

Nick introduced Alfonso to a girl, the sister of the girl he was dating. In his '48 Ford he would pick up the sisters, then Fonso. The fifteen-year-old black-eyed beauty loved Fonso. Making out at the local drive-in theater must have been exciting for him. You only know if you've been there.

I don't remember the girl's name, but I feel good when I think of him with his sweetheart in the back seat, kissing and hugging, then smoothing their hair and clothes when the movie ended and it was time to head home.

"Wake Up Little Susie" said it all—waking up after a couple of hours of hormonal excitement for my Alfonso. Don't laugh! Say instead, why not? Didn't he deserve as much?

Thank God for drive-in theaters. A generation was conceived in cars with the cool summer air drifting in through open windows, speakers piping in music, popcorn spilling, soft drinks being slurped between kisses. Who paid attention to the movie when love was in the air? Love and lust, they came together.

When the movie ended, the cars revved up, mufflers blasting, tires squealing and churning up dirt and gravel as they all headed for the exit. Sheer joy! Television ruined the drive-ins.

I praise the girl who kissed Fonso in the back seat. Whoever she was. I heard parts of the story one morning over coffee at a Village Inn with some of Fonso's friends. Nick laughed when he said it was really his date who had a crush on Alfonso.

Was Fonso to be a star-crossed lover forever?

"It didn't matter to me," Fonso said, smiling. The right or wrong girl, she was fine. We laughed. I looked at Alfonso. Not all those high school years had been a drag. Imagine him in the back seat with his sweetheart. She didn't last long, but bless her anyway. He came out of his shell, if only during those drive-in nights. *Blackboard Jungle, East of Eden, Giant, Rebel without a Cause.* Guys wanted to be as cool as James Dean in his red windbreaker. Where have you gone, Jimmy Dean? Our hearts have a place for you.

He was part of the fifties rock-and-roll and rhythm-and-blues generation. Fonso knew the lyrics to a lot of the songs: "Why Do Fools Fall in Love" by Frankie Lymon and the Teenagers; Bill Haley's "Rock around the Clock"; "I met my thrill," from Fats Domino's "Blueberry Hill." Those songs were the poetry of his coming of age, and they complemented the poetry of his oral tradition, the stories, feelings aroused from llano wind and river song. It was all building up inside.

It was a great time to be alive! Time for my Alfonso to feel joy! He was trying, but he was handicapped, and that truth wouldn't leave him.

My God, I wish I knew everything that was churning in his heart.

What if he had been given a chance? A real chance. Ah, no need to speculate on that. Destiny is what destiny is. You can't change fate that's written in the blood.

A poetic instinct was growing in his soul, a flourishing essence that had been evolving and expanding since Agapita pulled him from his mother's womb.

Most formative was the crucial out-of-body experience he went through as he lay paralyzed in the water after that fateful dive, face down, unable to move, waiting to drown. His soul rose up in a column of light, and it looked down at Alfonso floating immobile in the water. How beautiful that must have been, Fonso's soul rising into the sky and looking down on the body floating in the water. If his soul had kept rising, Fonso would have died, for flesh cannot live without soul.

He couldn't hold his breath much longer. He was going to drown. A tranquil peacefulness came over him, an acceptance. The body lying in the water would die, and its soul would move on to universal soul. All was light. From starlight, mud of earth, and the blood of his parents he had come; to light he would return. He couldn't hold his breath any longer. It was time to drown his lungs.

Eliseo pulled him out of the water just in time.

Alfonso was full of memories, sorrowful for one so young. He talked about his stay at Carrie Tingley Hospital, the two months he spent there encased in a body cast, seeing the world as a turtle views the world. He had to learn to walk again, feed himself, dress, before he could finally return home. He was only sixteen. Memories make for introspection, and what he had gone through was molding him into the person he would become.

When he was older, the images of that difficult time haunted him. A sad memory, but you know, that book's been written.

Good or bad, experience makes us all.

Life was whittling a poet out of him, this boy from llano earth, son of owls and the river, an old soul full of the mysteries of the church, his mother's prayers. Like Whitman going forth, Alfonso was becoming everything he saw, felt, tasted, experienced. Hadn't Agapita told him so?

Dear K,

It was the summer of 1956 when Elvira, his oldest sister, or it could have been his sister Susie, who inquired into the state's rehabilitation program. She brought the information home and encouraged Fonso to apply. He read through the material, thought it was worth a try, and went to an interview. After a battery of aptitude tests, he was told by the case manager that he would make a good bookkeeper. If he enrolled in business school, the state would pay for his tuition and books for a year. He had taken bookkeeping in high school and was good at crunching numbers, so why not take them up on the offer?

But a bookkeeper? For crying out loud! Was there no inkling in the test results that our boy was destined to write novels? The tests and the case manager couldn't decipher the yearnings in Alfonso's heart. A test is static for time and place—it cannot know the position of the child's heart or the speed of the child's imagination. Everyone is a moving particle, never at the same place at the same time.

Fonso was stoic. Algo es algo, dijo el diablo. Something is something, said the devil. Why not try it? The state welfare program would rehabilitate him, make him a useful citizen. In a couple of years, he could be a bookkeeper working in the back office of some small business in town. He would be able to go home each afternoon feeling proud to be a taxpaying citizen.

God bless the state that helps the poor and crippled. Social equality at work, social justice. Alfonso would come to understand how important it was for the government to level the playing field for those in need. And the taxes he paid for the rest of his life would repay the state's investment a million times over.

But what of the books he was to write? Was it because of his accident that he went on to become a writer? No doubt the trauma affected every cell in his body; it had shattered his soul. To understand the meaning of that fateful experience, he began to read books that spoke to his longings. And later, he would record his own answers in his writings.

But in 1956 he was headed to Browning Commercial School. His mother packed him a lunch—a tuna fish sandwich spiced with a bit of green chile and a small bag of potato chips. That summer morning, Fonso walked the ten blocks downtown to school. He would walk that route for two years, carrying his books and lunch. He could buy a soft drink at school and sit with other students at lunchtime. He drew close to the Korean War veterans. The men, older than he by a few years, had stories to tell, and Fonso listened. Korea had been hell.

There's a little bit of positive in everything. Those walks from home to school and back made him strong, and years later, when he walked the streets of New York City, San Francisco, Paris, Madrid, and other foreign capitals, he would remember those years of walking to business school. He got to know intimately every detail on Sixth Street—the houses, the neighbors, the dogs, the Catholic girls at St. Vincent's Academy hurrying to class, the sisters shooing them so they wouldn't be late. Never mind the boy standing, staring. Don't be late.

The walk to school became a mantra. This was his destiny unfolding, as every person's destiny reveals itself in the simplest details.

So a rope had been thrown to one floundering in the river of life. He had a purpose: classes in accounting and homework at night. That first morning at school, he hurried upstairs to typing class. He sat at a desk in the back row and stared at the typewriter in front of him.

K, I assume you've seen a typewriter. Your grandchildren, however, have probably never seen one. Their computers have soft-touch keyboards and automated printers. They don't know what it was like to have to carefully insert each sheet of paper by hand before you could type on it, and to have to use that manual lever to move the carriage to the beginning of the next line.

At the front of the room, the young typing instructor gave a command. Challenged to go beyond sixty words per minute, every student in the room began to type, filling the room with the clatter of keys striking, the teeny bell ringing with each carriage return, the sound of pieces of paper being torn from the typewriter carriages and tossed away. All Alfonso could do was stare at the typewriter in front of him. His left hand sat useless on the keyboard, the fingers not agile enough to strike the keys.

He felt awkward. The others were racing ahead, each one with two hands on the keyboard, typing the day's lesson, a race to get better and better. They knew that future employers would ask, "How many words a minute can you type?"

The young instructor made the rounds of the classroom, smiling, approving. All was going well until she reached Alfonso.

"What's the matter?"

"I can't," he muttered.

"You can't strike the keys?"

"No."

"Did you try?"

"Yes."

The room grew silent; the students turned to look at Fonso. Ashamed. I guess that's how he felt. You know, not normal.

The teacher took his hand and placed it on the keyboard.

"My fingers can't move."

She stared at him for a while, not knowing what to do with a one-handed student in her typing class.

"Go see your advisor," she said. Why had they put him in typing class?

Fonso sought out his accounting teacher, T. J. Gabaldon. Earlier in the morning, T. J. had gone over Fonso's schedule and shown him the classrooms. A tall, handsome man, he was to become a savior of sorts.

"Let's see what we can do," he said. "Sit here at my typewriter. Show me what you can do."

Fonso put both hands on the keyboard. His left hand hung limp.

"You can't press the keys with that hand, but you can with your right hand. When God gives you a lemon, make lemonade," T. J. smiled. "Let's make lemonade."

"How?"

"Try placing the fingers of your right hand on F, G, H, and J. Those will be your home keys. Now, try reaching up and down the keys. Good. Now stretch right. Good. Now left with your little finger. That's a little harder, but you'll get it. It will take time, but you can do it."

Yes, he could—he would learn to type with one hand. The following morning he sat in typing class, and like a wounded turtle he slowly typed out his first typewritten poem. *Now is the time for all good men to come to the aid of their country.*

Sixty words a minute? That would never happen, but he could type.

Here's my point. All those novels he was to write would be typed with one hand. Thousands and thousands of pages. He started his first novels on a Smith-Corona portable, using carbon paper to make copies. Try a year of writing on one of those old typewriters, and you'll get my message. Later he bought an IBM Selectric. That was like heaven. During his fellowship with the Kellogg Foundation, he was given a Kaypro II, one of the first portable computers around. Years later he bought the word processor he still works on today. A history of pressing stories out of machines that were never intended for one-handed typists.

He breezed through his classes, from beginning bookkeeping to cost accounting. T. J. was a great teacher, an imposing figure standing at the blackboard lecturing. In his right hand he held the chalk, while in the other he held the book and a white handkerchief. Why always the handkerchief? Fonso looked closely: T. J.'s left hand was missing the three middle fingers. He covered his handicap so well that most of his students never knew.

Beside teaching, T. J. kept records for a few businesses and bars

---

along Central Avenue. He hired Fonso as his assistant. Fonso's job was to pick up the weekly receipts, run the totals, and enter everything in T. J.'s business ledgers. What an education was in store! Imagine Alfonso walking into the local watering holes to pick up the week's tabs. He could sit at the bar and have a beer while the receipts were delivered from the back room. Those afternoons in the dark, cool bars, he overheard many a conversation by the movers and doers of the city, big-shot politicians and attorneys, and he got many a smile from some of the prettiest prostitutes in Alburquerque.

The city was wide open in the fifties—certainly not a Chicago, but open for business on the Rio Grande. Come one, come all, City Hall proclaimed. We'll look the other way as long as you pay your taxes. That was the Alburquerque Fonso knew, a rough-and-ready city, growing, feeling its oats. Fonso knew downtown from his years in the barrio. He and his friends often walked from the barrio up lively First Street to the YMCA. They went to movies at the State, Sunshine, KiMo, and Chief theaters. Now he was sitting in bars where politicos made deals, drank the best scotch, and swore they could buy anyone in City Hall.

Everything comes to an end. Two years later, Alfonso walked into school early one morning, looked around, and felt a strange emotion. Sadness filled him. Slowly, he walked through the classrooms, touching the business machines he knew so well. He said good morning to the secretary in the office. Always so kind, she looked tired that day. Everything in the building looked old and worn out. A whisper told him this was no longer for him. There's something out there waiting for you, a voice said. He walked out and didn't return.

Who had whispered? A guardian angel? Or his inner spirit, bidding him to move on?

T. J. had recently retired from teaching to become the business manager at the Girls Welfare Home on Edith Street. Fonso asked him for a job, and T. J. hired him. It was a perfect fit. And because of it, Fonso was finally able to enroll at the university in 1958. T. J. let him plan his classes around his working hours, and he made enough to pay tuition and books. No loans or grants for my poor boy, just work and school. The family had bought a '58 Chevy, so he had transportation. In that car he and Eliseo drove to México City a year later. There they met up with Arthur and Jimmy. They were young men in search of adventure. México City was enormous, fascinating, an art capital, with murals by the great Mexican artists in Bellas Artes, the Zona Rosa loaded with beautiful women. Fonso was becoming a wanderer in search of his destiny. Later, he and Patricia would take many trips to México, learning to love the country and its people.

He had a car, a job, and classes that were opening up new worlds. In the material world things were looking up, but inside Fonso was stepping into an abyss. He was questioning fundamental religious truths. Could he find the inner convictions he needed to survive? How much of the past can one leave behind and still be part of historical continuity?

During those first difficult university years, Fonso carried the weight of the world in his heart. What was the root of his malaise, the moral incertitude he felt?

"I learned to think for myself," he said.

That's it! He learned to think for himself.

He was reading and wrestling with ideas that didn't fit his old Catholic worldview. The old teachings weren't compatible with what he was learning. He had to decide: Do I stay in that safe, ordered world that I grew up in, or do I go my own way? What is right or wrong, sin, heaven, hell, the role of the church in my life?

Can I strike out on my own?

He did, and that brings us to the sorrow he felt. You see, he would leave the teachings of the church, but what of his mother? Would he no longer believe as his mother believed? He had to wrestle with that.

He walked alone on a perilous path with no end in sight, no sense of what he would discover. The old way had been secure; faith was prescribed: one simply followed the rules. Now he had to discover a new faith. But in what? The existential man.

During those early university years, he lived in that dark night of the soul that philosophers describe. Questioning God's plan, if there was a plan. Sometimes the depression got so bad he thought of ending it all. His family didn't know the destruction of faith he was wrestling with. He carried his feelings inside, attended classes, kept his part-time job, saw his barrio friends on weekends, read late into the night searching for answers, all the while wondering if he could go on.

Do you see where I'm heading with this, K? A picture of an artist as a young man. One portrait shows Fonso carrying on with daily activities: family, work, and school. This is the picture family and friends saw. They did not know his internal struggle.

The books he was reading were opening up new horizons, and the new ideas conflicted with old dogmas. It was a turbulent time for Fonso. He was on a new and tortuous path.

K, I'm very tired today, but here goes.

Fonso didn't read much literature during his years in business school. It might have seemed at the time that he had taken a wrong turn. Where was the force of destiny to turn him on the right road? Or was that time a hiatus, a time of rest for the wounded Alfonso? Accounting classes came easy for him, and that could be a trap. So many young people take the easy road, get a job, make a little money, and never reach their full potential.

He enjoyed hanging out with the Korean War veterans. One wounded warrior took Fonso under his wing. Easygoing Sylvestre had been shot during the Chinese offensive. He took classes mostly to get the monthly check, and when it arrived, he hit the bars in the South Valley and along Central. Some weekends he picked up Fonso, and so Fonso's education on the dark belly of the city continued. Sy was happy-go-lucky, always laughing, always sipping from a half-pint of mint gin. His friendly, open personality and the fact that his family had roots in the South Valley meant he knew everyone in the bars. There was never any trouble.

"Nothing is lost," Fonso liked to say. What he was learning about Burque's nightlife would be used in novels not yet written. Drugs, fast women, and bar fights. Fonso watched, soaking it all in.

I find it interesting that during that time Fonso was helped by older men. Sy and T. J. when he was in business school. His professors at the university also became father figures, guiding him through the world of literature. Dr. George Arms had been his teacher when he was a grad student, and later became his colleague when Fonso went to teach at the university. When Dr. Arms retired, he invited Alfonso to meet him for monthly lunches at the Faculty Club. What an honor! Congeniality with the most prominent professor who ever walked the halls of academe.

In 1963 he got his degree. He taught junior high at a South Valley school. He was recruited by Joe Griego, a World War II vet; the two became friends. With other teachers at the school, they met Friday afternoons for beers. Some weekends they went fishing in the northern Pecos River. In winter the South Valley irrigation ditches were stocked with trout, so together with Felipe and Ed they fished in the morning and drank beer in the afternoon. The group became lasting friends. When he taught at Valley High, the teachers he admired and went to for advice also were older men.

These men were to be an important part of Fonso's education.

Why did he choose them? Was he missing a father at home? Martin had aged, and Fonso found it difficult to talk to him. There was mutual respect and love, but little communication of the kind Alfonso needed. His brother Laute, who had been of great help during the barrio years, was busy raising his own growing family. The barrio days when Laute had played football with the gang were over, and Martinito and Salomon had moved to California. Fonso fell in with men who provided the kind of friendship and experiences he could never have with his father.

How many young men have gone through this? A father at home who doesn't, or can't, communicate with his son. Or absent fathers. Boys becoming young men with only their mother or grandparents to guide them. If they're lucky. Single parents, a new phenomenon.

Don't get me wrong; Alfonso understood the age difference between him and his father. Martin was nearly fifty when Alfonso was born—a ripe age for the time. He had worked hard on the ranches and provided for his family. He had built their home from scratch, but he had no formal education. What he was able to do, he learned by experience. He told fabulous stories and taught Fonso how to work with tools around the house, but he didn't know the world Alfonso was experiencing.

In a nutshell, there was none of the deep communication Fonso craved. He understood. It was only later in life that he wished he had known his father better. What had Martin done during those years in the service? What demons drove him to the occasional drinking binges? These and many other questions he wished his father had answered.

Dear K,

Today I feel a silence in the air. It's Martin Luther King Day. We grieve the fallen leader, we celebrate the man for all he did. 1964 was a pivotal year for minority cultures in this country, and I don't mean the Beatles invasion. The Mexican American community had a more pressing social agenda than following the Beatles on the *Ed Sullivan Show*.

César Chávez and Dolores Huerta founded the UFW, and their fight for campesino rights helped spearhead the Chicano movement. Students, teachers, and working people organized and marched, demanding the equal rights they had been denied for so long.

In 1972 Fonso would be in the thick of the movement, book in hand, attending Flor y Canto conferences, meeting the artists who painted the murals at the San Diego–Coronado Bridge, enjoying long talks with the activists. The struggle for social equality and the blooming of Chicano and Chicana art came together. Teatro Campesino performed one-act plays on flatbed trucks for campesinos in the fields. In the early seventies, Ishmael Reed created the Before Columbus Foundation, and Fonso was there, helping to spearhead a multicultural literature that demanded its rightful place in American literature. It was a glorious time to be alive.

We did create a revolution, he said, as Agapita had predicted.

Alfonso's father had entered the service in 1917, learned to march and shoot a .75 rifle. He returned to work for Anglo ranchers on the llano. He knew enough English to be the mayordomo of a big ranch, but like most Nuevo Mexicanos of that era, he didn't possess enough language skills to completely enter the new Anglo economy. When suddenly all credit transactions and laws that regulated commerce were written and spoken in English, many Nuevo Mexicanos were left out. A few learned to work with the Anglo entrepreneurs and take part in the new political entities, but all over the state, many lost the land grants that had been awarded first by Spain, then later by the Mexican government.

History was being written in a new language. Better get to school, Juanito.

A new way of doing business swept over the state. At the end of the day, many Nuevo Mexicanos were still shut out from the bank's credit, and their kids were disciplined in school for speaking Spanish. It grew more and more difficult to hold on to a four-hundred-year-old culture in the face of the overwhelming new Anglo government. Education was the key, and that meant assimilation, a force that began to change so much of traditional Nuevo Mexicano cultures.

Hispanic families are close-knit support systems, but life in the city took its toll on Alfonso's father. Once a proud man who had worked on the llano, in the city he felt useless. By default, the mother became the head of the family. She watched over Alfonso, fully aware of her son's struggle. He never complained, but she felt his pain. What of his future?

She was a strongly religious woman, and still she wondered about the role of destiny in life—and for her, destiny meant God. It was God who ruled over every life.

Had God failed her? Why had He punished her son? Or was she being punished? The God of her ancestors was present in every moment; His fingers stirred the fate of every life. She believed in the church, communion with the saints, and life everlasting. Her faith was as strong as her love for her family. She attended mass, kept the holy sacraments, prayed the rosary nightly, implored the saints to take care of her family.

But sorrow had entered her heart—the painful sorrow that mothers know intimately. In the end, she kept her faith. God would provide.

She massaged Alfonso every night, trying to revive the strength in his weak limbs, making sure he stayed warm that first winter after the train accident. I know Alfonso felt her pain. Did her sorrow somehow pass into him and shape the man he would become? Is it the mother who molds the son and not the father? In Alfonso's case, how could it be otherwise? It would take a long novel to fully acknowledge his mother's care. So much of her love was a silence she carried within. A book of sorrows.

The History of My Heart was the book Alfonso was writing. A lost manuscript. Instead you have these letters, my scant recollections of his life. He planned to write a travel journal, recording the trips he and Patricia had taken over the years.

Early in their marriage they visited Yellowstone, later Guaymas, then San Francisco, where he was awarded the Premio Quinto Sol for *Bless Me, Ultima*. In later years New York, Paris, Stonehenge, Frankfurt, Athens, Istanbul, Spain, Portugal, Egypt, China, the Amazon, Macchu Pichu, Africa . . .

Will I ever get to the travel book? Her photo albums are scattered all over the house. Kids have their own lives, they don't seem interested.

Love engenders love. He had love at home, but would he be a loving man? Could he, one day, climb out of his shell? He did when he finally found Patricia, a beautiful and loving woman—but I keep getting ahead of the story.

The sixties—ah, the sixties.

At the university we ran around with a few young women. Fonso dated a girl from Española, later a young woman he met in art class, a very bohemian New Yorker. She smoked pot and sipped wine during class breaks. He later dated Theresa for a few months, but in the end love didn't bloom from those relationships. Like the rest of us, he was dating, exploring his sexuality, but what did we know? What if you got a girl pregnant or caught syphilis?

The high school coaches had lectured us about syphilis and gonorrhea, the dreadful diseases of that era. They came with sex. A guy had to be careful. Sex became taboo. We weren't supposed to enjoy sex, we had to be careful. I'm sure girls felt the same. If something happened, we were told to get to a doctor and get checked. Catholic guilt and the fear of catching a disease put a clamp on Fonso. I wonder how many others lived with such concerns.

You don't hear much about venereal diseases today. Today it's AIDS. The epidemic has hurt so many. In parts of Africa it's still a scourge.

Part of growing up was wasting our youth. I think the guys who married right out of high school were better off, settling down. But then, they missed out on the crazy Saturday nights we lived through. Anyway, we mostly stayed close to the Casa Luna ladies. They were safe, but even those relationships didn't last. People faded away. *In the end—*

When you're young, breaking up with the one you love can be tragic. You think you've found true love, and then the person leaves. The affair ends, sometimes for a reason, sometimes just a silent good-bye. Losing the person you loved, or think you loved, is painful. Sometimes a love story has a beginning and a middle, but no end. Or a tragic end: the bottom drops out. That's the way it was. Still is.

The many loves of Alfonso. Perhaps that's what I have to write. Isn't that true of everyone? We look for enduring love. If we find it, we don't want it to end. To part from the person we love can be devastating. Does it bring sorrow? When love dies, the soul feels a little death.

Alfonso was learning to live with his handicap. Still, he didn't share the story of his injury with the young women he met. Would things have been different if he had been more open?

He wasn't so different. Don't we all hide parts of who we really are? Who can you fully confide in? Can you let your hair down and reveal who you really are? Deep inside. We all have the need to come out of our protective shells and tell our most hidden secrets to the one we love and trust. We search for that special person. Love is exposing our soul to someone who understands our joy, our pain, our sorrow.

There were no counseling sessions for Alfonso. He was on his own. He had family and friends, but otherwise he was on his own. Besides, does telling your story to a counselor really work? Don't we always hide something, even from the shrink? Did you confess all your sins to the priest or keep one back? Have you been hiding a dark secret? The secret you can't tell, the shadow within.

Many years later, Alfonso and his wife visited Pastura, the village on the llano, Alfonso's Eden. A place where things were good until the train accident. On a dare, he had reached for the forbidden apple.

I'm hiding something from you—I think you sense that.

The llano was his Eden, its plants and creatures his first companions, the wind his brother, the sky an embracing mother. He looked at clouds and learned to tell the weather, listened intently to the calls of coyotes and owls, their cries constantly announcing a change in life's struggle. Herds of horses ran roughshod, breaking open the wild earth, the vaquero's curses a joy to his ears.

In Santa Rosa de Lima's grocery store, his mother bought enough groceries to last a month: five-gallon tins of lard, fifty-pound sacks of flour, pinto beans, potatoes. His father often butchered sheep, fresh meat. Good, healthy home-cooked meals served up with plenty of mother's love, nourishing.

Now the beauty of the village was no more. Eden had fallen into disrepair. The houses once home to the old families were crumbling. Weeds covered the dirt streets. Even the wind sweeping across the village cried a sad song. Gone . . . a long, lonely gone.

Bereft of people, the village was dying. Two or three young families lived in their grandparents' homes. They drove daily to Santa Rosa de Lima to work in the tourist industry, cleaning motels or making sandwiches at fast food restaurants. Some worked at the prison or the new hospital, a few in the schools or City Hall. The gas stations had changed to self-service, so even those jobs were gone. A lot of things were gone, replaced. Such is the nature of things: they disappear. In the process, people suffer.

And the earth suffers. Fracking for natural gas was next, new scars on the land to keep the economy going, the water table threatened. Giant wind turbines now dotted the mesa around Pastura del Santo Niño.

The owls began to disappear.

K, the history lost.

Some cattle ranches survived, but because of growing foreign competition, the once-thriving sheep ranches were smaller and fewer. Deserted villages dotted the llano, their names a litany of poetic Spanish. A few families remained, clinging to the land in spite of droughts, clinging to hope, but many moved on. Alfonso's family moved, seeking work in the city. The Nuevo Mexicanos were the new Okies in their own land.

Alfonso and his wife stopped in front of the village church, Our Lady of Sorrows. It, too, was crumbling, the door closed. The cemetery next to the church was overgrown with weeds. Pausing, Alfonso pointed at a tombstone.

"My brother Salomon. U.S. Navy. He was named after my mother's first husband, Salomon Bonney. From that marriage came Salomon and Elvira. I have a photograph of Rafaelita carrying two-year-old Elvira. She wears a long black dress, black hose and shoes. It's the style of the time, but it could be her mourning dress. Her husband died a couple of years after their marriage. Dates and years are lost. Her black hair is cut short."

Fonso's wife put her arm around him. "In one generation, so much family history lost."

"Yes. My mother also had twins who died shortly after they were born. We don't know where they're buried."

"How sad," his wife whispered.

That's the way it was. Unmarked graves across the land, the harsh land they loved. Bittersweet was the nurturing it provided. He told his niece Belinda and Edwina that he wanted to buy a tombstone for the twins, Teresa Candelaria and Juana Clorinda. He wanted it placed it in the cemetery as a remembrance. But could he? He was getting along in years, bothered by bone problems, the childhood injury dragging him down. Besides, who visited the deserted place anymore?

They paused in front of faded crosses. Ortega, Bonney, Campos, Tapia, Anaya, Romero . . . a history of the people if one only had time to unravel it.

Why? Let the dead rest.

They paused and listened to the voices of the dead.

The faint voice of a woman rose in the breeze that moaned over the cemetery: "I told my kids I wanted to be buried here, with the rest of my family. The kids moved to Alburquerque, but I don't want to be buried there. No one to talk to. I know everyone here. I made my First Communion in this church, I was married here, all my friends are buried here. The kids moved away to work, but I never forgot my querencia. This is my earth, it gave us strength, it made us who we are. 'Bury me here,' I told my kids. 'If you don't, a curse on you.'"

"She got her wish," Alfonso's wife whispered, smiling.

"Yes."

A man called. Tapia, the mayordomo who lived nearby, ambled over and greeted them. He opened the church so they could look inside. Doves cried in the belfry, and bat guano spotted the floor.

"We don't have mass anymore," he told them. "The priest stopped coming. Too dangerous. The walls are crumbling. See the exposed adobes? Rain washes them down. Earth to earth. We need to plaster the walls, but nobody comes to help. In the old days, every Día de San Juan the people came to plaster the walls. The men would make the mud right here. They carried wheelbarrows full of mud to the women. The women did the plastering, you know. Everyone worked, laughing and making jokes, and when the work was done, we had a big fiesta. The women brought food; the men butchered a borrega and roasted the meat. There was lots to drink. We had a good time. The church looked new. Like it got a new face. The mud smelled sweet, like wet earth after a rain. Now, nobody comes."

A strong man, Tapia, but when he spoke, they could tell he was remembering those long-ago days when the church was plastered. He could hear the voices of the men calling and laughing, and the women answering, kids and dogs running, vaqueros riding in from the llano to look the young women over. If they found a querida, they would work alongside the girl; if they didn't, they would just eat, drink, and move on to Isidro's Cantina.

He was remembering.

No más la memoria queda, the voices moaned. Only memories are left.

Alfonso remembered mass in the church, the scent of lighted candles and incense, people flocking to the mystery of the mass, filling the small church with their faith.

Aroma of the faithful, the human scent of bodies that worked hard all week and found one day of respite on Sunday. Prayers mixed with candle smoke that rose to the ceiling.

"Up there is heaven," the priest said.

"I don't know," Agapita said, mulling over the priest's words, spitting out a bit of weed caught between her teeth. "I think heaven is here. This earth is all we know. Some make it their hell. Who am I to judge. And work," she added. "You were put on earth to work."

The men worked on the llano or hired out as highway crews, patching and resurfacing Highway 66, or they went into town to work at gas stations or construction jobs. When there was no work in the vicinity, men threw heavy tarps over their trucks and journeyed into the cotton fields of West Texas, returning with a little money in their pockets.

Alfonso remembered the three sons of Benito Campos, his cousins, returning from work in the fields, their pockets jingling with quarters, nickels, dimes, and crumpled dollar bills. His eyes grew wide. Imagine, boys with money in their pockets. They had seen the world beyond the village, towns like Clovis, Portales, Muleshoe, and they knew the highways that connected those towns. They knew Anglo names, names Alfonso had never heard. They said they went to work in Tejas instead of Texas.

They spoke like grown men. The toil of work lined their faces; muscles and sinews knotted their arms, their hands as tough and weathered as the vaqueros of the llano. They didn't attend school. They couldn't read or write.

"I envied my cousins," Alfonso told his wife. "Their pockets were full of coins. They had gone beyond the llano. That year my mother taught me the catechism in Spanish so I could make my First Communion. I could read."

The small village church was full of memories. Everything about the place of his birth held memories. Remnants of the small garden they had kept behind their home were hardly visible, once-tilled rows now overgrown with weeds and plastered down by years of summer rains. Green once thrived here.

"I carried water from the windmill," Alfonso said. "All summer long I carried buckets of water to the plants. The garden was green. We ate the best vegetables. The peach tree branches drooped with ripe peaches. Then . . ."

Perhaps it was best not to return to the home of his birth, nor to look at the dead garden reclaimed by time.

Alfonso's father had asked a rancher who ran cattle near Agapita's hut to watch over the old woman. One day the man arrived in Santa Rosa de Lima saying he hadn't seen her for a few days. He was afraid to look into the curandera's home, so Alfonso and his father drove to her adobe home on the llano.

"We found her lying on her bed," Alfonso said. "Instead of death, the room held the scent of vanilla. A sweet perfume, like I later smelled on the bark of Ponderosa pines. Her face so peaceful, she looked angelic. In my mind I could see her greeting death. She made coffee, lit a cigaro, and she and La Muerte sat visiting, enjoying the coffee and the breeze that came through the open door."

What did they talk about? "Is there coffee in heaven?" Agapita might have asked La Muerte.

"Quizás que no," La Muerte answered. "But for you I will ask el Señor to make an exception."

The empty coffee cups sat like silent witnesses on the table. Maybe she and La Muerte had a conversation about Agapita's life, what she had done, what she had left undone. In the end we all leave something undone, don't we? There is never enough time.

The sorrow of departing.

¿A dónde van los muertos, a dónde, dónde van?

Alfonso and his wife climbed up the hill to where Agapita's remains rested. "I hope she told La Muerte how she helped me, how she set my bones straight, as well as she could. Her hands worked magic. I would be worse off if she hadn't taught my mother how to massage my hand and foot. Yes, worse off . . ."

So many memories.

"I asked her once, 'What is the meaning of life?' 'Life is like a river,' she said seriously. My innocent eyes grew wide and I repeated, 'Wow, life is like a river?' She started laughing so loud, it set a nearby covey of doves to flight. Her eyes watered from laughing. Once more she had pulled my leg. When she stopped laughing, she said, 'I don't know the meaning. No one does. Live one day at a time and enjoy. Experience life. Be thankful. The end will come of its own accord, neither predestined nor thought out. It just comes. What you do is all there is. Be kind, Alfonso.' I hope I have obeyed her command."

"You are kind," his wife said, comforting him.

They climbed the hill to the cairn. Beneath the pile of rocks rested Agapita's remains.

"We weren't alone the day we buried her," Alfonso said. "Ranchers showed up and dug the grave. Women from the village came singing alabados, hymns for the departed. I was thankful for the procession of women in mourning who made their way up the hill. They hadn't forgotten the good that Agapita did for the people of the llano. This hill was her favorite place. Many a time when I came to bring her a rabbit, I found her here, looking out at the world. She heard songs in the wind, Comanche songs from long ago, Mexican corridos, vaqueros singing while they herded cattle, the songs of lonely sheepherders on the llano. Sad lyrics, ballads full of tragedy. She had lived through it all, and now it was done. She would lie and listen to the wind sweeping across the llano. At night the songs of coyotes and owls would serenade her."

A rancher and his son came with picks and shovels and tore down her hut so the adobes, like her body, would melt back into the earth.

"I suppose," Alfonso said to his wife with a sigh, "that after I am gone, no one will remember her. No one will come to sit here and listen to the wind. A rancher looking for stray cattle might pause and wonder at this pile of rocks, Who lies beneath? Whose earth is this? All will be forgotten—"

Is being forgotten one of the sorrows of life? I think so, because the minute you become aware that everything you ever did will be forgotten, you feel a sigh deep in the heart.

It is the soul telling you someone has been lost. Never to be reclaimed.

K, I sigh as I write this letter. Remembering.

K, a critic came down like a wolf on the fold—

¡Pendejo! What did he know? He didn't understand Alfonso's novel. I guess every writer feels angry when his work is criticized. The novel was laid bare, examined, peeled apart, a flaying of flesh from soul. A crude autopsy. What good does it do to tear apart a story that contains a universe, then lay it on a plate like the head of John the Baptist? Leave soul and body intact!

Forgive me, I'm wrong, of course. Critics do play an important role in the study of literature. A critic can be a guide, leading the reader into all the nuances of the story, or so my friends Bruce-Novoa and Cantú have said. Critics point out important information in the nooks and crannies of stories, tidbits of meaning the reader might have missed. A good critic can set the context, reveal some of the history surrounding a work, point to allusions, symbols, relationships, and reveal the life of the writer if that helps shed light on the story at hand.

A good critic is a shaman, shining light on the soul of the story and thus creating a whole from pieces.

Light, it's all about light. If a story is illuminated, it can grow, as plants grow in sunlight. A critique should be an organic thesis drawn from the natural world. A good story can be read and studied many times, and it will grow and grow, like a well-nourished tree offers its fruit year after year.

The public's reception of Fonso's novel was enthusiastic. He was invited all over the country to lecture and read from his work, especially California, which at that time was alive with the early Chicano movement. Protests for equality, students shutting down universities. ¡Sí se puede!

Then a Marxist professor criticized the novel. He saw no political value in the cultural traditions Alfonso described. The worst thing he said was that Ultima was Alfonso's imaginary friend. What gall, reducing the history, cultural traditions, and spiritual values of most

Mexicanos to fantasy. "Materialism over soul" was his slogan.

Ultima an imaginary friend? Ridiculous! A few listened to this professor from a California university. He preached that all literature should describe dialectical materialism, Hegel's call for the working class to destroy capitalism and evolve into a classless society. Thesis, antithesis, synthesis. True equality. Anaya's novel doesn't attack capitalism, the professor complained.

The class grew silent until a student timidly raised her hand and said, "My grandmother was a curandera. The story reminds me of her. Why can't a story be about a curandera? I know you told us how capitalism keeps us down, but sometimes a story is just a story."

"Or a cigar is just a cigar," a pícaro in the back of the room chortled.

"Don't bring Freud into this," the professor fumed. "If you get lost in your ego, you lose sight of your oppressors!"

Before he could cut the discussion short, another student spoke up. "My father was cured by a curandera. A horse kicked him and hurt his leg really bad. We thought it was broken. We lived on a rancho. A curandera set his leg. She took warm cow shit, smeared it on his leg, and wrapped a cloth around it, really tight. Like a homemade splint. It worked. The bone healed. He can walk."

Another student raised her hand. "Our village had a curandera, Doña Rosa. She delivered babies, including me. We didn't have a doctor, so she helped the women. My mom would have died without her."

The class nodded. Dialectical materialism was losing ground. It wasn't the only theory by which to review literature.

Our culture is a colorful colcha, as Sabine Ulibarrí used to say. It has all the colors of the rainbow. Alfonso's novel was a colcha, a quilt describing a way of life in Hispanic New Mexico in the 1940s. And the most beautiful square on the larger-than-life quilt was the figure of the curandera, Ultima. She cared for the well-being of Antonio's family. Around her, each square on the quilt illustrated some aspect of Nuevo Mexicano life and history. Plus, as many said, it was damn good reading.

Our curanderas were the first spiritual feminists, Fonso wrote. They took on nontraditional roles. Some didn't marry; they spent their time learning traditional ways of healing. They knew herbs, ointments, prayers. They lived outside the box. They cured soul.

The professor was partly right, after all. A revolution was needed to stop the exploitation of Mexican American workers. That's why the Chicano movement was born. Strong, committed Mexican Americans fought for their rights. In Los Angeles, high school students walked out of their classrooms, demanding courses relevant to their culture and history. Across the country, university students demanded Chicano and Chicana studies, and after a prolonged struggle, those programs were finally instituted.

And it came to pass that a man rose up and shouted, "¡Ya basta! Enough!" The workers followed him, marching out of the fields, calling, "¡Sí se puede!" The Chicano movement was born.

Fonso's novel was read by students who were helping feed farmworkers on strike, and by those demonstrating for equal access to education. Affirmative action was born from those protests; the society took on a hue of equality. If things come a little easier for minorities of color today, remember that it took a revolution to achieve so many rights that now are taken for granted.

Hand in hand with the political struggle came a flourishing of the arts. Stories, poems, songs, art, and theater described Mexican American culture. Embedded in the stories and poems by Chicanos and Chicanas was a call to action.

¡Huelga! The cry rang out and spread like ripples across the nation. Wherever a strike occurred, one found people from all walks of life marching. The sons and daughters of the *Grapes of Wrath* Okies and *Salt of the Earth* Mexican copper mine workers had not forgotten their history. Once more they took to the streets. Fathers and brothers, mothers and sisters, workers and students, all committed to the cause.

If you look at the photographs of the Chicano protest marches of that era, you might spot a curandera here or there, marching alongside the workers, carrying huelga signs, raising the banner of la Virgen de Guadalupe, holding cardboard placards on which were hastily written excerpts from the teachings of Gandhi and Martin Luther King Jr.

Curanderas with their bags of herbs, aspirin, and water bottles ministered to swollen feet, aching muscles, and those losing hope and falling by the roadside. After all, every mother is a curandera, every mother is a medicine woman for her children. Women encouraging the young.

I can hear those strong women calling: "Ándale, get up, let's go. ¡Sí se puede! Only twenty miles to Sacramento."

Dear K.

You asked why I brought Ultima into the picture if the story is about Alfonso and Agapita. *Bless Me, Ultima,* 1972, that story blessed my path . . . now it's Agapita, 2016 into the future. The same story repeats itself, or it's the same story with a different beginning. Both lead to the same ending—or do they?

Are you trusting me? You know these are the recollections of an old man. The narrator is confused, or the narrator is missing. The story is writing itself. That's the best place to be when the story is just flowing.

How in the hell was I supposed to know the ending of Alfonso's novel! Most writers don't know their story's ending when they start on page one. After all, the creative imagination should take over and just go. Fonso said the creative imagination is soul, and soul creates.

Readers asked Fonso, "Did you know Ultima was going to die at the end of the novel?"

"No," he answered. "The story led me to its proper ending." Didn't I say the story wrote itself? Story is an organic process, constellating in the brain, passing through heart, nerves, and muscles, down the arms to the hands. One hand in Fonso's case. The ending is the fruition of the story. What happens happens, because that's the way it has to be. In one of Antonio's dreams, he sees Ultima in a coffin. The force of the story and the need to restore harmony in the community prescribed her death.

Some readers have told me they cried when they got to the end of the novel. Catharsis. They had not anticipated her death. And they cried at the end of the movie. I attended the 2012 premiere at the Lensic Theater in Santa Fe. The entire house stood and clapped; there were a lot of wet eyes.

Why did Ultima have to die? Some craftier writer would have kept her for a sequel.

Alfonso went for the truth. Did he know that forty-plus years later he would write Alfonso's and Agapita's story? Of course not—Wait a minute! What if he knew, not consciously, but what if this story was in his mind as he was writing *Bless Me, Ultima*? No, that's not possible. I don't believe that. But just suppose for a minute that Alfonso's and Agapita's story was constellating itself in his mythopoetic memory. In other words, what if, unbeknownst to him, Fonso's and Agapita's story was swimming around in his imagination forty-plus years ago?

It makes sense. There's the boy and the curandera in both novels. Ultima is the curandera in the first novel; she is Antonio's guide as he awakens into that crucial time when he first sees beauty in the world. He realizes he is part of the natural world, in nature, in God. Ultima tells him he will write his story, the story of the people. "Your soul will create myth," she instructs.

"When?"

"Someday."

Always someday. Writers, and creative people in general, are haunted by time. There's never enough time. The same is true for everyone.

No, I don't believe Fonso knew this story when he was writing *Bless Me, Ultima*. That's too much to ask. Too much to accept . . . because then that means everything that *will happen* to us is swimming in our imagination from the minute our imagination comes alive. And since the creative imagination is soul, and individual souls are connected to each other . . . I'm getting lost, the lost narrator expecting too much of himself.

I'm not the only one who's lost. We are all of one essence. Is there a universal soul for our species? My church taught that God is that all-encompassing essence. Also my mother.

Our entire life is written in our blood, Fonso said. So life is the process of revealing those stories we have stored in our cells. We experience one story at a time as we go through life's passages. Each person's story is writing itself.

Is our DNA loaded with our past, present, and future?

Everybody's soul in sync with universal soul? Not predestination, but simply that we are everything that's ever been or will be.

Did Fonso know Agnes was going to drown?

Never mind. These are the musings of an old man who lost his wife. I still talk to her. As we get older, we talk to ourselves, we speak to the dead. It's no wonder those around us think we're crazy. We speak aloud to the departed we loved, love.

"That old man's talkin' to hisself. Loony." Let's change the subject.

Maybe it's just easier to plot a story. Some writers make an outline of their stories from beginning to end, then just write the scenes in the list. One chapter at a time. Fonso believed that a story should grow organically, like a tree growing from seed to roots to trunk and leaves, not knowing how far it will go, but driven by a sense of its potential. The potential of the story is equal to the author's potential.

Soul is organic; hence stories from the soul should be organic. The world of nature and its spirit is all we know. Nature is indifferent, some say. Earth and its weather and the universe and its unfolding don't give a damn about us puny humans. And yet, nature is our greatest teacher. We are bound to the universe by our organic composition. We must be connected.

Is there anything benign in nature, you ask? Beauty. Yes, there's beauty in nature. Our earth is magnificent, and so is the universe. There's beauty in ocean tides, sunsets, the Grand Canyon, Yosemite, the Amazon, the vast variety of flowering trees, tiger eyes burning bright, butterflies—

Nature pleases us with its ephemeral beauty. But there's a catch. A Catch-22. It is we who create beauty in what we see, feel, touch, hear, smell, imagine. For most of our evolution, our ancestors didn't give a damn about the earth's spectacular beauty. They only wanted to know where to find animals they could hunt for food. Hunter-gatherers. Survival. In the most spectacular forest, they were bent down gathering seeds and berries to eat, not hugging trees. Appreciation of nature's beauty is pretty recent. Once he had leisure time, Mr.

Caveman might have awakened one morning, looked at a glorious sunrise, and said, "Gosh, purty."

Agapita taught Alfonso to live in nature's beauty. The people of the village also lived in beauty, in spite of the hard work and poverty. "Gracias a Diós," they would say at sunrise, sunset, or when the sweet perfume of the llano wafted across the plain. The aroma of rain. There was beauty in their lives.

I get tired of easy stories. Those who plot their stories, the same story over and over. We have our mythmakers, from ancient times to the present, gifted writers from the South and West, the Harlem Renaissance and the Chicano movement, white feminists and feminists of color. Earth shakers. Every community has writers who expose human nature to the core.

And movies today? Don't get me started. Too many technical fantasies. But I have to say, the movies for children are far more colorful than the black-and-white movies we grew up watching. And they do present stories. It's a child's time to be alive if they like movies. But so many movies still don't reflect our ethnic communities. I mostly watch public television and late-night telenovelas. Football on Sundays. The big television moguls claim they provide a healthy diet, but a lot is junk food. Thank God for public television.

Am I getting fuzzy? I hear a murmur. My heart speaks to me in murmurs. Murmurization, scientists call it, poetry swirling in my thoughts mixing with the beep-beep of the machine measuring electrical pulses in my heart. Is this the poetry for our time, technology commingling with messages from the heart? Science and poetry recording wave movements. In nature, flocks of birds move as one unit, swirling and dipping, down and out, hundreds moving as one wave. Large schools of fish also move in synchrony, thousands swimming as one dark cloud. How do they do that? How do they know when to turn in unison?

Now, the murmurs in my heart move to the loves I once knew. Waves of emotions, memories, soul murmurs.

Dear K,

You say you guessed early on I was writing the letters, and you let me continue. Why? Yes, my compadre Dionisio showed me your request months ago—or has it been years? I wrote the first letter in July of last year . . . I think. Now autumn is upon us with its finery of gold. From the porch I see the river cottonwoods turning bright yellow. I yearn to go up to the Jemez to see the aspen shimmering in the season's slanting sunlight. Grandfather Sun is traveling south toward Machu Picchu. Soon winter will settle over the Rio Grande Valley.

Then the promise of spring. I love spring. In spring Mother Nature exaggerates, filling the air with millions of seeds, pollens, ants scurrying, apricot blossoms, the smallest forms of life coming out of their nests, the first spring butterfly bursting out of its chrysalis. Dandelions bloom, telling us nature is an extravagant mother. She only needs a few dandelion seeds to propagate, but no, she sends millions of seeds out into the wind on fuzzy helicopter wings.

Here! she shouts. Here is my abundance! Go, seeds, and find fertile earth! Create new plants for me! Same with the fluffy white seeds of June cottonwood drifting in the wind. Millions of seeds to make one tree. It's the same with men and women. The feminine imperative: Give me all the sperm you've got. From just one, I will create.

The Big Bang must have been an expression of that feminine singularity. In the womb of nothingness, a particle wrapped in the membrane of love exploded and created time/space. That tiny particle was the universe dreaming, and the sac that held it together was love. Just as soul is wrapped in flesh, the God particle was wrapped in love. The feminine universe coming into being, stretching, groaning, growing, much like babies create their space and time as they grow. Out of the universal womb, a new time was being born. One particle full of potential created the abundance we call the universe.

Our earth is a microcosm of the universe, and here on this grain of sand wedded to the sun we are part of nature's abundance. Constant creation, endless diversity, season after season, from sea slugs not yet seen by man to an exotic bird just discovered. What beauty! There is beauty in nature's creations; we ourselves are part of that beauty.

We are nature's creatures, evolved from earth-womb. We wondrous beings enhanced with spirit, we children of Mother Nature, we give thanks for this drama in which we play a role. We're petty players, to be sure, but we are transporters of soul nevertheless. What is our tragic flaw? Why are we born into this life-web? Some prophets preached that we are to have dominion over the earth. I think not. We should be caretakers, and yet so often we go astray. Our tragic flaw must be a seed of destruction we picked up along the evolutionary road. Deep inside beneath the trappings of civilization lies that dark seed. Holocaust.

We are too proud, filled with hubris, a pride that often wounds nature's creation. We destroy nature in its many elements. Like Cronus gobbling down his children, we feast on nature's bounty like gluttons.

Nature exaggerates: She does not lay only one egg, but thousands. There is not just one kind of fish, one kind of butterfly or bird or beast. There is not just one kind of tree, but myriads; not just one aspen leaf, but a forest of gold.

Patricia and I used to drive up the Jemez Mountains to enjoy the colors that come with the changing season. Every autumn, as soon as we heard the call of Canadian geese and sandhill cranes, we would drive up into the aspen forest, sit at our favorite lookout point, eat our lunch, and enjoy the beauty of the mountain. Gold aspens framed by green pines, an exaggeration so pleasing to our souls, we reveled in the time. Of the mountain and time, we alone on the mountain, wrapped in the beauty nature gives so lavishly to her sons and daughters.

Everything was magical then. Before Patricia went away. Now nothing is as it used to be. I haven't been to see the aspen in years. It's not the same going alone. The seasons come and go. I lose touch with time when I'm writing. Time changes as we age; it seems to disappear so fast. But I can make time stand still! I can beat time down! Cronus devoured his children, but he can't devour me! I conquer time by writing stories! A story captures time and stops it in its tracks. I, the creator, can stop time!

See what I mean about pride . . . forgive me. No one can beat time; with sister space, it rules the universe. Time/space, a truth as old as the Big Bang. The books that hold our stories will eventually crumble, turn to dust on library shelves no longer visited. Like the deserted library at Ephesus. The universe will continue expanding, unaware of the lost species that once wrote books.

Ha! Do you understand my obsession? How I came to be a writer. That wanting to preserve the beauty of my people in my stories. Do you understand? I could not let Father Time erase the spirit of my gente, the llano, and the river. I fought back! With my fragile stories, I fought back! With my craft, I dared tell time I could hold it still.

What gall. What pride. Time, in these pages I will hold you still! I am not alone. The prophet on the mountain meditates on stopping time, the woman deep in prayer stops time. Meditation and prayer stop time, a desire for timeless being, getting closer to the essence of God. Lovers stop time. The orgasm of love stops time, if only for a few precious moments. In that ecstasy when the sperm and eggs of procreation are spilled into the womb, we imitate nature. Nature is in constant orgasm, constantly giving birth. One season ends and a new one is born; October aspen leaves fall and turn to dust to feed the web of roots that is the aspen family.

We imitate nature. We storytellers are in constant birthing, each story the ecstasy of orgasm born in the creative imagination. Deep in the most creative activities exists the orgasm of spontaneity, release, sudden flashes of insight, soul revealed.

Soul revealed. Remember that, K.

We reveal soul with each story, song, or poem we write. Even the most sullen artist is a lucky person, revealing soul to share with others. This is the mystery Mother Nature teaches us. Be constant in your creations.

But I'm interested, why did you ask my compadre to write what he knew about me? Why seek his point of view? A third-person point of view? What could he reveal about me? I find it interesting you went that route. He's not much of a writer, you know. He came to me and suggested I should write you and pretend the letters came from him.

"Tell her things about yourself that you haven't shared before," he said. "It can be your autobiography, something to leave your family."

I protested. "I never intended to write my autobiography. The novels and stories I wrote are my life. Why bother family and friends with more?"

"But you wrote fictions," he said. "In letters you can tell the truth, be more honest—"

"I am honest!" I shouted in his face. "Fiction deals with the truth. The *Iliad* and the *Odyssey* are true to the culture they represent! So are *Paradise Lost, Don Quixote, Snow White*, the Muppets! Stories must be honest; if not, we're lost as a storytelling species!"

Boy, was I pissed off. My compadre telling me I could be more honest by writing nonfiction instead of fiction. I calmed down, I knew he didn't mean it. I guess he felt that my autobiography could reveal more details of my life. I agree, but even autobiography is filtered through the writer and thus becomes an approximation, a fiction.

"You say everything is fiction," he countered. "You can't mean that. There's reality. People write about what happened. Experiences are real."

I laughed. The eternal conundrum. Ten people describing the same event would create ten different stories. So which story would be the *real* one? Which do you believe?

"All ten are real," he answered, not realizing the trap he had fallen into.

"Uh-huh. Ten realities. That's like having ten universes. Which universe are we in? Is life real or an illusion? Are we awake or asleep?"

He pushed me and I tottered back, almost falling. "There! That's real," he shouted.

Again, I laughed.

He was acting out the well-known Chinese story that happened between a Zen master and the novice. The master was teaching the novitiates that we really don't know if we're awake or dreaming. The novice slaps him. If he cringes and wakes up, he was dreaming.

"It doesn't work," I said. "How do you know you didn't push me in my dream?"

"I'm not in your dream," he fumed. "I believe stories are real."

I agree. In stories we communicate our innermost desires and aspirations, the truth of life. The story reveals the heart and soul of the storyteller and his community; it's a *true* approximation.

"Bah! You stay in your dream. I'm real!" He beat his chest. "See!"

"Not according to the new quantum physics, which tells us that when an observer looks at an object, he changes it."

"Just by looking?"

"Yes, and he changes himself. Quantum photons reflected from any object enter the observer's brain and his nervous system. Ipso facto, he is changed forever. When I write, I am constantly changing the entire universe within the story. It's as if the universe is exploding with light, photons bouncing all over my writing room and entering my eyes, imaginative photons shooting into my brain. Don't tell me that doesn't change me. Like Whitman going out and saying he became everything he encountered on the road, I am changing. And change isn't only in the old world of physics; there's a new physics being born. The smallest particles in the universe are changing us every millisecond."

"But that's just light," he complained lamely.

"Light is everything. It's all we've got. We live in light, gobble it up daily. Bless the light."

"But you can't change reality!"

"I don't have to change reality. Reality is constantly falling apart, changing itself. It's a law of nature, the law of Humpty Dumpty. No one can put reality together again. Everything is constantly changing, and we are changing along with what you call reality. Nothing is static. In the quantum universe, 0 and 1 can appear simultaneously, not as separate bits but as qubits. We live in the age of paranoid physics. How stable old Mr. Einstein's theory of relativity seems today."

"But I'm not falling apart," my compadre insisted.

"You were young; now you're old. The stroke you had has you bent over. Your muscles and skin are sagging—"

"Okay! Okay! So I'm aging! I don't like the idea that everything falls apart, but it's true. Is there sorrow in this? I feel sad that I'm not like I used to be. Is that why you called the letters *The Sorrows of Young Alfonso*?"

"The title seemed to fit," I replied. "I had to return to the llano, where I started with Ultima, but I didn't want to repeat myself, I didn't want to write a sequel. There are a million details to my life, as there are in the life of every person. One is never done with one's own story. I was born and raised in the llano of Santa Rosa de Lima, the Pecos River, and the valley of Puerto de Luna, the village of the Santo Niño—or was it Pastura del Santo Niño? Those beautiful, dramatic landscapes created dramatic people. Yes, the people lived epic lives; in spite of poverty and difficulty, they lived in a poetic language. I wrote Ultima's story, and now I needed a view of place and people through Agapita's eyes. What were the forces that formed me? The forces of truth, beauty, and goodness."

"The diving accident changed your life. You keep coming back to that."

"Yes. So much of my life hinged on that out-of-body experience. I dove into the water, lost consciousness for a few seconds, then floated to the surface. I couldn't move a muscle. I waited; one of my friends would come, but what if they thought I was playing, joking around? When no one came, I knew I would have to swallow water and drown. That's when I saw my soul slowly rise into the sky. It looked down on my body floating immobile in the water. I was a kid, only sixteen, I didn't know what was going on. But there it was, part of me leaving my body and rising about thirty feet into the sky and looking down on me. My soul ascending."

"It could see?"

"Not with eyes as we see, but it could see. My soul rose in a column of light. It looked down and saw me floating in the water. It saw everything around me: my friends, the car, the rushing water, all bathed in gold light. I held my breath. I was going to drown."

"Where do the healers come in?" he asked. "From Ultima down the line to Agapita?"

I sighed when I answered him. "I was remembering . . ."

My recovery from the accident meant I relied on healers who affected my life. First the doctors at the hospital, neurologists, nurses, therapists, my mother, curanderas, all working to help me recuperate. Like Humpty Dumpty, I had fallen apart. Could I be put together again? First, attention was paid to the physical, relearning how to walk. I had to put my body back together. Then there was the spiritual part, learning to collect the parts of my shattered soul, creating harmony again.

"The curanderas helped," he said.

"Yes. In our community there have always been healers like Ultima and Agapita who helped the people. Those women passed their power into me. By plucking me from my mother's womb, they blessed me. I became a shaman. Like them."

"Was your mother a curandera?"

"All mothers are curanderas. My mother used a few of the common herbs curanderas use. The women shared plants and roots, osha and yerba del manso, manzanilla, some from the northern mountains, some from the river or the llano. Some common remedies she bought at the store, like Vicks and Mentholatum for colds. And she knew prayers. She cured me with prayer and with the nightly massages she gave me after I got out of the hospital."

"You called curanderas our first spiritual feminists. What did you mean?"

"We know there are persons who have practiced the healing arts since time immemorial. Shamans, priests, medicine men and women have been helping communities since the first cavewoman rubbed bear fat on her husband's tired shoulders. Women have been taking care of babies since Eve placed apple peelings on her baby's forehead to ease his fever."

"So that's why she wanted the apple. Was she a curandera?"

"All women are curanderas."

"Which one did she cure? Cain or Abel?"

"It doesn't matter. Cain wasn't born bad; it was something in the world that brought on his jealousy. Envy and jealousy, the two great passions that destroy so many."

"So this whole chingadera started way back then?"

"Yes. Our curanderas, or medicine women as they're described by some anthropologists, are part of that long line of healers. They devote their lives to helping people. Some don't marry, they are so focused on their craft. Their work requires a lot of energy, bodily and spiritual energy. They know what to take from nature to effect cures; they have intimate knowledge of community rituals and the working of soul."

"All that power," my compadre said, "could be misused."

"Yes. There are ways of directing energy and knowledge into negative channels. We see that happening all over the world, but those doing evil are not curanderas. As my mother used to say, evil people sell their souls to the devil."

My compadre nodded. "I remember my grandmother saying that. She believed there was a devil out there. Lots to learn," he whispered. At that moment, my compadre looked sad.

"It is a specialized subject," I said. "A history of caring for community. Even modern medicine came out of that tradition. In fact, our doctors are better doctors when they work with the spirit of love the old healers possessed. I've been to many doctors in my lifetime, and yes, modern medical technology is a wonder, but often just the caring touch of a doctor works wonders."

My compadre agreed. "Yes, I know what you mean. How do you

fit all this in? You're not a curandero. You write books."

"Ay, compadre, don't you know stories are powerful healing agents? Books can cure a broken heart, lift up the depressed, point a confused reader on the right path, fill the soul with knowledge."

"I see. So the accident led you to write?"

"That and a million other things. It could be no other way."

"I suppose we all look for the causes that have led us this way or that. Cause and effect."

"So we're back to destiny. Is there a greater power in charge of our lives? Or do we invent gods to give meaning to our lives?"

"You call it soul. Soul is everywhere?"

"Yes. It's as organic as the universe. Or universes. Even before the Hubble telescope sent us pictures of far-flung galaxies, we sensed the existence of other universes. We were born to dream."

"Your speculations are getting too thick," he laughed. "Are you going to let me read your letters?"

"They belong to K."

"Maybe she'll put them in a book. Or on the Internet. Anyway, I couldn't have written what you wrote. I didn't know Agapita, Agnes, your friends, the llano, the Pecos River. I would have made things up—"

"Exactly! Fictions, approximations. We're back to that."

"Well, I'm glad you did it. You got closer to the truth. Truth at the heart of every story."

"And a lot of sadness."

"Yes. There is an intrinsic sadness in life. For all the beauty this earth offers us, for all the joys we may experience, there is a sadness at the core."

"Sorrow?"

"Yes. Especially if you have suffered the stings and arrows of destiny."

"In Ultima's story you called it *la tristeza de la vida*. The Spanish phrase fits. The sadness of life."

Our Socratic dialogues were done. My compadre said goodbye. It was time for his medications, he said. "I'm falling apart," he mumbled. I don't know if he went away wiser, but he was certainly changed. As we are all changed through our most simple interactions. Just by looking at each other, we are changed.

K, I don't know if this final letter ties up any of the themes I've written. Sometimes there is no satisfactory conclusion. I can go on writing till I'm dead, such is the force of the creative imagination, the soul. Do what you will with the letters. If you want to share them with others, that's fine.

I should make it clear that in spite of the sorrows in my life, I did know times of great joy. So many experiences contained a core of joy within. When you feel depressed, look for joy in your life, feel it deep. Joy is a passion. It will pick you up. I felt joy in my parents, family, friends, the earth's beauty, my wonderful and beautiful wife. So much to be thankful for. Soul moves on. It does not die.

This is the way my letters end, not with a bang but with a sigh.
Be kind.

With love, Fonso

Dear K,

You seemed disappointed with my last letter. You expected a resolution to the story . . . perhaps have all the dramatic complications in my life worked out, all my many and complex experiences made simple . . . tying up loose ends, a happy ending. Isn't this what we expect of literary works? And here I presume my letters are a kind of literary work.

Let's see, what other novel do we have in the form of letters? I can't think of one right now, but one will come to mind.

I am tired. I've written myself out, but the minute I think that, my mind starts churning with ideas. I make notes on whatever bit of scratch paper is handy, then hurry to my desk to write. A writer is never done; these letters are never-ending. I could go on and on, each thought, each memory, a chapter in my life.

I'm an old man now, with the troubles that ensue with age. What sorrows come when we get old? I lost Patricia a few years ago, and the grief I felt was a kind of sorrow. Being so close to someone for so many years makes the parting very difficult. Anyway, that book is written. Don't know if you read it. Best stick to the subject at hand, the sorrows I knew as a young man. As I wrote the letters, I had this feeling that what I went through is what so many young people experience. I don't mean life's details; those are different for everyone. I mean the emotions. Growing up is an emotional journey.

What of the letters you wrote to me? Should I share those with others? Will you? I have the urge to keep writing. I write Sumerian cuneiform on clay tablets, American English on silicone chips.

What's the difference? I can write because farmers are out there farming. God bless farmers.

There I go again, the brain will not rest. Every conscious moment is filled with neurons firing in the brain, dredging up memories, synaptic connections we call those little threads of protein that connect one neuron to another. Is that all we are? One protein talking to another? I read that in the DNA ladder, 0 and 1 can occur simultaneously, promoting growth. We reflect on the larger connections of life, one experience to another, as out there in cold space wisps of dark matter connect one galaxy to another, storms of galactic winds sweep across the universe . . . everything is connected one way or another.

We haven't learned that yet. We are destroying our planet, cooking Mother Earth.

So many ideas to write about. The thoughts I have in just one day are enough to fill a five-hundred-page novel. Everything I read seems to be grist for whatever I'm writing. I like to read about science, trying to understand what makes me tick. What sends the universe on its way. Looking for a lost god behind every universal law, behind every quantum particle. Look at green, I tell myself. The secret of the universe is encoded in a leaf. Leaves of grass, leaves of the cottonwoods that grace my Pecos River, my Rio Grande, the Jemez River. The most efficient transfer of energy occurs in a leaf. Chlorophyll is magical. Curanderas knew that when they collected medicinal herbs. There is power in the leaf.

Connections, maybe that's all there is. But what if our marvelous brain firing a million electrical impulses every second can't make sense of all the connections? I feel that now, part of getting old. Sometimes we're too focused on one thing and do not see reason and rhyme in the greater picture. What is the greater picture? God's vision. I called God nature. It came from my years of roaming the llano and the river, years with Ultima and Agapita.

What keeps us integrated? Soul. Yes, I believe in soul. Soul has its own electrical energy, but scientists haven't found a way to measure it. It's just as well. Let's leave soul in the care of truly holy people who are aware of its power. They know that soul conducts the harmonies of brain and body. Soul's energy connects flesh to God, as it should be.

And we are all truly holy people, caring for soul.

I sat outside in the morning sun, looking for the first flocks of geese and sandhill cranes this mid-October. The stupendous cumulus clouds of summer are gone, those deities of rain that rise over the mountains and ascend to cool the valley. Now ice-crystal clouds sweep across the sky, this New Mexican sky that is unique among the earth's skies.

We New Mexicans are lovers of sky and clouds.

I feel old now. It's harder to look back and remember the myriad details of life. Perhaps I should have written more of my university years. There's a novel there. Maybe I'm forgetting how to write a novel. Characters appeared and told me the right way to proceed. It all used to come so easily. Oh, there was a lot of hard, grueling work to every book, but there was vision in what I wrote. The stories came from my creative imagination, but they also seemed to come from a greater power. That's why soul is universal, it attaches to universal memory. Now I feel that time is destroying order. I like that. I like being part of the universal law that tells us that sooner or later things fall apart. I am no Quixote, I am Humpty Dumpty, falling apart. God save my soul.

Maybe that's why there is no resolution in my letters. There is no hero at the end announcing that good will triumph over evil. Ultima said good will always win, and Sonny Baca, my private investigator, was usually victorious at the end. Can Alfonso be a hero for our time? Does he reflect the suffering of the children in a world gone mad with war fever and misguided religious fervor? If my letters are a plea for sanity, then writing them was worthwhile.

I'll leave it to you and the readers of my letters, if you decide to share them with others. That's how it should be: share the sorrows of young Alfonso. It is the reader who will make the connections in the end, and be satisfied or not. Find purpose or not. Remember, the observer of any artistic work changes the work, and in turn is changed by it.

The fabric woven by our connections to others becomes a beautiful tapestry, a wondrous reflection of being human in nature. Every iota of the universe fits into the meaning we seek. What is life? Why are we here? Each one of us contributes to the colorful cloth. And out there, far beyond our scope of seeing, the organic elements of the universe continually add to our Joseph's coat of many colors. We are not alone—we never have been.

You are not alone, K. Children will come to enrich your life, then grandchildren. Evolution continues. Pray for a bright future. No one is alone. I think the poet expressed it best: *No man is an island . . . Every man is a piece of the continent, a part of the main.* Listen to our poets, they search for truth. We are all connected to each other and must take care of each other. Agapita was right: the world is full of sorrow, but caring for each other will lessen sorrow. Reach out and connect to community. I tried to do that in the life I led and the stories I wrote. My parents practiced kindness, and so did Patricia. So do all the good people on earth.

A blessing, Fonso

Also by Rudolfo Anaya

Bless Me, Ultima
Heart of Aztlan
Tortuga
The Silence of the Llano
The Legend of La Llorona
The Adventures of Juan Chicaspatas
A Chicano in China
Lord of the Dawn: The Legend of Quetzalcóatl
Alburquerque
The Anaya Reader
Zia Summer
Jalamanta: A Message from the Desert
Rio Grande Fall
Shaman Winter
Serafina's Stories
Jemez Spring
Curse of the ChupaCabra
The Man Who Could Fly and Other Stories
ChupaCabra and the Roswell UFO
The Essays
Randy Lopez Goes Home
Billy the Kid and Other Plays
The Old Man's Love Story
Poems from the Río Grande
Isis in the Heart

Children's Books

The Farolitos of Christmas
Farolitos for Abuelo
My Land Sings: Stories from the Rio Grande
Elegy on the Death of César Chávez
Roadrunner's Dance
The Santero's Miracle
The First Tortilla
Juan and the Jackalope
La Llorona, the Crying Woman
How Hollyhocks Came to New Mexico
How Chile Came to New Mexico

Edited Volumes

(ed. with Antonio Márquez) *Cuentos Chicanos: A Short Story Anthology*
(ed. with Simon J. Ortiz) *A Ceremony of Brotherhood, 1680–1980*
(ed.) *Voces: An Anthology of Nuevo Mexican Writers*
(ed.) *Tierra: Contemporary Short Fiction of New Mexico*
(ed. with Francisco A. Lomelí) *Aztlán: Essays on the Chicano Homeland*